Book
Capta
Regency N
By Ashley Gardner

THE HANOVER SQUARE AFFAIR
A REGIMENTAL MURDER
THE GLASS HOUSE
THE SUDBURY SCHOOL MURDERS
THE NECKLACE AFFAIR
AND OTHER STORIES
(COLLECTED STORIES)
A BODY IN BERKELEY SQUARE
A COVENT GARDEN MYSTERY
A DEATH IN NORFOLK
A DISAPPEARANCE IN DRURY LANE
MURDER IN GROSVENOR SQUARE
THE ALEXANDRIA AFFAIR
(AND MORE TO COME)

Also by
Ashley Gardner

MURDER MOST HISTORICAL
(ANTHOLOGY: INCLUDES A SOUPÇON OF POISON)

Kat Holloway Mystery Series
A SOUPÇON OF POISON
A DOLLOP OF DEATH

The Thames River Murders

Ashley Gardner

Captain Lacey Regency Mysteries
Book 10

Chapter One

June 1818

The letter, neatly folded at my plate, looked innocuous enough, but I had a sense of disquiet about it.

The letter had come through the post, my name and direction carefully printed by hand. *Captain Gabriel Lacey, South Audley Street, Mayfair.*

An auspicious address, though not my original. I'd married it. Six months ago, I had been living in straitened circumstances in rooms above a Covent Garden bakeshop. At New Year's I had married Donata Breckenridge, a young widow, and moved into tasteful splendor.

The previous master of this house, Lord Breckenridge, had been a brute of a man, and a boor. Did I feel a sense of triumph that I had awakened with the beautiful Donata half an hour ago, while the foul Breckenridge was dead?

I did, I am very much afraid.

I breakfasted alone. Donata slept on upstairs,

weary from her social engagements of the previous night. Her small son from her first marriage, Peter — the current Viscount Breckenridge — took his breakfast in the nursery, and my daughter had not yet woken. In the family, Peter and I were the early risers.

I eyed the letter for some time, filled with a sense of foreboding. I'd received two rather nasty missives in the last weeks, unsigned, purporting me to be an imposter — in fact *not* the Gabriel Lacey who had left my Norfolk country estate more than twenty years ago with a regiment posted to India. I was a blackguard who'd come to cheat Lady Breckenridge out of her money and leave her destitute. If I did not heed the writer's warning, leave a substantial sum for him in a yet-to-be determined meeting place, and disappear again, he would denounce me.

I, of course, showed these letters to my wife at once. Donata had great fun with them, and was busy trying to decipher the handwriting. A jealous suitor, she proclaimed, though she had no idea which one. Could be dozens, she'd said, which unnerved me a bit, though I should not have been surprised. Donata had been quite a diamond of the first water in her Season.

I finished my ham and slice of bread, toasted to near blackness as I liked it, and took a long draught of coffee before I lifted the letter and broke the seal with my knife.

I make so bold to write to you, Captain, to beg a favor. I have a problem I have been pondering for some time, and would like another opinion. Sir Montague Harris, magistrate at Whitechapel, suggested I put the affair before you and see what you make of it. You would, unfortunately, have to travel to Wapping, but there is no

*way around that. If you would prefer to discuss the matter
first, I am happy to meet you in a place more convenient to
explain.*

Yours sincerely,

*Peter Thompson
Thames River Police*

"Barnstable," I said to the butler, who hovered
nearby, waiting to serve me. "Please send for a
hackney. I am off to Wapping this morning."

***

Barnstable, who was a stickler for appearances,
wanted to rouse the coachman to have me driven
across London in the Breckenridge landau. I
forestalled him, seeing no reason to wake the man,
Hagen, who'd been out until four driving my wife
from place to place. Nor did I wish to roll into the
seamier parts of London in a luxurious coach with
the Breckenridge crest on its side.

A hackney would do. Barnstable made sure one
halted at our front door, a plain black coach, shining
with rain. I asked Barnstable to convey to Donata
where I'd gone, in case she woke before my return,
and I was off.

The coach had only reached the end of South
Audley Street when the door was flung open again.
The vehicle listed sharply as a large man climbed
inside, slammed the door, and fell onto the seat
opposite me. He gave me a nod.

"Mornin', Captain."

"Mr. Brewster." My hand relaxed on my walking
stick, which had a stout sword inside it. "I would
have hoped Mr. Denis had ceased sending a minder

after me."

Brewster folded his thick hands across his belly and returned my look blandly. "Mr. Denis pays me to follow you. When you dart out of your house at nine in the morning and leap into a hackney, I can't but help wondering where you're off to. If I didn't find out, Mr. Denis would not be pleased."

James Denis was not forgiving of those who disobeyed his orders. I had to concede Brewster's dilemma.

"I am going to visit a man of the River Police," I said. "Perhaps not an errand you'd wish to take."

Brewster made a slight shrug. "I go where you go, Captain."

Brewster was a criminal, a thief and possibly a murderer. James Denis, an even greater criminal, ever plotted to have me under his thumb. The association between us, however, had become much more complicated than that. My ideas about Denis had changed, though I had no illusions about exactly what sort of man he was.

The journey across London was tedious, its streets clogged with vehicles, animals, and humanity living as hard as they could under the cloud of smoke twined with mist from the river.

We moved along the Strand, then Cheapside, then through the heart of the City's financial prowess at Cornhill and Leadenhall. We turned southward around Tower Hill and so to the docklands.

Wapping was in the midst of these, with tall ships lining the wharves, the forest of masts and yardarms stretching down the river. The bare rigging moved as the ships rocked, the vessels straining to be released to the freedom of the sea.

I'd sailed plenty myself in such ships, my longest

voyage being to India when I'd been young and in the army, to fight in Mysore. I'd dragged my delicate first wife across the ocean with me. That she would not have the eagerness to see an exotic part of the world at my side had never occurred to me.

A similar ship had taken me to Norway, then to France, and finally to Iberia, to fight battle after battle in the unceasing wars. Since I'd returned to England in 1814, an injury denying me the glory of Waterloo, I'd been land-bound. The sight of the tall ships stirred in me a longing to explore parts unknown.

For now, I turned my back on the ships and descended from the coach in front of the narrow house that was an office for the Thames River Police.

Formed by merchants and ship owners tired of cargo being stolen from the holds of moored ships, the Thames River Police patrolled the river, watch over the ships and docks, and apprehend thieves. While the river was their jurisdiction, they did sometimes help the magistrates and Runners throughout London with investigations.

I entered the house to find a small room filled with desks, maps of the river, and pigeonholes crammed with scraps of paper. A wiry young man scampered into the back when I removed my hat and gave my name.

Brewster did not enter the house behind me. He remained outside next to the hackney, leaning on its wheel and narrowly watching anyone who passed. He had no intention of letting the hired driver leave, he'd said, in case I needed a quick departure, but neither had he any intention of voluntarily walking into a house full of patrollers.

Peter Thompson came through a door in the rear of the room and held out his hand to me. He was a tall, bony man with lively eyes in a thin face, wearing a frock coat and breeches that hung loosely on his limbs. So he'd looked every time I'd seen him. He was only minus his frayed gloves this morning, clasping my hand with a bare, callused one.

I'd been in the office to which Thompson ushered me before, long ago, when I'd investigated the affair of the Glass House. I'd met Thompson not long before that, when his men had pulled the body of a young woman out of the water and asked my help identifying it.

Thompson's room hadn't changed. He had a desk and chair for himself, a stool for any visitor. I remained standing, remembering that the stool was less comfortable than leaning on my walking stick.

"Thank you for coming, Captain." Thompson also remained standing, a man who disliked to be still. "I hesitated to write to you, but this has been weighing on my mind for some time. Puzzles intrigue you, so I decided to ask your opinion."

While I'd gained something of a reputation for ferreting out things that were none of my business, I had to wonder why a man of Thompson's repute would ask for *my* help. He had plenty of young, sturdy men at his disposal to assist him in investigations.

"It is an old mystery, I'm afraid," Thompson said. "I must not lie to you—my superiors have told me to let it be. If no one has come forward in all this time, we are to make a mark through it and continue with more pressing matters. But I dislike leaving a thing unsolved."

"And you recalled that neither did I," I supplied.

The corners of Thompson's lips twitched. "You have a tenacity I admire, Captain. I believe you are the exact man for this little problem."

"You've piqued my interest," I said. "As you knew you would with your cryptic letter. Now I cannot leave here without knowing the whole of it."

"For that, I must show you." Thompson took up his hat and gestured for me to follow him out of the office. He led me from the house entirely, and around a narrow path between buildings to a yard in the back.

Brewster was not having me walk through tiny, dim passages with only a man from the River Police to protect me. He fell into step behind me, his stride even.

Thompson opened the door to another gray stone house, its bricks crumbling from years of exposure to damp, mist, and rain. A light rain was falling now, fog thickening until we stood in a ghostly atmosphere, the air gray-white around us.

Inside the door was a set of steps leading into a cellar. Thompson took us down these into clinging chill.

Candles burned in the darkness to light our way. Crates and boxes were piled in the room below, in front of open cupboards of filled pigeonholes. In spite of the cold, it was somewhat dry down here, no windows to let in the outside air.

Two young men stood in front of tall desks, making notes in ledgers. When they saw Thompson, they stood upright, at attention.

"Take some air, lads," Thompson told them. "Stretch your legs."

The two patrollers looked grateful and wasted no time hurrying up the stairs.

"They catalog things here," Thompson said, waving his hand at the ledgers. "Things we find in the river, goods seized from smugglers, evidence in cases, that sort of thing."

I glanced at Brewster. I wasn't certain that information about goods taken from smugglers was a wise thing to pass on to a known thief, but Brewster did not comment or even look interested.

"They catalog things more gruesome as well," Thompson said. He moved to a heavy, bolted door, and when he opened it, my breath fogged in the air that came out.

We looked into a chamber with a very low stone ceiling and thick walls, as though it had been carved into the banks of the river. The cold was enough to make my throat raw.

Shelves held wooden and metal crates and boxes, though not as many as in the outer room. Thompson lifted a crate from only a step inside the door and brought it out.

He set down the crate to close and lock the door again then carried it to a long table at the back of the main room. Brewster helped him lift the crate to this table, then Thompson used a long piece of metal to pry off its top. Thompson reached inside, lifting out a rolled piece of canvas.

"Will you move the crate for me, sir?" Thompson asked Brewster. Brewster lifted it down, clearing the table, now as intrigued as I was.

Thompson laid the canvas bundle on the table and carefully unrolled it.

"'Struth," Brewster breathed.

On the dark, stained canvas was a collection of bones. Human bones, clean and preserved.

Thompson started laying them out, one by one, until we gazed down at a near-perfect skeleton of a human being lying before us. The skull, which was mostly intact, bore a large gouge from the top of the head down to the right eye socket.

Someone had smashed a cudgel into this poor creature long ago and left him to die.

"Here we are, Captain," Thompson said. "I want you to help me discover who she is and what villain out there killed her."

Chapter Two

"Her," I repeated.

"That's what the coroner said at the time." Thompson straightened one of the hand bones, as though a whole, living woman lay there. "She was fished out of the river ten years ago, caught up on pilings, but no one ever turned up looking for her, and we were never able to find out who she was. We put out a report when we found her, but no one came forward. It's weighed on me for a long time. And then the other day, I thought — *this is something that the captain might be interested in.*"

Thompson read me well. I was unfortunately drawn to intrigue, especially when it involved a poor individual who couldn't fight back, or who had lost against a stronger opponent.

On the other hand, Thompson was optimistic about my abilities. A woman who'd been killed long ago, who was an unidentified collection of bones, and whom apparently no one had missed, would be a bit too cryptic a puzzle, I thought.

"That she was brutally killed is not in question," I said, touching the gouge on the skull. The bone was smooth under my fingers. "Though how do you know she did not receive these injuries from a fall? An accident?"

"I don't, not for certain," Thompson admitted. He fished from the box what looked like nothing more than scraps of cloth. "Her clothes had mostly rotted away, except for a few trapped pieces I managed to clean up."

I lifted a pale tatter of fabric that held a hint of blue. "Her dress?" I asked.

"I believe so, or undergarments. Also this." Thompson dug one more item from the box, a gold chain with a locket.

It was an ordinary locket, a small oval on a chain, the gold still bright even after years underwater. Whatever had been engraved on the outside, however, had been worn away, only faint scratches remaining.

I slid my thumbnail into the locket's crease and pried it open, but found nothing inside. If she'd kept a sketch, silhouette, lock of hair, or painting within, the river had long since destroyed it.

"That was fused around her neck," Thompson said. "No clasp. I had to cut it from her."

Interesting. "May I take these with me?" I asked, holding up the fabric and necklace. "If I can determine what sort of cloth it is, how common or how fine, we can at least conclude how wealthy was her family, which could narrow her to certain parts of town."

"She was a tart, most likely," Brewster said. "Killed and tossed into the river, no one coming forward to look for her. A lot of them don't use their own names, and no one knows who they truly are."

He spoke matter-of-factly, not condemning. In Brewster's world, a person made a living any way he or she could—he'd met his wife while she was a courtesan in a bawdy house.

Brewster might or might not agree that a tart deserved justice against her killer, but he wouldn't admonish me for taking on the task. As long as I didn't endanger myself, that is. If I were hurt or killed while Brewster was looking after me, Denis might be unforgiving.

"This locket is of very fine gold," I pointed out. "There's not a bit of tarnish on it. Grenville and his man will no doubt know exactly where it came from, or at least who made things like this."

The last time I'd helped Thompson identify a corpse from the river, Grenville's valet had recognized the jeweler's mark on the man's ring she wore, and we'd had the woman's identity within the night.

This time might be a little more difficult. She'd been lost for a long while, and if no one had come looking for her, Brewster might be correct after all. An anonymous woman, dying as she eked out her living.

"Also," I began. A thought had formed in my head, a way we might learn more about this body than her gender—I assumed the coroner had known she was a woman from the shape of the hips and other bones—and the fact that she'd been bashed on the head. "I know of a surgeon, a very good one," I said. "I'd like him to have a look at her. I'd value his opinion."

Thompson shrugged, as though indifferent. "By all means. This corpse is no secret. Forgotten, rather."

Brewster had a sharp gaze on me, guessing which surgeon I meant.

In March of this year, when my friend Leland Derwent had been badly hurt, James Denis had sent a highly competent surgeon to look after him. The man had saved Leland's life when all others had despaired of it.

I never learned the surgeon's name. I did not particularly want to. He had been transported for a crime and had returned to England, for reasons I also did not want to know. If he were to be caught, he'd be hanged. I doubted I'd convince him to come near a magistrate's house, but I could not think of a better man to view the bones.

I cleared my throat. "Would it be possible for me to take her away with me?"

Thompson's brows climbed high in his face. He rarely looked surprised about anything, but he stared at me in perplexity now.

"Where on earth would you take her?"

"Someplace safe, I assure you."

Brewster continued to watch me in silence. Thompson looked over the bones, pushed back his low-crowned hat, and scratched his head.

"Can your surgeon not come here?" he asked. "Would be simpler all around."

I cast about for some excuse. While Thompson was an informal man in many ways, I did not think he'd look the other way if a convicted felon, escaped from his punishment, were delivered into his house.

"He is of delicate constitution," I ventured. "The air would not agree with him."

Thompson looked amused. "Must be tricky for him to perform his surgeries then."

"He is retired." That was at least close to the truth.

"I will take good care of … her."

Thompson considered further, rubbing his lip, then he righted his hat. "I suppose I trust you, Captain. But take care. Without these bones, we wouldn't know there was a crime, a deceased person at all."

"Of course."

Thompson made no more comment, only began carefully piling the bones in the middle of the canvas, then rolling it up with the same gentleness.

He put everything back into the crate that Brewster, with a dark look at me, lifted for him.

"She's been kept fairly cold," Thompson said. He found a hammer on a cluttered workbench and pounded the nails into the lid again. He laid down the hammer and leaned an elbow on the top of the box. "Mind you keep her cool, now that the weather's turning warm."

It was not all that warm today, under a thick mist, but I took his meaning. Cold preserved, heat destroyed.

Brewster heaved the crate into his arms without being asked, but he did not disguise his distaste. He'd long thought I was mad, ever since the day he'd come across a valuable pile of silver objects hidden in my house in Norfolk. He'd offered to split the loot with me, but I'd insisted on returning the pieces to their rightful owner.

Thompson wrapped up the cloth and locket, which I placed into my pocket, then Thompson led the way out again.

I had the feeling of emerging from a tomb. The cold from the underground room fell away as we climbed out to the open air. Though fog prevailed, it was warmer outside, the dampness clinging to the skin. The two young men who had been working below looked disappointed when they saw us come out, and slunk back down to resume their tasks.

Thompson helped Brewster lift the crate into the coach. Thompson rested a hand on it a moment, as though saying good-bye to a friend.

"Thank you, Captain. Let me know what you discover."

No hurrying me. Perfect trust. Thompson was a man confident everything would resolve itself in due time.

We shook hands, then Thompson lifted his hat and disappeared back into the house.

"You aren't thinking of taking that home are ye?" Brewster asked, his look wary.

I imagined explaining to Donata that I had placed a pile of brown bones in her cellar for safekeeping. "No," I answered.

"Mr. Denis ain't going to like them either." Brewster's scowl was formidable.

"I know." I started to climb into the coach. Brewster put his hand on my back to help shove me inside but remained on the ground.

"I'll ride up top," he said. "I don't fancy sharing a vehicle with a dead body."

"Perfectly understandable." I settled myself into the seat and drew my greatcoat closed against the fog. "Tell the coachman to take us to Grosvenor Street."

Brewster's dour look fled, and his eyes lit. "So that's your idea, is it? I can't wait to see his face."

***

Lucius Grenville lived in splendor in Grosvenor Street, in the heart of Mayfair. His mansion's facade was unpretentious, plain even. Rows of uniformly spaced windows marched across it, each flanked by a pair of recently painted black shutters. The front door, also black, with a fanlight, held a polished brass knocker.

The unadorned exterior hid a house of magnificence. The homes of Mayfair, which shared common walls, might be one room and a hallway wide facing the street, but the bulk of the house ran far back into the property. Grenville's home was quite large within, containing lavish rooms on the ground and first floors for his guests, elegant private chambers above for the privileged few.

The footman who answered the door was Matthias, brother to the young man who now valeted for me. Matthias was tall, blond, and muscular, the epitome of the handsome footman Mayfair residents wanted seen at their front doors.

"He's not at home, sir," Matthias said after he'd greeted me. "But please come in and rest if you like, and I'll serve you something. Mr. Grenville's door is always open to *you.*"

He cast a glance at Brewster who'd climbed down to stand behind me. Matthias did not approve of Brewster, though he acknowledged his help in the past.

"That is kind of you," I said. "But I've come only to deliver something—to ask Grenville to keep it safe for me, to speak more concisely."

"Of course, sir." Matthias held the door open wide, never questioning. "We can put whatever it is in his collections room."

"Ah." I paused. "His wine cellar was more what I had in mind."

"Oh?" Matthias peered dubiously at the crate Brewster was now hauling out of the coach. "An interesting vintage?"

"You might say that."

Behind me, Brewster chuckled, his sour temper lightened. "Show us the way, lad."

Matthias opened his mouth to no doubt state that both Brewster and his burden should enter through the kitchen, then closed it. My friendship with Grenville occupied a place that didn't quite fit with Grenville's other acquaintance. Matthias gave a shrug, led us inside the front door, through the elegant hall, and down the back stairs to the kitchens and cellars.

Grenville's staff were working to keep up the magnificence of his household. Two footmen industriously polished a large quantity of silver in the servants' hall. Maids were in the laundry room, steam rolling out as they applied whatever magic they knew to Grenville's linens. The chef, Anton, hovered in the large kitchen, closely watching his assistant, a rather harried young man, as he stuffed a bird lying spread on a platter.

Anton glanced up when he heard our steps in the corridor, the displeased look on his face turning to rapture when he saw me.

"Captain!" Anton was a rather small man with a round stomach and stooped shoulders, but a wide, beaming smile. I have no idea how much of a martinet he was in his kitchen, but when it came to guests to feed, he was benevolence itself. "You are here," he announced. "Sit, sit. I will give you a *déjeuner* not to forget."

I bowed. "I thank you, sir, but I am here only briefly."

Anton's look turned scornful. "Nonsense. You are a gentleman. You have these ..." His fluttering fingers took in Matthias and Brewster "… to do your work, while you are fed by me." He shouted to one of the footmen across the hall. "Lay a place upstairs for the captain. He will dine."

Brewster lifted brows at me, but he trudged on after Matthias, taking his burden through the door to the wine cellar that Matthias opened for him.

Matthias nodded to me. "Go on, sir. I'll take care of everything. Mr. Grenville would likely have my head for bringing you below stairs anyway."

I was left standing in the kitchen with the good scents of Antoine's fine cuisine floating around me. I succumbed.

***

After the fine meal Anton forced upon me, alone in Grenville's dining room, I returned home.

I believe Anton enjoyed feeding me, because I was apt to eat everything in sight and praise it to the skies. With Grenville, Anton expected a certain amount of criticism; which he asked for to further his quest to be the best chef in the world. I simply enjoyed.

"Her ladyship is awake, sir," Barnstable informed me as I entered. "Asking for you."

I brushed dust from my sleeves. "I am hardly in a fit state to see her at the moment."

I had grime from the London streets embedded in my clothes, and who knew what dirt from the cellar to which Thompson had ushered me. Anton had let me wash my hands and face in a basin before I sat down to eat, but he was less scrupulous about my state of cleanliness than in wishing me to polish off every morsel.

Barnstable gave me an apologetic look. "She said she needed to see you the moment you stepped foot in the door."

"She will hardly thank me if I smear her pristine silk sofa with London's black mud. Send her word I will attend upon her once I've changed my clothes."

Barnstable's expression remained stoic, but I saw the flicker of dismay in his eyes. Donata was not a despot in her own home, but she did like her whims obeyed. I took pity on Barnstable.

"I'll tell her myself," I said. "I realize her delicate state makes her a bit impatient."

Barnstable's relief was apparent, but he only answered with a neutral, "Yes, sir."

The relief told me that Donata had been a bit peevish when she'd risen. She was in possession of a sharp tongue, which could sting if one did not know how to withstand her barbs.

I moved past Barnstable, who gave me a silent look of thanks, and up the stairs to my lady's chamber.

Donata Anne Catherine St. John, nee Pembroke, the daughter of an earl, widow of a viscount, and now simply Mrs. Captain Gabriel Lacey, reclined as gracefully as ever on a chaise in her boudoir.

Coffee reposed at her elbow as did an empty glass with a small amount of film clinging to its interior. Conclusion—she'd been ill soon after she woke.

The casual observer would never suspect it but for that glass with a draught to settle her stomach. Her color was high, her golden silk peignoir flowed over her limbs, and her dark hair was caught in a bandeau with careless elegance. The only thing missing was the cigarillo wafting its smoke about her face—she'd declared the things made her queasy when she was with child and had reluctantly given them up.

Donata held several letters in her hand and did

not look up when she heard my step.

"There you are, Gabriel. Barnstable said you'd gone out. Where on earth did you find to run to in the small hours of the morning?"

"It was nine," I said. "It is one o'clock now. Which is the small hours of the morning for *you*."

I did not move from the doorway, knowing I could not be surrounded by the best of odors, in spite of my contact with Anton's kitchen. Death has a miasma of its own.

Donata looked up. Her dark hair held a gloss that picked up the sunlight through the windows, burnishing a gold streak in it that matched her garment. Her fine-boned face held the arrogance of the aristocrat—her family's ancestors had graced this land from Saxon times, integrating themselves with the upstart Normans and continuing from there.

Her eyes were her best feature, in my opinion, dark blue and bottomless. When I looked into those eyes, my cares and pain fell away, and I drowned in her.

Few cracked the hard shell she'd formed around herself through years of unhappiness, but I'd found the way to the true Donata.

"Will you prop up the doorframe or come in?" Donata asked, an edge to her voice. "I do hate to shout across the room."

"I have been to Wapping and back in not the cleanest of hackneys," I said. "Let me change to something more suitable, and I will attend you."

"Nonsense, Gabriel. You are perfect as you are. Please, do come closer. If you fear to put dust on the furniture, you may stand, or I will have Barnstable fetch towels for you to sit upon. But I really must speak to you."

Her adamance made me curious. I had expected her to flap her hand and say, *Yes, yes, if you think it best*, instead of insisting I stay.

"What is it?" I came to her, but halted about six feet away. If her stomach was a perilous place, and I smelled of horse, dank cellar, and death, it might lead to a headlong rush to her basin.

She lifted the papers she'd been reading. "I've been perusing these letters again. The ones accusing you of being an imposter. I think—I am not entirely certain—but I might know who wrote them."

Chapter Three

The crease between Donata's brows and her lack of amusement with which she had previously regarded the blackmailing missives, gave me some disquiet.

"Well?" I asked when she paused. "Will you tell me a name?"

"Only if you will promise me you will not rush from here and stab him through the neck with your sword. You are rather precipitous at times."

Since I found the letters in bad taste but ridiculous, I did not think they'd drive me to murderous frenzy. I saved that for more worthy endeavors.

"I give you my word," I said. "I will remain calm until we know for certain who is the author of these profane letters."

Still Donata hesitated, as though debating whether to speak. "There was a man," she began slowly. "Before I married Breckenridge, I rather foolishly encouraged a gentleman into pursuing me, believing I'd marry him if he asked me. I was young and silly enough to think I could follow my heart in matters of matrimony."

"I am pleased you have come to your senses," I said dryly.

She flicked me a glance. "You know what I mean. I imagine you were full of glorious fantasies of romance and love when you were seventeen."

"Worse," I admitted. "I was twenty, and married the lady."

Donata knew all about that. I did not regret having a child with my first wife—I now had my beautiful daughter, Gabriella—but the marriage was a disaster on all other counts.

"Then you understand," Donata said. "I was besotted, as only a girl can be. He was a thorough blackguard, of course. But oh, so charming. Breckenridge was horrible in his own way, but from a respectable and ancient family, which made all the difference to my father and mother. If I had married with my heart, eloped with my charming gentleman, I would be destitute, ruined, and cut off from everyone I hold dear. Alas, such thoughts do not enter one's head at seventeen."

"Probably not." My daughter was eighteen, I thought with a qualm. Donata's father had been strong enough to curb her, powerful enough to set up an aristocratic marriage for her. How much power did I, a poor country gentleman and half-pay army officer, have to prevent my daughter from a foolish mistake?

"Are you saying," I went on, "that the writer of these threatening letters is your former inamorato?"

She gave me a look of scorn. "Matters hardly went *that* far. My love was innocent, though I am certain he had other ideas. But yes, I suspect him. He enjoyed flowery phrases, and these letters are rife with them. Besides, I can think of no other person who would wish to destroy my marriage to you."

"No?" I asked. "I can think of a good many."

Donata had been a wealthy widow, and her son was a viscount, possessor of vast tracts of property and piles of money. And who had sidled in to steal her from the gentlemen of the *ton*? A forty-odd year-old army captain, lame, with one suit to his name, who lived over a bakeshop in Covent Garden.

Three quarters of Mayfair was furious with me. They blamed Grenville for bringing a nobody into contact with their number, where I could meet a lady like Donata. They were entirely right, but that did not mean I'd give up my lady, tuck my tail between my legs, and scurry back to my damp, rundown house in Norfolk like a good country squire. Donata also had two cousins highly enraged that I'd cut them out of any chance with her.

"None who would send letters like this." Donata gestured with the paper she held. "There was always a little something mad about him. Probably added to his appeal — girls can be such idiots."

"What is this gentleman's name?" I asked again.

"Hmm." Donata's eyes narrowed. "I'm not certain now that I will reveal it. Not because I am ashamed, but you do tend to let your temper get the better of you, and you have the unfortunate tendency to draw the ire of the Runners."

"That is so," I said, keeping my voice quiet. "All the same, I wish you would tell me."

"I will think on it." Donata folded the letter and tucked it into a pocket of her peignoir. "I might be wrong, in any case. No use in you kicking a poor unfortunate who was minding his own business.

Besides, he might have reformed."

I doubted it. Once a roué always a roué, in my experience.

"Wherever did you go this morning?" Donata asked, the business of the letters finished. "Barnstable tells me you had a message then dashed out in a hackney."

"I did indeed. I am prepared to tell you all about it if I am allowed to make myself presentable."

"You do fuss so, Gabriel. Very well. Please be quick. I am too impatient these days."

I adjourned to my chamber, hurried through my ablutions, and let Bartholomew, my valet, tuck me into another suit. I owned several now, as my wife insisted that any husband of hers must look presentable.

I cared very little for clothing, but I had no wish to embarrass her, so I consulted Grenville, who referred me to a tailor who would dress me in clothes to suit me. As a result, I now owned several subdued, everyday ensembles, formal coats and trousers for elegant occasions, and several sets of riding clothes.

Returning to Donata's boudoir, I felt more confident taking a seat next to her.

Donata's room was entirely feminine, all ivory and gold, its furniture ornate and gilded, or elegantly plain. Ivory draperies trimmed with gold flowed at the windows, an ebony table at Donata's side held her coffee; a matching table at my side held mine.

I enjoyed coffee at any time of the day, and I readily drank it. A rich heat filled my mouth and warmed my stomach. I reflected that I was becoming pampered and soft, living in this luxury.

I related my visit to Thompson and what he had showed me, sparing her no details. Donata was resilient enough, even belly-full as she was, to listen without flinching. Indeed, she'd have taken me to task if I'd spared her any description.

I also showed her the cloth, which she stroked in curiosity, pronouncing it a rather well-woven cotton. The necklace too had been expensive, but we both agreed the clothes and necklace might have been gifts, or stolen.

Donata viewed the dead woman's trinkets without turning a hair. Only when I told her I'd taken the bones away in a hackney did Donata's eyes widen.

"Good heavens, Gabriel, you did not bring them here, did you?"

"Indeed, no." I drained my cup and clicked the delicate thing to its saucer. "I took them to Grenville's."

A spark lit Donata's eyes. "Did you? How delicious. What did Grenville say when you sprang them on him?"

"He does not know yet. He was not at home."

"His own fault then." Donata moved closer to me. "When you show them to him and discuss it, as you will, may I come too? I am most curious."

"A touch gruesome," I answered. "Better not."

Her look turned exasperated. "My dear Gabriel, I am not fragile porcelain. I have borne a child before, with great success. Peter is robustly healthy, terrifyingly so. I do not see what harm I can come to in Grenville's cellars."

"You are maddening," I said. "If I forbid you?"

"I will simply go myself when you are out."

In this day and age, a husband's word was absolute, and his wife was obligated to do exactly as he told her. I could prosecute my wife for disobedience, and I would not be blamed if I took my fists to her for defying me.

I knew, however, that Donata, possessing a natural air of command herself, simply thought such rules did not apply to her. She had no intention of meekly obeying me, and if I raised a hand to her, she had a powerful father ready to take me to task for it.

Or else, Donata had realized long ago that I would never hurt her, no matter how much she vexed me.

"Very well," I said, pretending to ignore her triumphant look. "I must find Denis's surgeon, and then we will go."

She was satisfied with that and thanked me tenderly, without words.

***

I had little idea where to begin hunting for the surgeon I had in mind, because I did not know his name, where he dwelt, and even if he remained in England.

I left Donata and looked about for Brewster. Brewster rarely entered my house, to the relief of those below stairs, who'd have to put up with him while he waited for me. Donata's servants considered themselves above such ruffians as Brewster and did not welcome him into their midst.

I asked the footman whose principal job it was to answer the door what had become of him. The lad pointed up the street and said, "Pub, sir."

I found Brewster in Oxford Street, in a public house he'd taken to, the Ox and Dog.

This part of Oxford Street edged between more genteel neighborhoods and the warrens of Soho and Seven Dials. Those who worked for the wealthy — coachmen, grooms, and the like — came here. Upright, hard-working people who, like Donata's servants, knew a bone-breaker when they saw one.

Brewster, however, had a knack for keeping to himself and fading into the moldings, quite a trick for such a big man. The clientele, however, had grown used to him and now ignored him.

This public house wasn't as old as some in London. Though it sported dark polished wood, settles around the large fireplace, and a scrubbed, flagstone floor, the house didn't sag at the seams, the windows were large and many-paned, and the whole place had a modern, cheerful air to it.

Brewster sat in the corner farthest from the door, his back to the wall, where he could observe the entire room from the shadows. A tankard rested in front of him, nearly empty.

The publican gave me a nod when I came in. I'd become as recognizable as Brewster, though the regulars weren't quite certain why a respectable-looking, military gentleman had such a pugilist-like acquaintance. I could feel the speculative gazes of the men in the tavern as I passed them—was Brewster my servant? Hired ruffian? Odd friend? Lover?

I paid no attention as I seated myself opposite Brewster and accepted the ale the publican put before me. I'd pay for mine as well as Brewster's, as had come to be my habit.

"I don't know where he is," Brewster said before I could speak.

"But your employer will," I replied. "Will you ask him to send the man to Grenville's house? I'm certain we can all practice discretion."

"No, I will not." Brewster locked his hands around his tankard. "You stick your neck out too far, Captain. His nibs will snap it off, one day, and I don't want mine coming off with yours."

"You only need to deliver the message. Mr. Denis will know *I* am the audacious one, not you."

Brewster's lower lip firmed in a way I'd come to know meant he would be intractable. "No. He's sent me to look after you. That means keeping you from endangering yourself from *him* as well. I have to say, watching you is more trouble than a whole flock of unruly sheep. You go off every which way. Leave it, Captain. That's my final word on it."

Chapter Four

"Very well," I said. "I will hunt down the surgeon myself."

Brewster's sigh nearly shook the table. "Will ye not listen to those with more sense than you? It's dangerous to go asking certain questions about certain people. Ye want nothing to do with the man."

I regarded Brewster in some perplexity. He was surly by nature, it was true, but he usually gave in and approached his master with my messages, deciding that if Denis grew angry at me, on my own head be it. This time, I read fear in his eyes. It made me wonder very much.

"I am seeking the surgeon's expert opinion," I said. "I have no wish to make a friend of him."

Regardless of whatever the surgeon had done to get himself sentenced to transportation, I had recognized competence, even brilliance, in the close-mouthed man. I knew that what secrets the bones had to tell me, he could reveal them.

"You're a fool," Brewster told me bluntly. "I'll have nothing to do with it. M' task is to keep you from harm, not let you race toward it."

"Better men then you have failed at such a task," I pointed out. "And I am still alive."

"Huh. Not for much longer, I'm thinking. Why do you want to go poking at old bones anyway? The poor lass is dead and gone. Nothing you can do."

I felt the stirring of pity I'd had when I'd looked down at the skeleton displayed so nakedly on the table. "Someone did that to her, took away her life, her chances. Whoever it is ought to pay."

Brewster obviously did not agree with me. He had been a help to me a time or two in the past, but he did not share my zeal for bringing culprits to justice. He, like most of the world, thought I should keep my long nose to myself.

"We are at an impasse then," I said. I drank the ale, which was a good brew, if a touch bland. The old public houses that looked as though they'd fall down about me often had the best ale in London.

"'Suppose we are," Brewster said.

"I will simply visit your employer and ask him for an address."

Brewster thunked his tankard to the table and leaned toward me.

"Now, there you go off again. I told you, I'm to keep you well and alive. If his nibs loses his temper and offs you, he'll blame *me*."

Did James Denis lose his temper? I wondered. I had seen him enraged before, but that had been a special circumstance, and the result of that rage had been deadly.

On the other hand, I'd witnessed a man set off an incendiary device in Denis's study, and Denis's sangfroid barely slip.

"You could refuse," I suggested. "When he tells you to look after me, you could ask that he give you another, less thankless, task."

"Huh," Brewster said. "Ain't worth m' life, asking something like that."

I took a final sip of ale and rose. "Then I'll be off. Perhaps I'll catch him in a good temper."

Brewster glanced at his tankard, aggrieved. "Now?"

"Indeed. If you must follow me about, then follow."

I gave coins to the publican, took up my hat and gloves, and tapped my way out to the street. Brewster, noisy with grumbles, followed.

***

I took a hackney to Curzon Street. Stumping up to the pub to find Brewster had taxed the strength in my weak leg, and I needed to rest it. That hurt my pride, but I had no wish to be laid up the rest of the day.

When we arrived at Denis's door, number 45, the stiff-faced butler informed me that Denis was not receiving, as he had another appointment.

I told the butler I would write a note. The butler assumed I meant I'd write the letter at home and send it, then realized I was determined to step into a room in this house and compose it there. He looked as aggrieved as Brewster but let me in.

I was rude, yes, and I'd never dream of being so highhanded in anyone else's house, not even Grenville's.

These men, however, had been happy to beat upon me a time or two, and had certainly threatened, hurt, and even killed others at Denis's command. I saw no reason to let them cow me. If Denis wished to use me, he would have to put up with me as I was.

The butler led me into a reception room which held a small davenport desk—a delicate, gilded piece with small drawers and a sloping writing surface. The desk could be easily carried to set in front of a sofa for the comfort of the writer.

The drawers held plenty of stiff, expensive paper, ink, and pens with nibs sharp and ready. Apparently, Mr. Denis expected this desk to be used.

Or perhaps he did not. This house was furnished and stocked down to the last detail, but much of it was for show. I never felt it was a true home.

I smoothed out paper, dipped the pen in the ink, and scratched a few words. The desk was slanted at such an angle that writing was comfortable. Perhaps I would suggest such a piece for Donata.

"Pardon me, sir," the butler said, easing his way back into the room. "Mr. Denis will see you now."

I glanced at the half sentence I'd penned, the ink already drying. I folded the paper and stuffed it into my pocket. I started to put away the ink and so forth, but another footman sidled in and began to do it for me.

I followed the impatient butler out and up the stairs, sensing his agitation.

I discovered the reason for his haste when we reached the top of the second flight, nearing Denis's study.

A cry of fear and pain sounded beneath me. Startled, I leaned over the banisters to see what was the matter, just as a man burst from a room on the floor below.

He was an ordinary-looking gentleman in a plain suit a man of business might wear. His brown hair, which was thick, stuck out every which way — from my vantage I could see the balding spot on the crown of his head. I could also see his beak of a nose on the face he turned up to me.

"Sir!" His cry was filled with despair.

Before I could answer, three of Denis's men caught up to him and bore him to the floor.

I started for the stairs. The butler tried to stop me, but while he was cast from the same mold as Denis's ruffian footmen, he was older, and I was quicker than he.

"Leave him," I snapped, hanging on to the railing as I charged downward.

The man they were beating was small and spindle-shanked, his old-fashioned knee breeches hardly adequate padding against their kicks. I put a strong hand on the broad shoulder of one of the footmen, and yanked him away.

The thug turned on me a look of astonishment, before he balled up a giant fist and heaved it toward my face.

"No." The sharp command from above, in Denis's silk-smooth voice, halted the fist in midair. "Bring the captain upstairs."

He gave no orders as to the smaller man, whom the other two footmen proceeded to beat and kick. I glared up at Denis.

"Surely he can be no more threat to you," I said. "Whatever lesson you intended to teach him is learned. If they go on, they'll kill him."

Denis's cold blue eyes found mine. I read in them great displeasure.

He waited while his footmen, paying no attention to me, got in a few more blows. Finally, he raised a hand.

"Enough."

The word was calm and not very loud, but instantly, the ruffians left off their pounding and dragged the small man to his feet.

The man was somewhere between thirty and forty, and had wide brown eyes that looked upon the world with friendliness. His face at the moment was covered in blood and bruises, a trickle of red at the side of his mouth.

"Thank you, sir," he said in a clogged whisper, not to Denis, but to me.

Denis made a curt gesture. His men dragged their hapless victim the rest of the way to the ground floor. They did not throw him into the street—no, that would attract the attention of the neighbors. A carriage had been pulled very close to the door, and Denis's men shoved the beaten man into it.

The coach pulled away, and then the footmen returned to the house, looking neither triumphant nor gloating. They were barely out of breath. They'd done their task; now they would turn to the next one.

"Captain, if you please." Denis's cold voice cut the air.

I hauled myself back up the stairs, shaking with anger.

"What sort of threat could such a small, harmless-looking man be to you?" I demanded as I followed Denis into his study.

The room I entered was barren but elegant, clean-lined, the furniture with delicate, tapered legs, the chamber free of the clutter that could fill the houses of the rich.

Denis must be one of the wealthiest gentlemen in England, but he shunned ostentation. The sole concession to luxury was a painting on the paneled wall, a portrait done in subdued but exquisite colors, the paint thick. The subject of the portrait was a painter from the Netherlands of the seventeenth century, a man with rumpled hair, a bulbous nose, and small black eyes, who looked as though he viewed the world with shrewd good humor.

I had not seen the portrait in this room before. Fortunate, I thought, that it hadn't been here when the incendiary device had exploded and ruined the walls. I wondered if the painting was a recent acquisition or had simply been moved from another room.

Denis seemed in a hurry, and impatient—for Denis. "Mr. Brewster has told me of your request," he said. "You might have saved yourself a journey. The answer is no."

"The surgeon's help would be invaluable," I said. "I need an expert, and he seemed to be."

"I cannot be expected to lay my hands on him at a moment's notice." Denis had not sat down, as usual, behind his blank-topped desk, nor had he requested that I sit. We faced each other in the middle of the room with Mr. van Rijn's portrait looking on.

I lifted my brows. "No?"

"No." Denis's look was severe. We were of a height, the two of us, though he was about ten years younger than me, and whole of body, while I leaned heavily on my stick.

"Well then," I said. "Give me his direction, and I will ask him myself."

"Not as simple a task as you suppose."

I waited for him to say more, but Denis closed his mouth and regarded me in stony silence.

I recalled what Brewster had said about the surgeon after I'd met him the first time.

When I had remarked, *He must owe Mr. Denis an enormous favor for hiding him,* Brewster had answered, *Or t'other way around.*

What hold did a convicted criminal have on Denis, who held the reins of any number of villains across Britain and the Continent?

"In that case," I said, "if you happen to chance upon him, perhaps you will mention that I would be interested in his opinion on a corpse. One that has deteriorated to bones."

Denis's brows flicked upward. "I see you have found yourself another nest of vipers to poke."

"Possibly. The woman was found in the river, near the docks at Wapping. Dead a long time. No one knows who she was or where she came from, but she was certainly killed."

"I see."

I could not decide whether Denis showed interest or not. On the one hand, nothing moved in his eyes. On the other, he didn't simply repeat his request for me to leave.

"If I can discover what happened to her," I said, not knowing why I continued to explain, "I might give her, and her family, a measure of peace."

Denis's gaze sharpened. He didn't speak, but I could almost hear his thoughts.

I had wondered and worried for years about my own daughter—had she been alive or dead? Gone forever? Denis had discovered the truth and used it to gain hold over me. I should hate him for that, but whenever my rage stirred, it quieted because *he had found my daughter.*

"I shall trouble you no more, then," I said, pretending to be as calm as he. "Good day to you."

"Good day, Captain." Denis's voice took a dry

note. I observed that he had never said he would actually pass on my message to the surgeon. Which meant he might or might not, as he chose.

I turned to go, but paused at the door the butler pointedly held open for me. "Who was the gentleman your men were so unceremoniously beating? The victim of your attentions?"

Denis's annoyance returned. "He is not so much a victim as a bloody nuisance." He eyed me severely. "As you are beginning to be."

"You have Mr. Brewster to trounce me anytime you command it," I said. "If you must teach me another lesson, I would be honored if you would let *him* do it. I have come to respect him."

Denis heaved a cool sigh. "Please go, Captain, before you try my patience too far. Else I will have all my hired help take you down the stairs and throw you out. Along with Mr. Brewster, who ought to keep you from me."

"Do not blame him," I said, bowing. "I am a slippery devil. Good afternoon."

I gave him another polite nod and left the room. It was not often I could leave Denis fuming, and I enjoyed it.

***

If I could not find Denis's surgeon to help me with the body, I would have to attempt to employ another to give me his opinion. Army surgeons were the only men of that profession I knew—I would go to the club formed by cavalrymen and ask about until I was directed toward one. I had known many on the Peninsula, but they had dispersed once the war was over, home to their families scattered all over England.

I returned to the South Audley Street house,

Brewster accompanying me in the hackney in a growling temper.

I looked forward to the evening, when I would be in the bosom of my new family. Gabriella had been spending a few days in the Berkeley Square home of Lady Aline Carrington, who was grooming her in the finer points of being a young lady, but she would be home this evening. I'd spend time with young Peter, Donata's son, of whom I was growing quite fond. Peter had the brutish strength of his deceased father but the sharp mind of his mother. I was pleased to be able to watch him flourish.

Before I could go to Donata's chamber and tell her what I had learned, Barnstable sought me out in my study, a pained look on his face.

Barnstable had crisp black hair that I suspected he touched with something from a bottle, a lean face, and intense brown eyes. He could display the greatest hauteur as a butler, but he was also a human being, very protective of his mistress and her family.

"Sir," Barnstable said, indignation in his eyes. "There is a *person* asking to see you."

I waited, but he simply stood and radiated disapproval. "Does this person have a name?"

The chill in Barnstable's voice could have sent frost up the walls. "I have put him in the back reception room."

Banished, that meant, to the chamber held for the least desirable of visitors. It also meant the visitor was a man of the middle or upper classes, or else he'd not have been admitted to the house at all.

"You did not answer about his name," I said.

"He has a card." Barnstable held it out to me between two fingers. Another mark of disapprobation—he delivered cards of Donata's visitors on a silver salver.

I saw why Barnstable hadn't wanted to tell me the man's name. The card bore, in plain black script, *Mr. Benjamin Molodzinski.* Likely Barnstable hadn't looked forward to wrapping his tongue around all the syllables. The card also proclaimed that Mr. Molodzinski had an office in a lane off Cornhill, in the City.

My curiosity was roused. An unusual name and an unusual visitor. I closed the card in my hand.

"I will speak to him. Thank you, Barnstable."

I descended the two flights of stairs from my study, my knee protesting, and reached the ground floor.

The rear reception room, a tiny niche of a chamber behind the stairs, had no windows. I wondered what the box of a room had been meant to be when the house was built, but presently it was furnished with uncomfortable chairs and dimly lit, to encourage the unwanted visitor to give up and quickly seek his way out.

My visitor today had waited. I walked in and stopped in surprise.

Facing me was the man Denis's men had pummeled then tossed into a carriage. His thick brown hair was snarled, and his face was bruised and bloody, one eye swollen shut.

"Forgive me, Captain," the man said. He drew himself up with what dignity he could. "I took the liberty of inquiring who you were and where you lived, and I'm afraid I followed you home. Will you speak to me, sir?"

Chapter Five

Of course I would speak to him. I very much wanted to know all about him.

I bade Mr. Molodzinski follow me from the reception room to the main drawing room.

We remained on the ground floor — I did not want to upset Barnstable's sensibilities by taking a stranger to the private rooms in the house. Nor did I want Mr. Molodzinski near my wife before I knew who he was and what he wanted.

It was Bartholomew, my valet, who brought in a bowl of water and cloths and doctored Molodzinski's wounds as he sat in a straight-backed chair, towels draped over him. The man submitted to the treatment with good grace.

"You may speak in front of Bartholomew," I said. "He is discreet."

Bartholomew shot me a grateful glance. He was as curious as I was, I could see.

"I wish to thank you for intervening for me,"

Molodzinski began. "It was good of you. And very brave."

"Futile," I said. "I didn't prevent them working you over."

"Ah." Molodzinski waved a hand at his battered face. "This is nothing I have not experienced before. My large nose tends to attract men's fists."

I had supposed, with his name, that the man would be foreign, but his English was as clear and succinct as mine, and possessed the slight cant of London. No one who hadn't grown up in this metropolis would speak so.

London, however, attracted men from all walks of life from all over the world. The long war with France had sent many a refugee to England's shores, and those families settled in and began to produce generations of children. Molodzinski's father might speak in a thick accent of some distant place on the Continent, but this man had grown up among Londoners.

Barnstable finished his ministrations but took his time with the bandages. He wanted to hear the man's story.

"I owe Mr. Denis money," the man confessed. "An ironic situation, as I am usually advising gentlemen about theirs. But I am afraid I owe him many thousands of pounds."

I wondered if Molodzinski had come to touch me for blunt. Before I could think of a way to politely put him off, the man smiled weakly.

"Mr. Denis knew I would not be able to pay him back such a sum for many years, so he was happy to take my services in lieu. Only, there I have been remiss in paying him. This afternoon, he was showing his … er … impatience."

"I see," I said. "You have my sympathy. I am also often remiss in rendering my services to Mr. Denis. He shows similar impatience with me."

"I thought so," Molodzinski said. "You were very good to try to stop him."

Bartholomew shot me a curious glance, wondering what on earth I'd done now. I quelled his look and returned to Molodzinski.

"What can I do for you, Mr. ... Molodzinski? Have I got that right?"

Molodzinski looked impressed. "You are one of the few Englishmen who do not tangle my name in their mouths. My family is Polish, though we have lived in London for several generations. I feel quite English myself, though plenty do not consider me to be so."

I understood why. While England's shores were a safe haven for those of many countries, at the same time, anything un-English was looked at askance. Also, if I understood aright, he was a Jew.

Grenville had plenty of men of Hebrew origin in the circle of his acquaintance, those who kept to their religion as well as those who had joined the Church of England in order to further their careers.

In this enlightened age, laws were strict with regards to any one not in the C of E. A Jewish man could not stand for Parliament, vote, or practice certain trades. They could, however, attend their own houses of worship—the synagogues—and were not barred from gaining vast amounts of wealth, as had the famous Rothschild family or Moses Montefiore, Rothschild's brother-in-law and successful businessman in his own right.

Molodzinski looked a man of far more modest means, though his clothes were well made and respectable enough.

"You have not told me why you sought me," I said.

Molodzinski looked surprised. "No? I beg your pardon, sir. I only wished to thank you for trying to help me. It was kind of you. But also to warn you. Mr. Denis is a hard man. Do not anger him, I beg you. If you were in his house, then you owe him as well. Extricate yourself from him as quickly and completely as possible."

Sound advice. I gave him a faint smile. "I am afraid your warning comes far too late. Mr. Denis has his hand well around my throat."

Molodzinski's expression turned to one of compassion. "Then I am sorry for you, sir. In that case, it was doubly courageous of you to come to my defense. If ever you need a favor, you have only to ask me, Captain. I am in your debt."

He stood and held out his hand. I took it, looking into eyes that were ingenuous and sincere.

Bartholomew had managed to put a bandage on his face, which looked awkward against his flesh, but Molodzinski's pride was undiminished.

I took his hand, felt his firm clasp, then the man nodded at me and took his leave.

Barnstable had unbent somewhat by the time we emerged, seeing that I'd received Molodzinski without concern, and he sent a footman running for a hackney. Bartholomew and I bundled Molodzinski into it. Molodzinski touched his hat, lifted his hand in a wave, then fell against the seat as the hackney jerked forward.

I was left wondering what on earth such a good-natured man had done to earn the wrath of James Denis.

***

My daughter, Gabriella, returned home from Lady Aline's soon after that, her eyes alight with excitement.

"I am learning quite a lot on the pianoforte," she said to me as I met her in the private parlor where the family usually gathered, though she and I were alone at the moment.

I watched Gabriella as she wandered about the room, too energetic to sit still. Her hair was glossy brown, a shade lighter than mine, but she had the Lacey brown eyes. Fortunately for her, she resembled her mother about the face, and had been spared my large, square jaw.

"This pleases you, does it?" I asked.

Gabriella turned to me and gave me a rueful smile. "I beg your pardon, sir. Lady Aline gives me so many attentions, as does Lady Donata, that it will quite turn my head."

"You deserve their attentions. You are a lovely young woman."

She was, I observed with a pang. I'd lost Gabriella when she'd been only two years old, a chatty, adorable girl who ran fearlessly about army camps or our tiny backstreet house in Paris.

I'd not seen her from the day her mother took her and fled until Gabriella had returned to London last year, a young lady of seventeen. She was grown now, and beautiful, but I still saw in her restlessness the quick mind and curiosity of that baby girl.

Gabriella blushed under my praise, made herself cease fluttering, and came to sit beside me.

"Father, I know that the attentions to me—the dancing instructions, the music masters, the endless lessons on how to address everyone from a scullery maid to a duchess—are to make me presentable enough to gain the favor of a gentleman once I am out. I am to marry whoever that gentleman is." Gabriella lost her delight. "Only, I am not certain I wish to marry. Not yet. I am very young."

Ladies in Donata's and Aline's circles wed at Gabriella's age and younger. I knew both women worried that if Gabriella did not "take" this Season, she might be left on the shelf.

The ladies and gentlemen not in the aristocratic circle, however, such as Gabriella and myself, might wait a bit longer for matrimony. A prudent father in the country gentry would seek the very best match for his daughter, even if it took some years.

I tried to sound comforting. "Do not let my wife and Lady Aline goad you into a marriage you do not want. Marriage is for life. Be careful whom you choose."

My words brought back her eagerness. "Oh, I shall, sir. I have no wish to run headlong into wedlock with a spindly gentleman with no chin, a hawk nose, and a sour disposition simply because he is the Baron of Nonesuch."

I could hear Lady Aline's decided opinions ringing in her words. Gabriella admired Lady Aline—a determined spinster—very much.

"There," I said. "You see? You have a sensible regard for these things."

Her face fell again, her moods as changeable as the wind. "But I hate to disappoint Lady Donata. She has been so kind to me."

Donata had devoted herself to Gabriella's come-out with the zeal of a Methodist trying to convert the masses of London from a street corner. I did not know whether Donata was enjoying herself because she might never have a daughter of her own to indulge, or because her first marriage had been so unhappy that she wished to guide Gabriella down a different path.

Whatever the reason, Donata had certainly thrown herself into the task.

"Donata only wants to see you content," I said. "She would be the last person to wish you married to the Baron of Nonesuch, unless he made you very happy indeed."

The smile returned. "Well, that would be a relief. She does give me reams of information every day on this gentleman or that, who his family is, why he'd make a good husband. No one too lofty, mind. Apparently, I am quite the nobody."

I raised my brows. "Donata said that?"

"She does not have to. Pedigree is all important in this endeavor, I believe. While I am a gentleman's daughter, I have neither title nor vast wealth to make me much of a catch."

Donata had already explained this to me, somewhat apologetically; Aline with her brisk no-nonsense approach to life.

"They wish to marry you off, because that is what ladies of their acquaintance do," I said. "A woman either marries and becomes a grand hostess or does not marry at all and lives quietly in a back room. But neither path must be for you. I am surprised at Lady Aline—she is quite proud of avoiding the married state herself."

"But she is the sister of a marquis, has much wealth, and many connections," Gabriella said. "I asked her, point blank, why she wishes me to marry, when she so adamantly did not. Things are different for her, she said. She has the leisure to never marry if she does not want to. Her father saw to that by settling a large amount of money on her."

Something I could never do. "Even so," I said. "Do not marry to please Donata and Lady Aline. It is a step to be considered carefully."

Gabriella leaned forward and kissed me on the cheek. "You are a wise man, sir. I will heed your words."

Again restless, she leapt up, ready to run from the room. Gabriella seemed to remember, at the last moment, that a young lady should not dash away from her elders until she had leave, and she hovered at the door.

I had risen from my seat when she hopped up, and I gave her a nod. "Go on, then."

Another sunny smile, a hurried curtsey, and Gabriella whirled from the room, her footsteps rapid on the stairs.

She left me with a lighter heart. I loved her so.

***

I did not hear from Grenville all day. Presumably he had not returned home—I felt certain he'd have sent a rapidly penned note, or turned up on the doorstep himself, when he learned of the corpse in his wine cellar.

I did journey to the cavalrymen's club in St. James's after I had told Donata of my failed quest to find the surgeon, to inquire about surgeons there. The elderly colonels I'd found only looked at me blankly, and I left disappointed.

That evening, I would attend the opera at Covent Garden with my wife and Lady Aline. As Gabriella was not officially "out" yet, she would remain home, which I thought ridiculous, but Donata was firm. Last year, when Gabriella had visited, we'd taken her about, but at the time, she'd been considered more of a tourist and a child than a young lady being readied to be presented to the *ton*.

I would be glad when Gabriella's come-out ball, planned for next week, was done with, and we could all breathe out again.

We traveled to Covent Garden in Lady Aline's coach, that tall, white-haired lady saying she felt honored to have such a handsome gentleman escorting her. She thoroughly approved of me, she said, since I was not tiresome and actually knew how to be polite to a woman of her advanced years. Donata only looked on, pleased that Aline, one of her mother's closest friends, and I got along so well.

Donata's box was lavish, and as usual, full of guests. At the interval, plenty of ladies and gentlemen visited to gossip away. Donata, in one of her extravagant headdresses, sat happily in the middle of it.

I slipped out, seeking a moment away from the chaos. Donata saw me go, and understood. She was in her element here, but knew I was not.

Under the colonnade outside, hopeful ladies of the demimonde smiled at me, but they recognized me and knew I was a devoted husband. That did not prevent them teasing me, however.

"Now then, Captain," one young lady said, slipping her hand into the crook of my arm. "Walk with me a bit, will you?"

She was several steps above a street girl—the kind Black Nancy had been. She reminded me more of Marianne Simmons, an actress who had taken up with protectors for survival.

This young woman had black hair and blue eyes, wore plenty of rouge on cheeks and on her bosom, and dressed in an elegant gown of blue lace and silk worthy of Donata.

"I emerged only to take the air," I said to her. "Nothing else. I would rather walk alone."

"No, you would not," she said, steering me from the piazza with a surprisingly strong hand.

"If you are dragging me off to rob me, I must warn you I have very little," I said. "My watch fob was given to me by my wife, so I must ask to keep that, though you are welcome to the few coins in my pocket. And to my handkerchief. My valet is quite adamant about keeping me in linens."

The young woman laughed. "Ain't you a one? I wish you *weren't* so interested in your wife, sir. You'd be lively. Perhaps when you grow tired of married life, you'll seek me?"

"If my wife shows me the door for hurrying away with you now, I will be back in my rooms above a bakeshop and hopelessly poor again," I said. "Shall you risk it?"

She only pealed in laughter again. She had been determinedly walking me around the corner to James Street, which led south into the large square that was Covent Garden.

This late, the vendors would have closed up and gone, to wait for early morning when their wares came in from the country. At the moment, Covent Garden would be home to the denizens of the night, ready to prey on the unwary.

I managed to detach myself from the lady as we walked down the shadowy street, but she grabbed me again in a firm grip. Another young woman closed on me from the other side, this one a street girl, and together, the pair dragged me on toward the square.

They must have known I would not deliberately hurt a woman. I was pondering making an exception in this case—they might be taking me to men who would relieve me of my watch, its precious fob, coins, and even clothes, which would fetch a good price with secondhand merchants.

I noted the absence of Brewster, who would be handy about now. Of course, he'd choose this instance to grow tired of following me.

The ladies drew me to a halt in the deep shadow of an arch in a corner of Covent Garden market. On the other side of this wall, ironically, was Grimpen Lane, where my rooms above the bakeshop lay.

"I promise you," I tried. "You'd do better to lie in wait for a wealthier gentleman."

My young lady in finery grinned. "Never you mind that. We've not brought you here to rob you. A friend wants to speak to you."

"Friend?" I could not imagine who they meant. I knew several of the street girls, most notably Felicity, a black-skinned young woman who had a ruthless streak in her. Felicity, however, if she wished to see me, would simply find me herself.

"He's not much for the opera," the young woman continued.

"If he wishes to call upon me, he has only to send a card," I said. "Or a letter. I can arrange to meet him in my rooms if he wishes anonymity."

She patted my arm. "He never said you were so amusing."

The street girl who'd come to help her remained silent, unsmiling. Behind the belligerence in her eyes, I read worry. I wondered very much.

"Captain." A terse voice came out of the darkness. "I had word you wished to speak with me."

I recognized the accent with its touch of the west of England, the man holding a hardness that was quiet but with an edge. As my eyes adjusted to the darkness, I saw the balding head and sharp face of the surgeon I'd met a few months ago, the one I'd gone to Denis to seek.

He did not emerge from the shadows, but I gave him a bow. "Well met," I said. "You are a difficult man to find."

Chapter Six

The surgeon did not speak as I told him quietly what I wished him to do. The courtesan and the street girl faded from us, disappearing into the gathering mists, as though they'd never been there.

The surgeon studied me with cold dark eyes as I described the bones and related how I'd taken them from the house in Wapping to store at Grenville's. I saw no flicker of interest, nothing.

"I'd be most grateful for your opinion," I finished.

The man watched me for a few more heartbeats, before he said. "We'll go now."

I recalled Donata's insistence than when I examined the bones again she come with me. However, I knew that if I asked the surgeon to wait while I dashed back into the opera house to fetch her, he would fade as quickly as the young women had done. I'd never see him again.

I gave him a nod. "I will find a hackney."

"I have a conveyance." He turned abruptly and

strode into the mist.

I hobbled after him, my stick making too much noise on the cobbles. Fog magnified sound in the square which, while it still had plenty of people wandering about it, was eerily quiet tonight.

I reached Russel Street to find the surgeon waiting by a dark carriage pulled by two bay horses. A coachman hunkered on his box, head bent against the fog. He looked nothing more than a bundle of clothes with a whip poking from them.

The surgeon opened the small coach's door. I put my foot on the step, preparing to haul myself inside when his hand on my elbow assisted me up efficiently. His grip was strong, his guidance sure. I sat down without my usual difficulty.

The surgeon climbed quietly in as I planted my walking stick on the floor. He glanced once at the stick, no doubt remembering I kept a stout sword inside it.

He said not a word to me as we trundled through foggy London from Covent Garden to Mayfair. We went by way of Long Acre, then to Leicester Square and Coventry Street to Piccadilly. North through Berkeley Square and so to Grosvenor Street, the coach halting precisely at Grenville's front door.

During this journey, the surgeon had not spoken. He'd not gazed out the window or at me, only fixed his eyes on some point behind me and remained silent.

When the coach stopped, the surgeon looked at me directly. "Go inside. Keep the servants away, then return and fetch me."

I nodded my understanding and opened the coach's door before the footman in Grenville's vestibule could do it for me. I got myself down as the lad reached me, and shut the carriage door before he could look inside.

Grenville was at home, the footman informed me, but dressing to go out. I knew just how long this process could take, and I knew that if I made the surgeon wait, or if Grenville commanded a servant to bring him inside, he'd simply leave. I had this chance and no other.

I handed the footman a coin. Servants expected gratuity from guests they assisted, though Grenville's had long ago forgiven me that obligation. The lad looked startled and stared at the penny in his hand.

"No need, sir," he began to say, but I shook my head.

"Send Matthias to me, if he is here. And go downstairs and have some ... coffee."

I tapped the side of my nose. The footman looked enlightened—I was asking for discretion, though he wasn't certain what for.

He darted off for the back stairs, and I waited in the cool staircase hall, hoping Matthias wouldn't be too long. I could give the order to Matthias to clear the ground floor and path to the cellar and be certain he'd carry it out without question—at least, he'd save his questions for later.

However, it was not Matthias who came down the stairs on light feet but Grenville himself.

"Lacey?" he called as he skimmed down the steps. "What the devil? You dash in here and leave a *corpse* in my cellar without so much as a note for explanation. I send word to South Audley Street demanding to know what you mean by it, and I'm told you're at the opera of all places. Damn it, man, what is it all about?"

Grenville's eyes were alight, but with curiosity, not anger. He'd once told me he'd befriended me because he could never be certain what I would do, and today I had only confirmed this conviction.

I decided to let his curiosity burn a little longer. "Come and see. May we enter your cellars? Or did you move the poor woman?"

"Woman, is it?"

Grenville reached the foot of the stairs. He was dressed to go out, in black pantaloons with buttons at his ankles, fine shoes, a pristine linen shirt and perfectly knotted cravat. Only his coat was wrong — a frock coat meant to be worn in the afternoon rather than a formal evening one.

He must have snatched up the first garment he'd laid hands on in his charge downstairs, which conveyed his agitation more than words ever could. The fact that he readily skimmed toward the backstairs without even thinking to change his clothes also betrayed his eagerness.

Despite Grenville's swift pace, Matthias appeared and reached the door to the backstairs before him — Grenville rarely touched a door handle in his own house.

"Wait," I commanded. I surged forward and gave Matthias the orders I'd meant to give before Grenville appeared — to clear the way so that none would see who entered.

Matthias obviously wanted to ask why, but he only nodded and slipped down the stairs to obey.

Not long later, Matthias led me, Grenville, and the surgeon through the eerily deserted passages that led past the servants' hall, the kitchen where Anton had accosted me earlier, and the scullery. Candles burned in holders and in sconces, lighting no one.

The wine cellar was illuminated by a few lanterns hung on the walls in anticipation of our arrival. The crate was where I'd left it, between tall racks that were half full of bottles. Some of the finest port and small casks of brandy reposed here, and I'd shoved a box of old bones among them.

Matthias, on my order, dragged it out. Grenville gestured to a table on the other side of the room, and Matthias lugged the crate to it.

"You can imagine what transpired when I had Matthias open this not an hour ago so I could look inside," Grenville said as Matthias maneuvered the crate to the top of the table. "He pried loose the lid, and a grinning skull looked up at us. I believe our collective shout reached the top of the house."

"You weren't that loud, sir," Matthias said. He took up an iron bar for opening crates of wine. "I imagine your voice only reached the kitchen." He busily loosened the lid and set it aside.

The surgeon had said nothing at all as Grenville and Matthias had chattered nervously. He'd remained in the shadows, several paces behind us. Now he came forward and reached into the box himself.

As Thompson had in the rooms under the magistrate's house, the surgeon competently laid out the skeleton. He did so more quickly than Thompson, never having to pause to decide what went where.

In less than ten minutes, he'd reconstructed the body of the woman, stretched out across Grenville's table, the brown bones small and pitiable.

The surgeon remained silent as he bent to study the body. When he needed more light, he snapped his fingers at Matthias and pointed to a lantern, which Matthias brought without question.

The surgeon took the candle out of the lantern, and leaned with it over the bones, cupping his hand to keep the wax from dripping.

The three of us watching didn't speak at all. I couldn't take my eyes from the surgeon as he nearly pressed his nose to the body, examining every single bone, every joint, every dried bit of skin that clung here and there.

"Female," he said at long last. "As you said. Young. Never bore a child. From a middle-class family, possibly a wealthy one. A healthy young woman, robust. This ..." He pointed to the crack in her skull "... no doubt killed her. No other signs of injury. She was struck hard, once, with a thin, blunt object. Poker, maybe. Or maybe an iron bar of some kind. Died almost instantly. Whoever struck the blow either was very lucky or knew precisely how to do it."

"The injury could not have been from a fall?" I asked. "Or something falling on *her*? An accident?"

The surgeon shook his head. "Her face would have been more crushed, with more splintering of bones. She was struck." He leaned closer to her. "I put her age about nineteen, certainly no more than early twenties. Where did you say she was found?"

"Wapping docks," I said. "Caught under a piling. Found ten years ago."

"Mm." The surgeon touched the woman's arm bone, rubbing his finger along it. "If she was in the water from her time of death, I'd guess she'd been there no less than a few years. Flesh deteriorates quickly and fish consume it in a surprisingly short time. She is nothing but bones—five years might be the outside mark, if she were thrown into the water right away. I can be no more accurate."

Grenville blinked. "Good God—it's accurate enough. How on earth can you know all that?"

The surgeon met his gaze, his eyes cold and remote. "That she was healthy, her bones strong, her body straight, suggest to me she was not of the working class. She has a family wealthy enough to feed her and care for her, and she did not have to do manual labor. State of her teeth tell me how old she was. I speculate she is not an aristocrat or gentry, because a great to-do would have been made of her disappearance. This suggests her family is not significant enough to have every detail about them printed in the papers."

I removed the necklace and strip of cloth Thompson had given me from my pocket. Donata had pronounced the cloth fine and the necklace delicately wrought gold, which supported the surgeon's theory that her family had had money.

Grenville took the necklace with interest. "A fine piece. Thompson is certain it belongs with the young woman?"

"It was around her neck," I replied. "Fused as one piece, he said. He had to cut it from her. Could Gautier help us with that, do you think?"

"I will ask him," Grenville said. He looked ready to dash away and find the man on the instant, but he steadied himself. "Anything else you can tell us about this poor girl?" he asked the surgeon. "Not that you haven't related a veritable stream of information already."

"She had a broken arm at one point." The surgeon pointed to a bone in her forearm that looked perfectly fine to me. "Possibly shortly before her death, though not immediately before. It was set well, mended cleanly."

Grenville let out a breath. "I suppose we could question every surgeon in the country to determine which one set the arm of a girl, say fifteen years ago? A bit daunting."

"No need," the surgeon said. "Only one in London helps breaks heal this cleanly. He must be an old man now, but if he is still alive, he might remember. Jonas Coombs. Tottenham Court Road."

I pursed my lips, impressed. "If Thompson had been able to consult you years ago, he might have found the woman's identity and solved her murder immediately."

For the first time since I'd met him, I saw something like humor flicker over the surgeon's face. "I was detained."

"Never mind—it's a help now," Grenville said. "I will inquire as to the whereabouts of Jonas Coombs of Tottenham Court Road. And put Gautier on the trail of this necklace. Mr. Thompson will have his mystery solved in no time."

I was not so optimistic, but then again, I'd had no hope we would come by so much knowledge so quickly.

"Thank you," I said to the surgeon. "I'll see you are compensated for your time."

"No need." The surgeon's amusement had swiftly faded. "My price is silence, Captain. See that you keep it.

Chapter Seven

We saw the surgeon upstairs, the house remaining empty and quiet from kitchen to front door.

The same coach and coachman waited. The surgeon nodded a good-bye to me and Grenville and got himself into the carriage, which rattled off into the darkness and fog.

"Well," Grenville said as Matthias shut the door. "That was worth missing Lady Longwood's soiree for. He's an interesting man."

"A dangerous one, I'd wager," I said. "Even Denis seems a bit cautious about him. Now, shall you rush late to your soiree or ask Gautier about the necklace?"

"Your sense of humor is remarkable, Lacey. Come along."

We ascended to the upper part of the house, Matthias disappearing down the back stairs, presumably to tell the servants they could emerge from hiding.

Gautier was in Grenville's dressing room, attending to a coat. The coat hung on a rack that put it at Gautier's height as he went over it with a pale-bristled brush.

"Sir," Gautier said as Grenville led me in. His look of disapproval at the frock coat Grenville now slid from his shoulders would have been comical at another time.

Grenville handed the valet the necklace without preliminary. "Could you find out who made that?"

Gautier, his interest caught, held up the chain to the light of the elegant triple-candle sconce behind him.

It was a simple gold necklace with an oval locket, the sort ladies wore as remembrances. Inside would be a miniature or lock of hair of a loved one — mother, sister, father, husband — but as I had observed, this locket was empty.

"An old piece," Gautier announced. "An heirloom, I presume. Not English, not originally. Though it *might* have been made in England, but from someone trained on the Continent."

"Where on the Continent?" I asked. "France?"

Gautier shook his head. "I'd say something German. Bavaria, perhaps, or Bohemia or farther east than that. Jewelers there copy French styles but in a different way. They like heavier pieces but at the same time not so ostentatious. This is well made, expensive."

"We're looking for its owner," Grenville said. "Would a jeweler in London know the piece? Even if it came from the Continent, perhaps the young lady or her family had it repaired at some point."

Gautier tried but failed to mask his enthusiasm. "I will inquire, sir."

"Good man. Lacey, I must attend this blasted soiree, but you will tell me everything tomorrow, won't you?"

"Indeed. As soon as my wife releases me from the dungeon for disappearing from the opera and not returning."

Grenville did not laugh. "Lacey, one thing you will learn about Donata is her equanimity. Every wife in the *ton* expects her husband will make himself scarce from her most of the time. I imagine she will take no notice of your absence."

I was not so sanguine, but I thanked him for use of his cellars and promised I'd return the bones to Thompson.

"Not at all," Grenville said. "Once I got over my shock, I knew of course that you were on a new adventure. But perhaps a note would be best next time, my dear fellow."

***

I could not make my apologies to Donata for leaving her behind when I reached home, because she had not yet returned. I speculated that she would be more disappointed in me because she hadn't been there for the surgeon's assessment than because I had deserted her at the opera house. Donata had many friends and a lively nature, and she'd scarcely miss me.

Brewster, on the other hand, was there to greet me when I descended from the carriage.

"Captain," he said. "You learn what you wanted?"

Bartholomew had the front door open, a fissure to warmth and light. I lingered in the dark fog. "I learned a great deal. I take it that you had something to do with the expedition?"

"Mayhap." Brewster's expression did not change. "We keep this 'atween you and me, Captain. His nibs don't need to know."

"Of course," I said at once, but I was surprised. Denis's minions rarely disobeyed him, and Brewster had been adamant about me not speaking to the surgeon. "Thank you," I added. Brewster had done this favor for me at considerable risk to himself.

"Aye, well. Knew you wouldn't let it rest, and would find trouble if you continued." Brewster touched his hat. "Night, sir."

"Good night. Give my best to your wife."

"Yes, sir." He remained stone-faced, and I could not tell if he were angry or pleased with my sentiment.

Brewster touched his hat again and faded into the shadows, and I entered the well-lit house.

As had become my habit, I ascended to the chambers of first Peter, then my daughter, making certain they slept and were well.

Peter was growing—he'd put on a few inches since I'd met him—and would soon move out of the nursery and into his own chamber. Not long after that, he'd begin school. It was to be Harrow for him, as it had been for me.

I straightened the covers over the sleeping boy, my stepson, and left the nursery.

Gabriella's room lay on the same floor as the nursery, her windows overlooking the back garden. Her bedroom was a pleasing chamber—it held a bed with four delicate, tall posts draped with embroidered hangings, walls in a pale cream with plaster medallions in an elegant frieze, sconces dripping with faceted crystals, a chest of drawers and bedside tables with walnut burl veneer.

Gabriella slept with one arm flung across her pillow, her cheeks flushed. She breathed easily and deeply, the sleep of one with no troubles.

Donata and Aline were keen to marry her off, to make a brilliant match that would be a triumph for them. But for now Gabriella was my girl, lovely, good-natured, with a lively mind. I would hold on to her as long as I could.

I smoothed her covers as I had for Peter, carefully so as not to awaken her, and returned to my own chamber.

Bartholomew readied me for bed and asked me what the surgeon had told us. Apparently, his brother had already sent word about where I had been.

I related the tale, and Bartholomew listened with his usual interest. "We're off again, are we?" he asked. "You will let me help, sir?"

The question was delivered in a tone of admonishment. He was not pleased he'd been left out of tonight's consultation.

"Of course," I assured him. "Finding this woman's identity will be quite a puzzle. I have to wonder whether her absence was reported to the Runners, but Pomeroy may have some information in that regard. And we will again have to comb through the shops of London to find all we can about a necklace."

"I'm your man," Bartholomew promised. He paused in the act of carrying my clothes to the dressing room. "You will take me with you before you go off investigating, won't you? Only, you do tend to rush headlong, sir, begging your pardon. And her ladyship, she'll blame me if anything happens to you."

I tied my warm dressing gown around me and gave him a severe look. "I would not dream of rushing headlong without you, Bartholomew. Now, good night."

"Sir." Bartholomew, looking pleased, retreated to the dressing room.

I settled myself by the fire to wait for Donata. I heard Bartholomew bustling about the dressing room as he put my clothes to rights, then silence as he at last slunk off to bed.

I indulged myself in a brandy and book. Donata had a small library, Grenville an extensive one, and the two between them kept me in reading material.

I liked books about history and the world best, and I was reading an account of Lord Elgin's travels to ancient monuments. I was more fascinated at the moment by Egypt than Athens, but I admitted the wonders of Greece were astonishing.

Donata was often late returning home, so I did not worry when she remained absent at two, then three. At four, I began to wonder; at five, when the sun began to rise, I left my chair and paced. At six, the June morning already bright, I was in my dressing room, heaving on my clothes.

I banged down the stairs to the unguarded front door. A footman was usually on duty to admit visitors during the day, but he'd either still be rising from his bed or downstairs helping prepare the house for the morning.

Barnstable, hearing me, emerged from the sunny dining room where he and a footman were laying out the breakfast things. "Sir?"

"Did Lady Breckenridge come in last night?" I demanded. "Is she tucked away somewhere, asleep?"

Barnstable, who had a fork in his hand, blinked but did not look unduly worried. "She sometimes stays with Lady Aline, sir," he said. "If she is out very late and does not wish to ride home alone."

"I see." My fears subsided the slightest bit but not very much.

"Shall I send someone to inquire, sir?"

"No, I'm dressed and will go myself. If she is well, I'll escort her home."

Barnstable's rising brows signaled to me that he did not approve, but my agitated state put me beyond caring how crass Donata's butler thought me.

I knew it was not the thing for a husband to go tearing across Mayfair looking for his wife, but trepidation gripped me, and I would not be easy until I found her. Donata would gaze at me crossly and tell me I deserved my worry for vanishing last night, but I would bear her annoyance as long as she was well.

I conceded to let Barnstable call for the coach. Donata's lady's maid, a Frenchwoman called Jacinthe, also had not returned, which made me hope Barnstable was right—Jacinthe would have stayed at Lady Aline's to take care of Donata's needs.

Our coachman, Hagen, could provide no information, as we had journeyed to Covent Garden last night in Lady Aline's conveyance. But he had not been sent for, nor received any word from her ladyship.

Hagen quickly and without fuss drove me to Berkeley Square. Lady Aline Carrington, sister to the Marquis of Weymouth, spent the Season in London in a lavish, rather modern house in Mayfair, while her brother maintained the older family residence in

Portman Square.

Aline defied convention by living alone — without companion, brother, mother, sister — but her reputation and opinions were so well-known that exceptions were made for her. Lady Aline had been a member of the bluestocking set of her day, and still was, writing pamphlets on the place of women in society, and setting the bastion of old-fashioned males of London on edge. She drew to her the most brilliant of people — artists, writers, lecturers, mathematicians, scientists, actors and actresses, musicians and singers.

Donata had been drawn early into her circle. These days, Donata and Aline more or less set the taste for London in music, poetry, and opera, while Grenville set it for art, gentlemen's clothing, food, and wine.

I'd met Lady Aline very soon after arriving in London, and had found a friend in her. At this hour of the morning, however, my friendship won me nothing.

A footman gazed at me stonily, unhappy I'd brought him upstairs from where the household was preparing for the day. He declared that Lady Aline by no means would descend to see me.

"If my wife is in the house, I will leave without fuss," I said. "If not ..." I made as though to move past him.

The footman, a tall, rather muscular young man, stepped in front of me. "Viscountess Breckenridge is not here, sir."

"Then I must insist on speaking to Lady Aline. I'll shout through the keyhole if need be."

"Her ladyship is not to be disturbed," the footman replied firmly.

Other servants were appearing, Aline's aged butler and several maids, all looking annoyed. An upstart captain of uneven temper demanding entry at six in the morning was not to be borne.

"I'll speak to your coachman then," I said. "I suppose I will not have to shout through a keyhole to *him*."

The footman scowled at me. "The coachman is not here either, sir."

"Then where the devil is he?"

The footman had been well trained, and was good, I knew, at being silent, decorative, and efficient, but he had reached the end of his tether. He was ready to throw me to the pavement.

The butler, no less put out with me, came forward. "If you will allow me to explain, sir. Her ladyship and the viscountess arrived here late last evening. Her ladyship descended, but the coachman drove the viscountess on. The coachman has not returned, but we know he has met with no accident. He sent word that he was spending the evening at a public house on the Brompton Road."

My qualms were not eased. Brompton was not a great distance—south of Hyde Park and not far from Tattersall's. But even so, why should Donata order Aline's coach to Brompton or thereabouts and not return?

"Did he say which public house?" I asked irritably. Aline's servants obviously expected me to run home quietly and wait for the return of my eccentric wife without fuss.

"The Hound and Hen," the butler said, tight-lipped. "The publican is his cousin. I will tell her ladyship you called."

They *would* throw me to the pavement in another

minute. I growled a thanks at the butler and retreated.

Donata's coachman, Hagen, sharing my concern for his mistress, readily drove me south to Piccadilly and west to Knightsbridge, then angled southwest on the Brompton Road. London began to turn to country here, with gardens and plant nurseries, cricket grounds, and farms in the distance.

The Hound and Hen, a pretty country inn, was on Brompton Lane. When we entered its yard, I saw Aline's coachman emerging from the house. I descended as quickly as I could, making my way to him before he could vanish into the stables.

"Sir?" Aline's coachman blinked at me in surprise. He was a large specimen of a man, filling out his red coat. He had a round face, canine teeth filed to points, a large nose, small eyes, and not much hair on his head. He made up for the lack of hair on top by growing a set of luxurious side whiskers.

Hagen had come off the top of our coach. "Don't *sir* him," he snapped. "You tell him where ye took the mistress."

Unlike Aline's man, Hagen was lean and ropy, with a leathery face, dark eyes, and a thick shock of brown hair. I always thought he looked more like a highwayman than a coachman, but he was a skilled driver and protective of Donata and her son.

Aline's coachman was much more good-natured, apt to tell a joke he'd heard or talk horse with me in a spare moment, but at present, he looked nonplussed. "I took her nowhere," he said in bewilderment.

"Then where is she?" I demanded.

"Answer him," Hagen said. He took a belligerent step to Aline's coachman, murder in his eyes. "She was with her ladyship, then you came here. What happened in between?"

"I set her down in Park Lane, as she told me," the coachman said. "She gave me quite a few coins and suggested I visit my cousin. She'd send for her own conveyance to go home, she said. Kind of her, I thought." He ended with a defiant look at Hagen.

I held on to my patience. "What house in Park Lane?"

"Near Brick Lane. I saw her go into the courtyard — she has friends there, she said."

Since Donata had friends and acquaintance all over London, this sounded plausible. Less plausible that she'd sent the coach away and hadn't bothered to tell Hagen and her own household.

"Her abigail descended with her?" I asked.

"Of course." Aline's coachman looked worried. "Is her ladyship well?"

"We don't know, do we?" Hagen snarled. "Why do you think we're asking ye?"

"I can take you to the exact place I set her down. I saw nothing wrong in it, sir. The viscountess was quite decided."

As only Donata could be. The best thing for me was to go home and wait for her to return, but my agitation would not let me. Why should Donata suddenly decide to visit a friend in the middle of the night and not arrange transport for herself to get home?

If she were any other woman, I might suspect she'd gone covertly to meet a lover. With Donata, I could not fathom her motive.

Though she'd been quite willing to not bother with fidelity to her first husband, who'd paraded his mistresses before her, I doubted she had taken up those ways again. Donata did not much like or trust men, with very few exceptions, and she'd declared it a relief to be married to a man who wanted to be with none but her. Besides, if she had been dashing off to a paramour, the rest of Mayfair would have told me about him.

I began to have other, more worrying suspicions about what she'd done. I turned to Hagen. "Let us go there and fetch her."

"Yes, sir." Hagen brightened, happy to be commanded to do what he wished to anyway.

He turned to the carriage, then his eyes narrowed, and he pointed a long finger at the back of the coach. "You there! I see you—get out of it."

Hagen charged toward the carriage, where I suspected someone had helped themselves to a ride by clinging to the back.

I did not expect the man who strode firmly into sight from the morning shadows. Although, I ought to have expected him.

"Captain," Brewster said. "If you're looking for your wife, I know exactly where she is."

Chapter Eight

Brewster spoke calmly, though he shot Hagen a fierce glance.

"What the devil?" I approached Brewster, barely keeping my temper. I wanted to strike at the man, though I knew I'd only land on my back with his boot in my stomach for my pains. "What are you doing here?"

"I saw you rush off early this morning," Brewster said. "'S'my job to follow you, innit? Almost missed you—had to hop on the back in passing."

Hagen did not look happy, both with the fact that Brewster had taken the liberty and that Hagen hadn't noticed.

"Where is her ladyship?" Hagen asked, fists balled. "If you've done somefink w' her ..."

"I haven't touched her." Brewster's face was calm. He directed his words at me. "She's in Covent Garden, Captain. In your old rooms, in fact."

"What the devil is she doing there?" I demanded

in a near shout.

"Couldn't say. Didn't ask her. She spies me hanging about the opera last night, and tells me to be useful and squire her to your rooms. Was to meet her in Park Lane after the music was done, and I'd arrange a hackney there. I did as she asked."

"And you said nothing to me?"

"This was after I said good night to you. Went back to the opera to keep an eye on her—and she gave me her orders."

"Even so." I gripped the head of my walking stick—which Donata had given me. "You could not send word to me?"

"Don't work for you, Captain," Brewster said. "I work for his nibs. If your wife asks me a favor on the side, that's her business. Not for me to go telling tales to the husband. But since you seem so worried, thought I'd better say she's well."

"Damnation." I yanked open the carriage door. "Hagen, please take me to Grimpen Lane. Get in, Brewster. I know you'll only follow—you may as well ride where I can keep an eye on *you*."

***

I found Donata breakfasting in my front room on a large repast from Mrs. Beltan's bakeshop. Brewster, likely anticipating a storm, stepped into the shop itself while I rushed upstairs.

Bread, a fresh crock of butter, ham, cream, coffee, and some sort of cake lay before her. When I entered—barreled through the unlocked door is a better description—Donata dropped the hunk of buttered bread she held, then let out her breath, hand to her heart.

"Really, Gabriel, I'm sure every beetle has fled into the nearest hole. I had hoped Mr. Brewster would be more discreet. I intended to return home before you woke."

"I have not slept." I slammed the door, sending loose plaster from the ceiling down to float upon her coffee. The window was open, letting in soft June air and harsh June odors. "I have been awake, waiting for your return."

Donata gave me a look of surprise. "Indeed, you usually do not wait up for me. I return home at three or four to find you fast asleep."

"I had something to tell you, and then you did not return. Did you not think to send word? Why the devil are you here?"

"To meet someone I did not wish to meet in South Audley Street of course." Donata lifted her dropped bread and fished plaster flakes from her coffee. "You do the same, do you not?"

"It is to do with the letters, isn't it?" I said, not bothering to lower my voice. "You confronted the man you believed wrote them. Bloody hell, Donata."

Color flushed Donata's cheeks. She laid down her bread and pushed to her feet. "Please do not swear at me. It is rather early for that sort of thing."

"What other words can I use? You leave your friends, instruct Lady Aline's coachman to set you down in an alley in Park Lane, and coerce Brewster into putting you into a hackney for Covent Garden. Wandering about London in the middle of the night, meeting a man who might be a danger to you —"

"Goodness knows, *you* never do the same." Donata's eyes flashed as she interrupted me. "Gone from the house at any hour as soon as you receive a message about something that might interest you. Meeting with ruffians, confronting criminals to tweak their noses when you disapprove of what they do, coming back to me battered and bruised. And I am to smile at you and understand."

"It is different for a lady!" I shouted. "London is dangerous, Donata. Or do you not know this, sheltered in your well-run house? It is not only for propriety that ladies do not wander about alone. That is a nice pretense. At every corner, you could be robbed, beaten, abducted, raped, and dragged off and murdered. It happens. I have seen the victims it has happened to."

My voice rose in volume with each sentence, until I was roaring every word, my fists balled, my blasted horrible temper coming out of me to bash itself on her.

Donata was nothing like my first wife. Carlotta, when she had enraged me, cringed and shrank from my outbursts, sometimes falling at my feet in sobs.

Donata's eyes glittered, blue-black and snapping, and her voice was ice-cold to my hot.

"I took far more precautions than you do, Gabriel. I was sensible enough to bring my abigail and Mr. Brewster to look after me."

"Brewster! A ruffian who likely has committed murder. You trusted your safety to him …"

"You do every day. He is a man for hire—I paid him to guard me. I also know he has orders from Mr. Denis to look after you. Looking after *me* aids that cause."

"Only until Denis decides to tell him to dispose of me! Recall whom Brewster works for, first and foremost. But you are leading me from the point. Why the *hell* did you decide to confront this letter-writer—alone, here? Did you think to rush him around the corner to Bow Street and accuse him of blackmail—"

"*If* you would let me explain, Gabriel, I would tell you I did no such thing. I confronted his wife."

The surprise of her words cut off the breath I was drawing for my next shout. I let my mouth hang open, which must have looked very foolish.

Donata's anger did not ease, but she took on a satisfied look. "She is a timid thing. I did not wish to alert this gentleman that I thought he might be sending the letters, and I could not openly meet with his wife. He would question her, so I thought to divert her to where we could meet in private. I did not wish Aline to know what I was about either, which is why I allowed her to drive me all the way back to Mayfair. I had the idea at the interval, when I could not find you, and spied this lady among the crowd. It worked very well. We had our chat, and I sent her home. By then I was so absolutely exhausted that I saw no reason not to avail myself of the bed here. I have Jacinthe, who is sleeping upstairs — I kept her up very late, and she needs the rest. Your landlady and her assistant very kindly looked out for me this morning."

Donata resumed her seat. She moved gracefully, but I noted a tremor in her hands.

"Bloody hell, Donata," I repeated. It was all I could think to say.

"Back to swearing, are you? Did you come in our coach? Leave it for me as you go about your business. I will be home as soon as I am finished with breakfast, and Jacinthe is awake."

"No, we will return home together." I scrubbed my hands through my hair as I paced the room. When I reached the window, I banged it shut, unable to take the combined odors of baking bread, the stale scent of the nearby market, and the stench of waste over it all. "This place is not fit for you. It never was."

"And yet, you lived here for years, too proud to take the hospitality of your friends."

I could have argued that when I'd arrived in London, I'd had no acquaintance whose hospitality I could count on. Colonel Brandon had returned with me, taking up residence in Brook Street, but as he had tried to kill me, albeit in a roundabout fashion, I did not fancy sharing a house with him.

I could have argued this, but then she'd have reminded me that I'd been befriended by Grenville and several other people in the meantime. I might have saved myself wretchedness, in her opinion, if I hadn't been enjoying it.

I had nothing more to say on the matter.

"We will return home together," I said firmly. "I will wait downstairs while you finish your breakfast."

Donata snatched up a knife, scraped it through butter, and slapped it across her bread. "You are a high-handed, foul-tempered, officious ... man ... at times, Gabriel."

"Yes." I ran a hand through my hair again. "Hence, I will wait downstairs."

"No, you will not. You will sit down and tell me where *you* ran off to in the middle of the opera. I know you find my acquaintance tedious, but I would have hoped you'd have made it past the interval."

Donata was furiously angry with me. I did not blame her, but at the same time, she had been foolishly reckless, and I was angry with her.

When Donata was at her most angry, she became cold, retreating into aristocratic hauteur. Her bursts of temper and acid observations were not pique, I'd come to know. The cool disdain meant fury.

I saw her trying to decide whether I was as bad as her first husband, a boor of a man who'd mostly ignored Donata when he wasn't humiliating her with everything he did. Breckenridge had been high-handed, foul-tempered, and officious, as she'd just accused me.

I'd ruined my first marriage because of my rages. My wife, weary of them, had fled with a man who was gentle with her. I was commencing my second marriage in the same fashion.

"Donata," I began.

"Say nothing more, please." Donata took a bite of bread. "I find myself ravenously hungry after my first sickness, and I would like to eat in peace."

The reminder that she carried my child increased my remorse. Whether she meant it to or not, I could not say, but I sank heavily into the chair across the table from her.

"It truly was a foolish thing to do," I said, my voice quiet.

"Mmm." Donata gave me a severe look as she chewed. "If you intend to sit there morosely, please tell me what you stayed awake all night to impart."

It took a few moments to calm myself. A small silver pot on a tray held coffee, but only one cup had been brought up. I rose, fetched one of the old, chipped porcelain cups I'd purchased in the market for myself long ago, and filled it with steaming brew.

Mrs. Beltan's coffee had not improved, but I sipped it gratefully. At one time, I'd welcomed it as ambrosia. Now I'd grown used to the fragrant stuff Donata and Grenville gave me. I was becoming soft.

"I found the surgeon," I began. "Or, rather, he found me. I took him to Grenville's—I had no choice in not waiting for you. I either entered the coach with him there and then, or he'd be gone, never to return."

Donata finished her bread and attacked a piece of ham. "When I'm in a more forgiving mood, I might say I understand. What did he tell you?"

I related how we'd entered Grenville's cellars and spread out the bones, how the surgeon had fairly quickly made his assessment. "Tomorrow — or rather, today — Grenville and I will question the other surgeon he named and trace the necklace she wore."

"I already gave you my opinion on the necklace," Donata said. "If she was that young, it was a gift from a parent, or a grandparent. Her death must not have been the result of a robbery. The gold in it alone should be worth a great deal."

"Indeed," I said. My ire was rising again. I had been wrong to rage at Donata, but she was not blameless. And yet, she continued to speak to me as though the problem were resolved, me put in my place.

I swallowed my irritation. "That is the whole of my news. What did you learn from the wife of my blackmailer?"

Donata took another bite of ham, swallowed. "Very little, if anything at all. Either I am wrong, and he is not involved in any way, or he has his wife so cowed she doesn't dare say a word against him. She was always a timid, rabbity thing."

"I take it you speak of the gentleman who you nearly married? Before you were paired with Breckenridge?"

"Yes. Conversing with his wife, I know I had a lucky escape — if Breckenridge can be called a lucky escape. Perhaps all men are brutes, and I have been deceiving myself."

I set down my cup. "Most gentlemen *are* brutish.

Some, like Grenville, learn to hide it well. I never have."

"I have always been aware of your uneven temper," Donata said calmly. "My nature is not the most placid either."

"I will never hurt you, Donata." I made my voice as gentle as I could, in spite of my continued anger. "Never. I give you my word."

Her eyes flickered, her body moving the slightest bit. She'd not expected me to say that.

"It is good of you," she said after a time.

"My father was a great bully, and beat upon my mother most of her married life. She was too weak to fight him, and I was too small to help her. I vowed I'd never be the same. I realized even as a lad that a strong man does not need to prove his strength against those who cannot match him."

Donata carefully laid down her fork. "I have always thought you strong. Especially after the moment you knocked my husband flat. I was delighted."

"And came to my bed." I remembered my dismay at finding her there. If I'd had no honor, I would have taken what she offered, but I'd turned away and left her, seeking sleep in another room.

She shrugged. "I misread your character at first, I admit. I was also not the mad adulteress you thought me. I simply did not know what to make of you. Brought by Grenville, but not his toady; no title in your family, but not cowed by those who possessed them. Hot-tempered, but turning your fists to those who deserved them. Injured but with more fire than any man I'd ever met. If I were to break my marriage vows, I wanted it to be with the army captain who'd showed the world what a horrible man my husband truly was."

I had misread her character as well. "I am honored."

Donata sent me a little smile. "I remember you being repulsed, not honored. I am pleased you gave me another chance."

"When you ceased trying to be shocking and allowed me to see your true self, I was happy you gave *me* another chance."

Donata's smile faded, and something entered her eyes I couldn't read. "Is that what we will do now?"

"You flitting about London in the middle of the night, worrying the hell out of me, is just cause for anger," I said, an edge returning to my voice. "When no one knew where you were ..." I cleared my throat. "I never want to feel like that again."

Donata's lips parted. Whatever guardedness was in her fled, and she came swiftly to her feet.

I started to rise, polite as ever, but her hand on my chest sent me back down. My wife landed on my lap, her arms going around my neck.

"I'm used to no one caring what I do," she said. "I had no idea you'd even notice."

"How could you think I'd not notice?" I cupped her face. "You are my wife. You carry my child. You are like the rarest porcelain, only much more treasured."

Her voice went soft. "Good Lord, Gabriel, you know how to melt a woman's heart."

"Promise me you'll take care. *Please*."

Her fingers on my face were cool. "Promise me you'll not shout at me as though I'm a boot boy. You are kind to *them*, I have observed."

"I promise ... that I will try." I could never quite tame the beast inside me.

Donata pressed a light kiss to the mouth that had raged at her. "Your bed is not very comfortable, as you have observed to me. But I think it will do."

I agreed that it would do very well for now. I carried her there, where we tested its comfort for much of the morning. I left my walking stick behind in the sitting room when I carried her to bed and never even noticed.

***

Brewster and Hagen were enjoying a companionable smoke when Donata and I at last made our way to the carriage waiting at the end of Grimpen Lane.

They passed a corncob pipe back and forth, discussing, with grunts, the merits of different tobaccos. It was the first time I'd seen Brewster have any sort of camaraderie with Donata's servants.

Jacinthe, the maid, had risen while Donata and I reconciled, and had taken a meal herself in the bakeshop. Jacinthe marched behind us, the disapproval on her middle-aged face showing she agreed with me about Donata's nocturnal adventure.

My wife and I were subdued on the way home. I had a warmth in my breastbone that seared when I thought of our hour or so in my bedroom, but also a worry. Donata was not a meek, obedient wife. She would do as she pleased, when she pleased, whether I liked it or not. I saw more storms in our future.

As the carriage moved past the tall houses of Piccadilly, I asked, "Shall we adjourn to Grenville's so that you might look at my grisly treasure?" It was after ten in the morning, and the road teemed with carts, horses, people, dogs—the metropolis going about its business.

"An excellent idea," Donata answered. "He

dislikes rising early."

"I will never become used to the idea that any hour before one in the afternoon is early."

"That is because you are country bred," she said decidedly. "Rising and retiring as the sun does. We in Town draw the curtains and light the lamps, making time as we like."

"And yet, to arrive before or after a certain hour in some places is not done," I remarked. "So you follow the clock to some degree."

"Only when we please. Call to Hagen and tell him to take us to Grosvenor Street. If Grenville is not awake, it shall be his own fault for missing my speculations on the corpse."

I complied. When we arrived at Grenville's plain front door, we found that he was indeed out of bed, and that Marianne Simmons was with him.

Chapter Nine

"Of course, Lacey, you would interrupt," Marianne said to me as Matthias ushered us into the dining room.

Matthias had told us, upon answering the door, that Mr. Grenville was not at home, then leaned closer and whispered he knew that Grenville would be incensed if Matthias turned us away. And so we were admitted.

Marianne and Grenville sat very close together at one end of the table, a lavish breakfast spread before them. Their heads bent to each other's as they made quiet comments, their words punctuated with soft laughter.

Marianne wore a flowing peignoir of gray shimmering material, its placket lined with lace. Grenville was, for him, in dishabille, in a long dressing gown called a banyan, with no waistcoat, the neck of his shirt loose.

When Marianne heard my step, her amiable look

fled, her frown set in, and she voiced her admonishment.

"I beg your pardon," I said, bowing. "We did not know we would disturb you."

Marianne spied Donata behind me, and her expression changed to one of neutrality and some caution. Marianne still did not know quite what to make of Donata.

On the one hand, Donata did not censure Grenville, or Marianne for that matter, for their public *affaire de coeur*, but then again, Donata was an earl's daughter, and although she was unconventional, Marianne was still a bit nervous around her.

Grenville looked slightly more embarrassed than Marianne to be caught in a private moment, but he surged to his feet and bowed to Donata.

"Never bestir yourself," Donata said to him. "Gabriel has brought me to look at the bones, as promised."

Marianne's brows climbed as Donata added another unfathomable facet to her character.

"Matthias can take us down," I offered quickly. "Anton would not be pleased if you rushed away from his breakfast."

"Indeed," Grenville agreed. He had recovered his aplomb and became his usual gallant self. "Are you certain, Donata? Please do not distress yourself with this bad business."

"I shan't." Donata turned away, her large shawl sliding to bare the glittering gold net over silk of her evening gown.

The waistline of the gown rode high under her bosom, the fashions of this Season perfect for hiding her increasing figure. She'd removed the necklace of heavy stones she'd worn to the opera — they now reposed in my pocket — but it was quite obvious that Donata had been out all night, and equally obvious that I had not.

Grenville, who set the standards of politeness for the *ton*, said not a word. Marianne did not either, though I was certain that as soon as we were in the cellars, the two would speculate about us.

Matthias led us off to the back stairs, retracing the route he'd taken us last night. This time, the servants weren't warned away — they moved aside and bowed or curtsied respectfully as we passed, but they did not let us slow them in their industry.

"I am pleased to see Grenville happy," I remarked as we moved through the servants' area.

Matthias shot me a look. "Miss Simmons, if you don't mind me saying so, sir, does take a bit of getting used to."

"She is uncertain of her position," I said. "Be patient with her."

"She can be kindhearted, when the fit takes her," Matthias conceded.

I feared that Donata would be sickened by the sight of the body. Her condition was already delicate, but when Matthias carefully lifted the sheet we'd draped over the pieced-together skeleton, Donata gave only one faint, sharp inhalation, and then went silent.

She touched her hand to her mouth, but not because she was ill. Tears glistened on her lashes.

"The poor thing," Donata said, her voice low. "I am ashamed of my curiosity now."

I looked down at what used to be a young woman, and shared Donata's pity. Matthias too, was somber.

Donata went on. "She was left, alone under the water, and no one came for her." She looked up at me, eyes full of compassion. "Please discover who did this, Gabriel, and unleash your temper on *him*. I will help you in the endeavor as much as I am able."

***

When we returned to the dining room, there were two more places set at the table and several additional covered trays on the sideboard.

"No need," I said. "We have breakfasted."

"*You* have not," Donata said. "Eat, please, or you will make yourself ill. I am already ravenous again, so I thank you for your kindness, Grenville."

She seated herself, nodding graciously at the footman who brought her coffee. I filled two plates at the sideboard, my stomach growling now, reminding me that I'd taken in nothing since last night before we'd departed for the opera.

Marianne had moved to another chair. From her glance down the table, she wondered whether she should remain in the room at all, but Donata showed no concern that she shared a table with an actress who had been little better than a courtesan.

The two ladies had been companionable enough when we'd traveled to Bath, or whenever Marianne shared Grenville's box at Covent Garden and Drury Lane, but this was his Mayfair home, a different venue. Grenville was defying convention for bringing her to his house—he ought to keep his ladybird in her separate lodging.

This told me first that Grenville cared very much for Marianne. He'd never have risked censure otherwise.

It also told me he was tiring of London and the close scrutiny of his fellow men. He was a traveller at heart, and I sensed him impatient to be away. I wondered if he'd take Marianne with him when he went.

"Gautier has already been a mine of information," Grenville informed me as I began to eat. "He has given me a list of jewelers who might repair a necklace such as the one found on the young lady, and he has already begun making inquiries. I expect to have a shorter list before the day is very old."

Donata clinked silver to porcelain, looking as at home eating in the elegant chamber as she had at the secondhand table in my rooms. "The Runners should employ valets in their number," she suggested. "Gentlemen's gentlemen certainly know more about trade in London than any foot patrollers."

"Gautier would agree, dear lady. Lacey, once we are presentable, I propose a visit to the man your surgeon suggested—Coombs was his name?"

I knew Grenville remembered the man's name precisely—Jonas Coombs—but it would hardly do for a dandy of the *ton* to betray he had much interest in anything beyond clothes, horses, and women.

"I believe Gabriel is avid to go immediately," Donata said. "Once Bartholomew decides that he is fit to be seen, Gabriel will return and rush off with you."

Grenville took a languid sip of coffee. "Lacey, I believe your wife is poking fun at us."

"As ever," I replied.

I reflected, as we continued to eat, and Donata and Grenville exchanged witticisms—many at my expense—how much my life had changed.

I'd returned to London in the throes of melancholia, some days barely able to leave my bed. I'd known no one, had very little to my name.

Less than four years later, I was seated at the dining table of the most famous man in London, married to a beautiful woman, all of us thoroughly casual.

Donata was breakfasting in finery from the previous night, I in whatever clothes I'd thrown upon my person before dashing out, Marianne with very little under her silken peignoir, Grenville in a state of undress he'd never in his wildest moments let anyone see him in.

Donata and I had celebrated marital bliss in rundown rooms in Covent Garden, and I suspected Marianne and Grenville had been engaged in similar activities before they'd emerged for their *petite déjeuner*.

Yet, here we all were, earlier in the day than anyone but me would rise, Grenville and Donata utterly comfortable, Marianne and I wondering how we'd landed there.

If I'd known four years ago that such a morning awaited me, I'd have been disbelieving.

But one never anticipates where life will lead. I knew that tragedy could follow hard upon happiness, and so I treasured the moment in that sunny dining room. I hugged it to me, and let it go only with the greatest reluctance.

***

Grenville and I paid our visit to Mr. Coombs of Tottenham Court Road after Matthias and Bartholomew had ascertained that the man, in fact, still dwelled there.

Mr. Coombs had retired a few years ago, but lived in his modest house, hiring out his front room to a younger surgeon he'd trained. Coombs's rooms were upstairs and in the back, where he lived alone, having been widowed two decades before.

Coombs was nothing like the surgeon who'd sent us to him. He was a soft man with thinning hair combed across his bald head, and wide brown eyes. He looked like a gentle cow who might amble inquisitively up to one and lower its head to be scratched.

"Captain Lacey and ... Mr. *Grenville* does this say?" Coombs asked in amazement, blinking at Grenville's card. "Not *the* Mr. Grenville from all the newspapers?"

"I am afraid so," Grenville said. He bowed, apologetic.

Grenville had dressed after his morning bath in subdued clothes—a somber coat, plain ivory waistcoat, straight trousers over ankle-high boots, a fashion he was bringing into style. Plain gloves and a high beaver hat completed his ensemble.

I'd considered leaving Grenville in the coach while I questioned Coombs, simply because having such a well-known man visit this corner of the city would be a sensation. Those who saw him would speculate.

On the other hand, Grenville had so much cordiality in him that he could put anyone, from princes to scullery maids, at their ease. He could charm and flatter, and every word would be sincere. I tended, in my impatience, to ask abrupt questions and put others' noses out of joint.

"Come in, come in, gentlemen." Coombs ushered us into a small sitting room that held two chairs near a fireplace, a table with another straight chair, and a bookshelf.

Only a few books reposed on the shelves, while the others were taken up by tools of his trade. A saw, a large knife, what looked like a long-handled chisel, forceps in several sizes, and other instruments I could not identify. Having watched army surgeons on the Peninsula cut off limbs, force bones straight, and hack open men to extract shot, seeing the instruments gave me a shudder.

A surgeon had picked rocks and pieces of bone out of my knee, talking to me cheerfully while he set my leg and sewed me up. I hated him at the time, cursing and swearing and vowing to kill him. He'd only grinned and kept working, and afterward, I'd apologized. The man had saved my life, saved my leg, and allowed me to continue walking about, if painfully. I'd been luckier than many. The surgeon had taken my apology with a breezy, "Happy to help, Captain."

Coombs noted my look and my walking stick. "Ah, Captain, I see one of my brethren has practiced our trade upon you. Never fear, I am retired, and not apt to pick up my hacksaw and go at you, unless of course, in dire emergency, you turned to me. Hardly likely, is it?"

"And yet," Grenville interjected smoothly, "I have been told there was none better at setting a bone than you, that it heals cleanly and seamlessly."

Coombs looked surprised. "Then you've come for my services after all. I have taught my apprentice well—I can have him examine whomever's broken limbs you need mended. You two gentlemen look whole, so I conclude you are petitioning me on another's behalf?"

Grenville continued. "I'm afraid the poor soul we've come to ask you about is already deceased."

Coombs's brows climbed. "Dear me." He turned from us, but only to open a door near the fireplace and call out to a person named Humphries to bring tea. He then removed a flask from his coat and took a quick drink. "Forgive me, gentlemen. I believe I will need some fortification." He held the flask out to Grenville in offering. "An indifferent liquor, but it coats the palate."

Grenville politely declined, but I accepted the flask, knowing that a shared drink of spirits could soften relations between men a long way.

The whisky was cheap and awful, and I kept myself from coughing when I handed the flask back to Coombs.

"Have another," I said. "I imagine you will need more fortification when I explain that we brought the deceased with us."

Chapter Ten

Coombs was more interested than shocked. He took another nip from the flask. "Indeed? And where is this deceased person? If you are not having a joke with me. I have heard that you young fellows of the *ton* make jests of odd things."

Grenville shrugged. "There are those who might find such a thing amusing, but we are in earnest, I assure you. All that were found were the woman's bones. If we show you the break, can you tell us if you mended it?"

Coombs scratched his head, disheveling his thin hair. "Perhaps. I've never been asked such a thing before, but I will make an attempt."

"Thank you." Grenville moved out to the hall and the stairs to signal Matthias and Bartholomew to bring up the crate.

I reflected that whoever the poor young woman was, she had been having more of an outing in the last few days than she'd had in the ten years she slept under the magistrate's house in Wapping.

Matthias pried open the crate and gently and respectfully lifted out a piece of canvas which cradled the arm bone that had been broken and mended.

Coombs took another pull from his flask and directed Matthias to lay the limb on the table. He pulled back the canvas and peered at the bone with professional interest.

"The body had deteriorated this much?" he asked, directing the question at Grenville. "She might have died long before my time."

Grenville gestured to me. "Lacey?"

I recalled what the surgeon had speculated as he'd examined her. "The guess is that she'd been underwater about three years before she was found. Possibly five. She was discovered ten years ago, which puts her death fifteen years back at most."

Coombs touched the arm bone, turning it to look at the break. "She mended cleanly, that is certain. Very straight, well-done. If I did not set this bone, then someone quite skilled did. It is a trick, you see, to hold the limb steady so that the break lines up perfectly. Bones fuse together again, as this one has, but if the limb is set badly, a person might lose use of it altogether." He glanced down at my knee, as though thinking that if *he'd* had charge of my leg, it would hang straighter.

"Did you set this one?" I asked. "She was a young woman, from a middle-class family, but likely one of decent means. That is all we know."

Coombs went silent. He brushed the bone as it lay on the canvas, then turned to me abruptly. "I would like to see the rest of her."

And so, once more, our lady was laid out upon a

table, bare and friendless, pathetic and forgotten. Coombs helped Matthias and Bartholomew place her bones appropriately, his good-natured expression deserting him as he studied the wound on the skull.

"Terrible," he said, shaking his head. "Diabolical. The blow killed her, did it not?"

"That is what Thompson of the Thames River Police believes."

Coombs took a step back from the table, chewing on the knuckle of his forefinger. "The River Police? They found her?"

"Yes," I replied. "Caught under a mooring in Wapping Docks. She might have gone in there, or from a ship, or been carried there by the current. We have no idea."

More gnawing on his bent finger. Then he removed the digit from his mouth. "I might not be able to help you, gentlemen. The set of the bone looks like my work, but who the young lady is, I cannot tell you. It has been too long … my memory is not …" Coombs's eyes narrowed, as though his thoughts had taken him another direction, but he shook his head. "My apologies. I cannot recall."

He was lying. He'd remembered something, but was reluctant to tell us what.

Grenville must have drawn the same conclusion, because he said in a patient tone, "I assure you, Mr. Coombs, what you tell us will go no further. We only wish to discover who this lady was and help Mr. Thompson bring her killer to justice."

Coombs glanced at me, taking me in from my thick hair that refused to lie flat, to my boots, and the walking stick that so firmly propped me up. After a time, he sighed.

"You are a military man, sir. I have more respect

for an army captain than I do for the Runners or thief-takers. I have thought of a young lady I treated perhaps fifteen years ago — I set her left ulna, as this one has been. I remember her, because it is unusual for a wellborn lady to break an arm, unless she is mad for riding. But this lady was not one for horses. I asked her."

I curbed my impatience. "The lady's name?"

Coombs chewed on his second finger this time, again taking me in from head to toe. "I hesitate to tell you, Captain, only because the young lady I am thinking of isn't dead. She is very much alive. Her father keeps a shop in the Strand. But other than her, any broken bone I've set has belonged to men young and old, or older women who are becoming brittle. I am very sorry that I cannot help you."

I frowned. My nameless surgeon had been very certain that Coombs had been the man to treat the injury. I trusted his assessment — I recognized intelligent competence when I met it.

"If you did not help this young woman, can you guess who did?" I asked. "A surgeon who would mend her this cleanly?"

"I am not acquainted with every surgeon in London," Coombs said. "Perhaps she sustained the break in the country and was attended there. Farriers often set bones when no one else is available. Whoever did it has great skill, I will admit."

I did not answer. I'd hoped our search would be as quick and simple as Denis's surgeon had made it sound, but I was back to uncertainty.

Coombs's apprentice banged his way in just then bearing a large tray with cups and pots. The man, already in his thirties, I'd judge, but with the gracelessness of a youth not grown into his body, jolted so much as he strode in that I feared the tea would slide off the tray and be lost.

The tray tilted precariously, and I saw Grenville poised to catch it. But the apprentice managed to set it down on the table near the bones.

Coombs gave his apprentice a stern look. "I hope you do not mind an indifferent repast, gentlemen. The lad is better at surgery than brewing."

The apprentice, far from looking offended, grinned, made us a bow, and retreated.

Grenville and I partook in a polite cup of tea — which was weak and bitter. Coombs dosed his with large dollops from his flask.

Coombs had nothing to add about the body that Denis's surgeon hadn't already surmised, and we took our leave. Bartholomew and Matthias carried the crate down the stairs, Grenville following. All three looked disappointed with our errand.

As the others climbed into Grenville's coach, a thought struck me. I told the coachman, Jackson, to wait, while I ascended to Coombs's chambers again.

When I returned to the carriage, the others had settled in. Coombs's apprentice cheerfully pushed me up inside and shut the door for me. Jackson started the horses, and we rolled into the mass of conveyances trying to push their way down the busy road.

"What did you ask him?" Grenville inquired. He held on to a strap above him as the carriage lurched, and looked as though he regretted sipping the bad tea. Grenville was prone to motion sickness.

"I asked him the name of the family of the woman he'd treated," I said. "There may be no connection at all, but I am curious. Odd that Coombs should set the arm of a similar young woman near the same time this woman's would have been done. How many young ladies of good middle-class families break their left arms and have them set by surgeons of equal skill?"

"I have no idea." Grenville's eyes began to sparkle, the carriage's jolting forgotten. "Did he tell you who she was?"

"Her father's name is Hartman, and he owns a watch shop in the Strand."

"Excellent," Grenville said. "As you speculate, it may lead to nothing, but we have so bloody little to go on."

"A broken bone and a necklace." I shrugged. "I believe we have had as much or less before. Shall we repair to the Strand?"

"Indeed." His motion sickness forgotten, Grenville tapped on the roof and ordered Jackson to head the coach toward the river.

***

Messers Hartman and Schweigler, watchmakers, had a shop at number 86. The building on the Strand Jackson stopped before was unassuming, with a plain door and a small window, a discreet sign announcing that this was indeed a watch shop.

The interior, when we ducked inside out of thin rain that began pattering down, was dim and workmanlike, befitting a craftsman's place.

Mr. Hartman obviously recognized Grenville on sight. He came from the back himself before the assistant could fetch him, a smile on his face.

"Welcome, sir. How very kind of you to call upon us."

"Quite." Grenville flushed.

In his zeal of questioning Mr. Hartman Grenville had forgotten that any time he visited an establishment, it gave said establishment panache. Grenville's patronage was as prized as a royal one — it could make or break the careers of hat-maker, glove-maker, tailor, watchmaker.

His arrival this morning, unannounced, would be remarked upon, and Mr. Hartman's reputation made.

Grenville, who was very careful about from whom he purchased his wardrobe and accoutrements, turned an uncomfortable shade of red. He glanced at me, as though wishing for me to help him, but I only rested my hands on my walking stick and enjoyed myself. It wasn't often I was able to see Grenville discomfited.

"I wish to make a gift," Grenville began. "Something for my good friend the captain here. He is soon to be a father. Well, for the second time."

"Ah." Hartman brightened. "My felicitations, Captain. A large family is a boon to a man."

I bowed. "Thank you. I am most fortunate."

"A timepiece is a wonderful gift, Mr. Grenville. Mr. Schweigler is the watchmaker here, and truly a skilled gentleman. He is Swiss, you know."

I supposed him being Swiss was significant, but I knew little about the watchmaking industry. I had a timepiece that had been my father's, a heavy silver thing from the last century, with a plain dial and a small key for winding it. It wasn't very valuable, as watches went — or my father would have sold it — but it ran well, though it easily tarnished, and I'd kept the thing out of habit.

I pulled out the watch in question and held it in my hand. I'd had it since I'd come home from the Peninsula, and my father's man of business had given it to me. I'd inherited it, the house in Norfolk, and little else.

"A venerable thing," Hartman said, his gaze going to it. "May I?"

I unhooked the watch from the chain Donata had given me for it and handed it over. Hartman slid an eyepiece from his pocket with the ease of long practice, opened the back, and peered through the lens to the watch's viscera.

"Finely made," he said, sounding impressed. "A Leroux perhaps?" He glanced at me hopefully.

I shook my head. "No idea. It was my father's."

"Well, it is exquisitely done. No hallmark — they didn't often do them in silver fifty years ago, only in gold. Still, it is a fine piece. Perhaps Mr. Schweigler can make one still finer."

"The finest," Grenville said. "The captain has been through much, wounded in the war, you know, and being forced to retire."

Now he was enjoying *my* discomfiture. I said, "Indeed. Mr. Grenville has been kind to befriend me."

Mr. Hartman regarded me with more interest. "Waterloo, was it?"

"Afraid not. I was wounded in the Peninsula, too hurt to go back into the field for the last show. Apparently, the Iron Duke somehow managed without me."

Hartman chuckled politely at my joke. "Please, gentlemen, be seated. My assistant will bring coffee, and we will discuss things."

He hurried out of the main shop through a door, leaving us alone.

"Well," Grenville said.

I couldn't help a short laugh. "I suppose you are purchasing me a watch."

"You must admit you need one. Your timepiece is not bad but it ought to be kept under glass, to be admired as a relic of a time long past. I should have given you one years ago."

"Forced it upon me, you mean."

"Do not get your back up," Grenville said. He seated himself in an armless chair with sinuous legs that had also come from the last century. "Or your pride. This is all in the line of duty. We must put him at his ease."

"Of course." If nothing else, we'd have made a gentleman happy with an easy sale.

The front room of the shop was small and dim, the only light coming through the window that gave on to the street. The chamber was more like a sitting room, with the old-fashioned chairs and a round, gate-legged table, and a small case with a glass top resting on the table. The case was empty at the moment, but perhaps Hartman displayed watches in it—an easy thing to carry away to the back rooms and lock up when the shop closed.

Hartman returned with his assistant, who carried coffee. Hartman was a rather large man, somewhat stout, but more solid than fat. In his younger days, he might have gone in for pugilism. He was in middle-age now, approaching his elder years, his thin hair iron gray. He wore a beard on his round face, neatly trimmed nearly to his chin.

The assistant was clearly related to him—son, nephew, or grandson—with the same round face, brown eyes, and solid body that would someday become soft. The assistant was clean-shaven, showing a cleft in his chin that perhaps his father—or uncle, or grandfather—also sported under his beard.

The assistant poured coffee into rather elegant

porcelain cups, left the silver pot on a tray, and silently retreated into the depths of the house.

"He is learning the business," Hartman said with an apologetic glance at the door the assistant closed. "He is not entirely happy about it, but he is young. My brother's boy. He wants to be a soldier, but the war is over, thank God. He wants to explore the world now, but my brother fears to let him out of his sight. I am trying to think of ways he can make journeys for me. I hate to break his spirit."

"I understand," I said. I sipped the coffee, which was remarkably good. Far better than the tea Coombs had offered us. "I have a daughter who is quite … spirited. She is about to make her come-out."

Hartman laughed, his salesman's demeanor relaxing slightly. "I have much sympathy for you, Captain. Daughters can be very worrying." His laughter faded a bit. "Very worrying, indeed."

Something flashed in his eyes, a darkness, a grief — only a flash, but I'd seen it.

I could not very well ask him if long ago, one of his daughters had broken her arm, and was she still alive without it being awkward. I saw Grenville's gaze flick to me and away. He was also trying to think of a means to introduce the topic.

I had an idea, though. Not very kind of me, but thinking of the young woman, dead and forgotten, made me impatient and angry. If this watch seller had absolutely nothing to do with the woman, then he would only be puzzled and curious, and we'd go away, having brought him some business.

Gautier had returned the necklace to Grenville, along with his list, in careful handwriting, of the shops that might sell similar pieces or repair old necklaces like this one. Grenville had handed the necklace to me, so I could take it back to Thompson to return to the boxes of evidence in the cold cellar.

I removed the necklace, which I'd wrapped in a handkerchief, from inside my pocket, laid it on the table, and opened the folds of linen.

"I know you sell watches, but perhaps you can help," I said to Hartman. "Have you ever seen a piece such as this? Or know what jeweler would be able to tell me about it?"

I had been studying the necklace, its simple gold chain and smooth locket as I spoke. I looked up into heavy silence as I finished.

Hartman was staring at the locket, his gaze fixed, his face so white I thought he would fall into a dead faint. His dark eyes blazed like obsidian among the stark white, his lips bloodless.

"Where …" Hartman reached a hand forward, his fingers stiff, movements slow. He stopped shy of touching the locket, as though he feared it would sting him. "Where did you come by this?"

The words barely came out of him. I lifted the necklace and laid it across his fingers.

"It was around the neck of a young woman found in the river," I said. "She died, nearly fifteen years ago."

Hartman stared at the necklace on his hand, his chest lifting in a tight breath. Grenville was on the edge of his chair, poised to catch Hartman, who surely would fall.

Just as I reached for him, Hartman collapsed back into his seat. He brought his hands, clutching the necklace, to his face, and began to weep in long, gut-wrenching, wordless sobs.

Chapter Eleven

Grenville and I exchanged surprised looks. I felt a touch a remorse — Hartman was weeping with abandon, his self-assurance gone.

"Mr. Hartman," I said gently.

"Perhaps some brandy for him, Lacey." Grenville removed a flask from his pocket and handed it to me. His was silver, beautifully engraved, a contrast to Coombs's rather battered, plain one.

I did not think Hartman would be able to hold the flask himself, so I tipped a good measure of brandy into his coffee and lifted the cup to him. "Drink."

He would not take his hands from his face. Hartman's entire body shook, sobs catching in his throat, choking him. He began to cough, couldn't catch his breath.

I thumped his back. Grenville rose in alarm. I hit Hartman's spine with the heel of my hand, and finally, he gave a gasp and began to breathe again.

"Drink," I repeated firmly.

This time, Hartman took the cup in his shaking hands and poured the lukewarm liquid into his mouth.

More coughing, but his color grew better, and finally he drew a long, ragged breath.

"She is dead, then?" he whispered.

Grenville returned to the table. He pulled a chair close to Hartman's and sat, taking Hartman's gnarled hand.

"We are not sure who she is," he said gently.

Hartman's look was one of terrible despair. "My … daughter. Judith. She's been missing for fifteen years."

Grenville and I exchanged a glance. Hartman took another gulp of coffee, this time without choking. He held the necklace tightly, not wishing to relinquish it.

"Your pardon, sir," I said. "It is possible the woman who wore it stole it from your daughter. As Mr. Grenville says, we are not certain."

Hartman stretched the chain between his hands. "It was joined around her neck when her mother gave it to her. It has only been cut once." He pointed to a broken link. "When it came off her."

"The young woman who was found had broken her arm at one point," Grenville said.

Hartman nodded. "Yes." His eyes screwed up, more tears pouring down his face.

Grenville continued in his gentlest tone. "We've visited Mr. Coombs, the surgeon. He said he set the arm of a young lady about that time, but he claims she is alive and well."

"No." Hartman pulled a handkerchief from his coat sleeve and buried his face in it. "We told him, when we went to him, that she was her sister. They look much alike. We decided to do so to let no one know her shame."

Her shame? A broken limb was no cause for shame, not that mine didn't embarrass me. I sensed Hartman meant something deeper.

Hartman mopped his face. "Forgive me, gentlemen, but I must close the shop."

He rose, tottered to the door and locked it, then pulled the curtain across the front window. When he turned back, his breathing was better, but the utter grief in his eyes smote me.

Grenville had risen. "We will go, then. We are so sorry to have caused you distress."

Hartman stopped, looking at us in some bewilderment. "How ... how did you gentlemen come to know of this? You are not Runners — well, I know Mr. Grenville is not."

"Mr. Thompson of the Thames River Police asked me to help him," I said. "He had never been able to discover who she was. I have found people before, and so he confided in me." I was puzzled. "You did not know she was dead before we told you — did you never report her disappearance to the Watch? The Runners? There would have been a hue and cry ..."

"No." Hartman shook his head emphatically. "We looked for her, of course, did our best. But we did not want the Runners. They are dear, in any case. We searched ..."

He'd not wanted to give up, I saw. He'd clung to hope all this time, forcing himself to go on with his life.

"By reporting her, you might have discovered the truth long ago," I said.

Another shake of the head. "*No*, Captain. We did not want the Watch or Runners blundering into our business. They could not have helped in any case.

Not if she were dead already." He hesitated. "Where is … she?"

I hid a flinch. At the moment, Judith Hartman was a jumble of bones in a crate sitting inside Grenville's carriage.

Grenville said, "We'll see that she is returned to you, sir."

Hartman stuffed his handkerchief into his pocket and wiped his eyes with the back of his hand. "For the first time, I am glad her mother is gone. Judith's vanishing already killed her once." He let out a long breath. "Now, gentlemen, if I can ask you to leave. I must …"

He glanced about the shop as though not certain what he needed to do. I took up my hat and walking stick and gave him a bow.

"Of course," I said. "I am terribly sorry to have upset you, sir. If I had known, I would have broken it more gently."

Hartman shook his head. "No, no. I am grateful to you for this knowledge. For this." He held up the necklace he still clutched.

"If you would like to speak to Mr. Thompson," I said, "and tell him what you know, it might assist him to find who killed her."

"No," Hartman said abruptly. Deep anger flashed in his eyes. "I do not want inquiries into our private affairs. She is gone. Nothing to be done. Please go, Captain."

I bowed again. "If you need any help, Mr. Hartman, any at all, please feel free to call on me."

I removed a card from my pocket and laid it on the table. Donata had caused new calling cards to be made for me, ivory rectangles smooth and clean, with my name in fine black script. I took out the small, silver pencil that went with a silver-backed writing book she'd also given me—to help me make notes when I solved things, she'd said. I'd been grateful, but also reflected I had much more in my pockets now to steal.

I quickly wrote my Grimpen Lane address on the back—if this man craved privacy, I doubted he'd want to arrive at the large and well-populated South Audley Street house.

I pushed the card across to him with my gloved finger. Hartman made no move to take it. I gave the man another nod and departed quietly with Grenville.

Not until we were in his coach, and Jackson had headed us along the Strand toward St. Paul's Churchyard and the long journey to Wapping, did Grenville let out a breath.

"So," he said.

"So, indeed." I studied the tall and rather drab houses we passed, the throng of humanity wafting down this busy thoroughfare. "The poor man."

I'd watched Hartman's reaction with sharp pain in my heart. For years, I'd not known the fate of my daughter, and I know some of what he felt.

I'd looked for Gabriella, but been unable to afford a long search. The war with France hadn't helped—Carlotta had left with a French officer, and I'd not been able to scour that country for her. By the time the war had ended, thirteen years after Carlotta had fled with Gabriella, I had given up all hope of finding her.

My only comfort had been that she'd gone off with Carlotta. If Carlotta had intended to desert her child, she would have left Gabriella with me in the first place. This gave me some assurance that

Gabriella would be looked after.

As it turned out, Carlotta's French lover, Major Auberge, had cared for my daughter and raised her as his own. He'd taken care of her, I hated to admit, better than I had been able to.

Even so, Gabriella had been my child, the love of my existence, and not knowing where she was had torn a hole through me.

"I want to discover who killed her," I said. "Hartman should not have had to suffer like that. She shouldn't have been killed."

"I know, old man. I agree with you." Grenville rested his hands on his walking stick. "But where to start?"

"Hartman and his family. They must know why Miss Hartman was walking along the Thames docks, or where she'd gone the day or night she'd disappeared. Had she been meeting someone? Running away from someone? Why on earth would Judith want to pretend to be her sister when taken to a surgeon to have her arm set? Why did Hartman call it *her shame*?"

"All very good questions. All the same, I am not sure Hartman will embrace you into his family and let you interrogate them."

"I had no intention of interrogating," I said stiffly.

"You do become zealous, Lacey. Hartman, as you must have surmised, is a Hebrew. Such men do not welcome outsiders into the bosom of their families. While the Rothschilds, Goldsmids, and Montefiores attend my soirees and invite me to theirs, they would not wish me to delve too much into their private lives and their personal business."

"Not many families would," I said. "No matter what their origin."

"Yes, but ..." Grenville searched for words. "In my experience, Hebrew fathers are particularly guarded about their daughters. More so even than Englishmen. If you wish to discover the truth, you might have to do it without the assistance of Mr. Hartman. Might have to fight him for it, even."

"Surely he would want to know. And bring the man — or woman — to justice. I certainly would, were it my daughter."

Grenville gave me a deprecating look. "If it were your daughter, my dear Lacey, you would hunt the man down and wring his neck yourself. You know this."

True, I'd be too impatient to let the wheels of justice turn in their course. When Gabriella had been endangered a year ago, I'd gone after the man who'd hurt her — Auberge and I had given him a good beating. Hartman, I thought, might feel the same.

"I will find the culprit, beat him black and blue, and drag him to the Runners," I said. "I will leave it up to Hartman whether he wishes to prosecute."

Grenville looked doubtful. I did not finish that if Hartman didn't want to prosecute, I'd happily bring suit against the killer. And, if that didn't work, dispatch him myself. Pomeroy might object, but at this point, I did not care.

At last Grenville gave me a nod. "Very well," he said. "You know I will do all I can to help. Where do we begin?"

***

We started by journeying to Thompson in Wapping and returning the crate. I'd left the necklace with Hartman — I did not have the heart to take it from his hands to sit in a box in a cellar.

Thompson was out when we arrived, but he came

in as a patroller ushered Grenville and I, and Bartholomew and Matthias, the two brothers carrying the box, into his tiny office.

Brewster had followed us, I'd seen as we'd climbed from the coach. How he found me wherever I was in the city I had no idea. He might have jumped onto the back of the carriage as he'd done when I'd gone searching for Donata. However he'd done it, he now leaned against a crumbling brick wall opposite the magistrate's house, folded his arms against the rain, and waited.

"Good Lord," Thompson said after I had told him what we discovered. "I knew you were the man for this. And Mr. Grenville."

"All too glad to help," Grenville answered.

Thompson rested his hands on top of the crate. "Indeed, I will send her back to her family to be given a decent burial. I'm afraid the magistrate here cannot help with any sort of coffin, or …"

"I will take care of that," Grenville said smoothly. "I will contact my funeral furnisher and give him instructions."

Thompson looked grateful but at the same time wary. A middle-class man like Hartman might not welcome the ostentation of an expensive funeral master—who provided coffins, bearers, horses, mourning decor for the home, and many other services. A funeral for a man of Grenville's class and a shopkeeper would be widely different.

"Instructions, I said," Grenville went on. "All will be in good taste. He will send a coffin here, and a conveyance for the young lady to be returned home."

Thompson conceded. "As to finding her killer …" He sighed, his bony shoulders sagging. "If Mr. Hartman has no wish to prosecute, little can be done even if we discover who killed her. If that killer is still alive. It was a long time ago."

"*I* will prosecute," I said. "Too often I have seen men ruin others, either by outright murder or in a roundabout way. I've had to stand by and do nothing."

I tasted my anger, remembering Jane Thornton, the first young woman whose circumstances I'd investigated; Lady Clifford, whose husband had made her miserable; and the death of one of Denis's men at the Sudbury School, where Grenville had been nearly murdered himself. I'd found out many things, but had been too poor, or the circumstances had been too complex, for me to bring the ones who should have paid, to justice.

Now, thanks to Donata, I had money of my own. I disliked spending much beyond what I needed, but I believed she'd have no objection to me funding a prosecution for the murder of Judith Hartman. She'd been moved by the young woman's death as well.

Thompson only observed me with his dry intelligence. "As you wish, Captain. I will not tell you the road might not be easy. I have the feeling you'd bypass any objections."

We took our leave then. I touched the top of the crate before I went, and made a silent vow to the sleeping girl inside to find her killer.

I swallowed on sorrow, bowed to Thompson, and followed Grenville out into the rain.

***

It was not done for a gentleman to call on his funeral furnisher. They called on the gentleman instead, at his home. In this instance, however, Grenville was impatient and wanted it done. I had no objection.

Grenville's family used a man whose premises were in a lane off Houndsditch in the City.

Houndsditch did a thriving trade in clothing of all kinds, from secondhand clothiers to tailors for the middle class, to rag men in their constant search for castoffs. Many of these ragmen and secondhand clothiers were Hebrews, and I studied them as I passed them by with more interest. I was suddenly being thrust into their world, which I had scarcely noticed before.

Any man I'd met of the Hebrew religion had been no different than I was, I'd observed — in fact, many came from circumstances far better than mine and blended into London life more seamlessly than I did. True, I was able to vote or stand for Parliament, had I been reckless enough to do so, and they were not — but how did that make me a superior man?

It did not, in my opinion. A man's character and honor made him stand above others, not his religion or strata in life.

Grenville, far superior to many on all counts, descended in the turnoff between Houndsditch and Aldgate with as much poise as he did alighting from a carriage at Carlton House.

A young man sitting in the yard, working on a black headstall in his lap, dropped his tools with a clang and bolted into the house as Grenville strolled toward the door.

"Sir?" The funeral furnisher emerged, settling his coat, and fixing a gaze of great surprise at Grenville. "It is not time for you to partake of my services yet, surely. You're in fine fettle, Mr. Grenville."

Chapter Twelve

The funeral furnisher was not what I expected. The idea of a man who made a living burying people gave me the picture of a thin, rather cadaverous person, with gray hair and dry, papery skin. Instead, this furnisher was stout from good meals, had black hair and long side whiskers, and a twinkle in his blue eyes that spoke of a merry nature.

"No, indeed," Grenville said. "My health is robust thus far. Though one never knows. Today, I have come to ask a favor for another."

"I could have called upon you." The man looked hurt. "You had only to send for me."

"Unusual circumstances, Mr. Wilkinson."

Wilkinson shrugged and gestured us into the house. Instead of the sumptuous parlor I'd imagined, we went to a very plain sitting room with dark-paneled walls and straight-legged, shield-back chairs.

Without preliminary, Grenville explained the

errand. Mr. Wilkinson's ruddy face showed sympathy.

"The poor lamb. You leave it to me, Mr. Grenville. I'll take fine care of her. Now, does the family want a walking funeral, or a carriage? I have some new headstalls in—with ostrich plumes that are the most beautiful, straight, well-dyed things I've ever seen. Quite stylish. And the finest cloth for draping the parlor. You give me some indication of what he wants, and I will arrange it."

"I am afraid I don't know," Grenville said. "I promised to deliver the young woman home. After that, it is up to him."

"I understand. I understand. Grief is a difficult thing. That is why so many leave the choices to a trusted friend, like yourself."

"If he does want more, you send the bill to my man of business," Grenville said. "Thank you, Wilkinson. I know she's in good hands."

We rose and took our leave. Wilkinson, whose head came up to my chin, peered at me with professional interest.

"We never like to think of bereavement," he said. "But consider me when the time comes, sir. Giving loved ones the send-off they deserve is important, I think. And for yourself, sir, if you forgive me. Though that day I am certain is far in the future."

I'd never been sized up quite so frankly for a coffin before. I had known a coffin-maker in the army with an eccentric sense of humor, who would measure officers before battle to make sure he had enough boxes with the right dimensions. Since the officers he put his ruler to usually made it back in one piece, it became a mark of good luck to have him come at one with a tape measure.

I made my bow to Wilkinson and followed the very amused Grenville out.

"He's quite proud of his business," Grenville said as we rolled away. The rain had ceased, all to the good. I had an appointment to ride in the park with Donata's son. "But very skilled at it. The processions he arranges go off with aplomb and never drift into the vulgar. He is rubbing his hands, counting the days before I fall off the twig. It will be the grandest event London has ever seen, he says."

"Then your demise will cheer at least one person," I said. "The rest of us will be morose."

"I am certain I will have enraged enough men with my haughtiness by then that there will be a line of rejoicers," Grenville said. He sighed. "I grow weary of this life, Lacey."

"You long to be off."

Though the rain had ceased, a dampness pervaded the town. London was awake and alive, men and women, horses and carts moving through the streets in a great press, regardless of the weather. High brick walls hemmed us in, cutting off any view but stone and humanity.

"I do," Grenville said. "Dr. Johnson observed that when a man is tired of London, he is tired of life, but I am missing the rest of the world. One can only remark upon the cut of another man's coat so often. Although the bright green thing I saw upon the back of young Lord Armitage last night made me choke. And then I felt old. He is twenty-three, uninterested in the opinions of a man of forty. He, like Wilkinson, looks forward to my departure."

"Stop." I gave Grenville a stern look. "You are plunging into melancholia—I know the signs. Go home and make your plans for your Egyptian excursion in the winter. I have told you I will accompany you, and I will."

Grenville brightened. "You're right, Lacey. That will be just the thing. The weather there is appallingly hot, even in January, and there is dust everywhere, along with poisonous snakes and insects. You will heartily enjoy it."

"I believe I will," I said.

We talked of places in Egypt we'd visit and what I looked forward to seeing, as the carriage wedged its way through the damp press of London and dropped me at my front door. I took my leave of Grenville, feeling better, and went to find Peter to go for our ride.

Hyde Park after a rain, when the sun was beginning to emerge, was a fine place. Trees and brush sparkled with raindrops, the air had freshened, and the open expanse of the park was invigorating after the narrow streets of the metropolis.

It was not yet the fashionable hour, when the entire *haut ton* would turn out in carriages and on horseback to parade in their finery and greet one another with wit both pleasant and biting. Peter and I had a stretch of the Row to ourselves, though others were walking or trotting horses in the distance.

Peter was a good rider — he'd been given instruction at an early age and already he had a quiet seat, a steady hand, and knew how to move with the horse. Ostensibly, I was furthering his riding education, but the truth was we both enjoyed our afternoon rambles in the park, the men of the household together.

Peter was slightly downcast today, though I did not realize this until our first half-hour had passed. He was usually a cheerful chap, nothing at all like his churlish father—or perhaps the absence of that overbearing father had brightened his disposition.

"What is it?" I asked him when I noticed he didn't laugh as quickly, or seem as interested in naming and describing others' horses. "Something bothering you, old man?"

Peter didn't answer for a time, as though debating what to tell me. "Mother is going to have a child," he burst out. "Nanny said."

Peter was six years old, tall and sturdy for his age, and could converse without nervousness with adults he knew. I saw his mother in this. Donata talked, as she called it, *man-to-man* with Peter instead of behaving as though he were a strange creature from a land she'd long ago left behind.

I sometimes forgot that Peter, already a viscount, was in truth a bewildered little boy.

"She is," I said. "We were going to tell you so. In a few days, in fact. Make a celebration of it."

"I don't have a father," Peter said abruptly. "Not anymore."

"I know." I'd been there when Lord Breckenridge had been pulled out of brush and bracken, stone dead. "I'm sorry about that."

"Mother says you are to be my father now, even though you aren't really. That is, if you and I are willing."

"I'm certainly willing," I said in all sincerity. "If you'll have me."

Peter frowned, his small face screwed up in uncertainty. "You'll be the true father to Mother's child. You won't need me."

"Ah." I thought I understood what was bothering him. "You think when I have this new little one, I'll forget all about you."

"Won't you?" Peter was struggling to keep the wistfulness from his question. Males in England had stoicism drilled into them from an early age. "Mother never liked my father. No one did—I didn't like him either, really, though I don't remember him much. So … maybe … you won't like *me*."

The sins of the fathers are to be laid upon the children, so said the Bard in *The Merchant of Venice.* Well did I know how trying it was to be the son of a man most people, including his own family, despised.

"You are not your father," I said firmly. "I truly believe God gave us free will, Peter. You need be nothing like the late Lord Breckenridge. I respect and esteem you, lad. You remind me far more of your mother, and you know I care very much for her. Another child will only add to our family, not take away from it."

Peter watched me, doubtful. Another rider, his greatcoat pulled close against the chill the rain had brought, came toward us at a slow lope. We'd have to cease this conversation and nod to him, speak to him if he were an acquaintance.

"Think of it another way," I said. "Gabriella is my daughter, and now your stepsister. I have room in my heart for her, and you, and another child. You and Gabriella get on well, don't you?"

"She's very kind," Peter conceded. "Though she's much older than me."

"She's a kind young woman." Could I help it if pride rang in my voice? In the decade and more of her life I'd missed, she'd become a sweet-tempered, sunny-natured girl. Loosening her to meet the young men of London filled me with dread. "You will have to help us raise our new child to be as kind and thoughtful as Gabriella."

"I will?" Peter looked more interested. "Do you think it will be a little girl?"

"I hope so," I said. "The world needs more ladies. They're so much softer and more cheerful than us."

Peter's grin flashed. He enjoyed it when I spoke to him thus, as men together.

The other rider was nearly upon us. I turned, ready to tip my hat and greet him if need be.

The rider went low in his saddle and urged his horse toward us at a rapid pace. I stopped in surprise. It wasn't done to ride hell for leather when the park began to fill with the elite, though I sometimes shocked the denizens with a good gallop.

I recovered my surprise in time to see the man, muffled to his nose, his hat pulled over his eyes, ride hard for Peter. He swung something down beside his horse—it appeared to be a bag with a weighty object inside.

He was going to knock Peter from the saddle. My body knew this before the thought could form.

The crackling of gunfire came back to me, the scents of smoke and the roar of men in the middle of battle. I'd fought those who tried to smack me from my horse, cut me down, shoot me, trample me. I'd survived by being ruthless, fast, and trusting my instincts.

As the lingering din of war sounded in my head, I shoved my horse between the rider's and Peter, driving my mount at the approaching man's, forcing him to turn.

The rider's horse shied; mine spun and smacked his hindquarters into the other, ready to kick. The rider kept to his saddle, though his horse swayed. He righted the beast, and let fly the sack at me.

It had indeed been filled with large rocks, as I

found when it struck me. If I'd ducked, it would have flown over me and hit Peter, and so I took the full brunt on my back and side.

The impact, though I tried to roll my body to mitigate the worst of it, sent me from my horse. I landed hard, on my shoulder and bad leg, cursing as gravel cut my face.

Out of the corner of my eye, as I lay in fury, I saw Brewster emerge from the trees that lined the Row and hurtle toward the rider. He reached the horse and got his hands on the man's coat, but the rider struck out at Brewster. A knife blade flashed, Brewster let go, and the rider and horse skimmed away.

A pair of small boots landed next to my face. "Papa." Peter's worried voice sounded. "Are you dead?"

Through my pain and frustration, a warmth flooded me. He'd called me *Papa*. Not *sir* or *Captain*, or any of the formal monikers by which he'd addressed me thus far, but an acknowledgment of how he wished to regard me.

The moment ended when Brewster inserted himself between me and the rest of the world, going down on one knee.

"Bleedin' 'ell. You alive?" He turned me over to see my glare. "Thank God for that. Don't know what I'd tell his nibs."

His hard face took on a look of relief. Whether for my own sake or the fact he'd not have to report to Denis that he failed to keep me alive, I couldn't say.

Other riders were stopping, as did a sleek, two-wheeled curricle. "Who the devil was that?" The rather large and long-nosed countenance of the second Baron Alvanley peered down from his seat, his hands competently on the reins. "I had no idea there were highwaymen in Hyde Park."

William Arden, Lord Alvanley, was fairly young, not quite thirty, but he'd already had a distinguished army career and was firmly in with the Prince Regent's set. Grenville found him witty and entertaining, but Alvanley was ever trying to push Grenville aside as the successor of Mr. Brummell.

"What happened, Lacey?" Alvanley went on. "Shall I fetch someone?" He looked disapprovingly at Brewster, obviously too much of a ruffian to be my servant.

"I will be well," I said in some irritation.

Brewster's strong hand under my arm got me to my feet. Peter, trying to hide his tears, handed me my walking stick.

"I'm all right, Peter," I told him reassuringly. I rested my gloved fingers on the boy's shoulder and felt him trembling.

Alvanley's tiger—a young lad hired to tend the horses when the driver of a curricle or phaeton was away from the vehicle—had leapt down at Alvanley's command and caught my horse.

The boy, not much older than Peter, led my mount, a strong bay with a thick black mane, back to me. The tiger patted the horse in admiration before he handed me the reins.

I'd need a leg up. Before I could ask, Brewster was next to me, cupping his hands to heave me onto the horse. He pushed so hard I nearly slid off the other side but caught myself in time to save me that embarrassment. Brewster boosted Peter into the saddle of his smaller horse with more gentleness.

Alvanley, still on the box of the curricle, called to me. "Did you catch who it was? We should have the

Runners on him. A man can't go about knocking gentlemen from their horses."

"No." I peered in the direction the rider had disappeared, but of course, he was nowhere in sight. "He was too covered. Could have been anyone."

Peter spoke up. "Fine bit of horseflesh."

He was right—and the fact that the horse had been a good one should narrow the field. Horses were expensive, well I knew. I'd only been able to be a cavalryman because of the generosity of Colonel Brandon, who helped fund my horse, tack, and uniform. Only a wealthy man could afford a well-bred horse.

"An Irish hunter," Peter went on. "Red with two white stockings, and a star on his forehead."

"Jove," Alvanley said to him. "You have an eye, Breckenridge. I had better watch out when you start your stable."

Peter flushed but looked pleased.

Alvanley took up his reins, and his tiger jumped to his seat. "That will be it. Find the horse, and you find the man. Good day to you, Captain. My best to Mrs. Lacey and Mr. Grenville."

With a polite nod, he slapped the reins to the horses' backs and they walked on. Brewster watched him go, then turned to me.

"Who was it, Captain? You must a' seen."

"I assure you, I was more interested in keeping the man from hitting Peter," I said in irritation. "He was well dressed, but he could have picked up his clothes secondhand and hired the horse. We know nothing."

Brewster made a huffing noise. "We know one thing. He was after hurting you or the lad. Best you take yourselves home, Captain."

I had to agree. Peter, looking nervously about, drew his mount in close to mine, and we rode to the mews behind South Audley Street, our contentment shattered.

***

Peter wasted no time, once we were home, seeking his mother and telling her of our adventure.

I had never seen Donata as distressed as I did now. I'd taken Peter up to her private parlor, where Barnstable said she waited for us. Once Peter, who'd recovered his fright, excitedly blurted out the tale, she went down on her knees beside him and caught him in her arms.

Peter succumbed to her embrace, somewhat puzzled. "I'm all right, Mama. Truly. The captain was there."

Donata looked at me over Peter's head. "What the devil happened, Gabriel?"

"Nothing Peter hasn't already told you. It must have been a madman. Came at us, tried to strike Peter, but I blocked the blow. I'm only sorry I didn't knock the blasted man down myself."

Donata returned to hugging Peter tightly. "Who would do such a thing to a child? To my boy?"

I had a few ideas, but didn't want to mention them in front of Peter.

Peter patted Donata's back, still uncertain about his mother's outpouring. "I am very well, Mama. And hungry."

Donata released him with a little laugh, but remained on her knees beside him. "Aren't you always? Very well, run along and have Nanny give you plenty of tea and bread with extra jam and honey."

Peter grinned and gave her a loud kiss on the

cheek. "Thank you, Mama!"

He dashed from the room. Bartholomew, waiting outside, swept Peter onto his big shoulders and carried him up the stairs.

I watched them until I made certain they reached the top floor without mishap, and Bartholomew and Peter had ducked into the nursery. I closed the door to find Donata sitting on the floor, her silver and ivory striped skirts flowing about her.

"Love." I joined her, rather painfully, on the carpet, and put my arm around her. "He's all right. Peter is a sturdy lad."

"He is *my* lad." Donata leaned into me, her usual bravado gone. "Thank God for you, Gabriel." She closed her eyes, her hand straying to my thigh folded next to hers. A few moments later, she opened her eyes again and regarded me in concern. "Are *you* all right? You fell. Were you injured at all?"

"Ah, now you remember to ask about the fate of your husband."

"Do not joke. Not now." Donata's hand tightened on my leg. "You seem to me so … indestructible, Gabriel. The only reason I ever remain strong is I think of you, and your courage. I could not bear to have that taken from me."

Chapter Thirteen

I sat dumbfounded. I'd never heard Donata speak so, not with this ragged breathlessness and using such words. I pulled her closer.

"Dear lady." I kissed her temple. "When I met you two years ago, you already possessed great strength. What sustained you before I did?"

Donata wiped her eyes with the back of her hand. "Anger and bitterness. It wasn't strength; it was striking out in defense. You have anger too, but beneath it all is a constant sense of honor, of right and wrong. It drives you. I had lost that compass. You gave it back to me."

My dumbfounded state continued. I knew Donata had fondness for me, or she'd never have agreed to marry me, but I had not known any other reason.

I also had no idea how to answer. I was not an eloquent man, not like Grenville, who had the correct words for every occasion.

"I never realized I was such a paragon of virtue,"

was all I could invent to say. "I fancied myself a bit of a rogue."

Donata raised her head, a spark of her usual liveliness returning. "I did not say *virtuous*. I mean you have convictions and follow them, no matter what anyone else says and thinks. It is refreshing in a world where what others say of one is thought to be all important. That is an entirely different thing."

"True," I agreed.

"You are not virtuous, Gabriel. Thank heavens. Virtuous men are pompous and tiresome."

"Then I will endeavor not to be. Tiresome that is. Or virtuous and pompous."

Another look from under her lashes. "I thank you for that. Now, tell me who you think tried to bowl over my son. I have changed my mind about it being the gentleman I fancied as a girl. He has become rather portly and fractious, and could never have performed such feats of horsemanship. And too parsimonious to hire others to do so, according to his wife."

"Who inherits the Breckenridge title?" I asked. "After Peter, before he grows up and has sons himself?"

Donata answered readily. "One of Breckenridge's horrible cousins. I'm not certain he or his brother would try to shove Peter aside to inherit, however. Both Romulus and Remus expressed great relief when Breckenridge sired an heir."

My forehead puckered. "Romulus and Remus?"

"That is what I call them. Robert and Winston St. John. Robert is the elder, but only by a year. They are rakehells of the worst kind, are happy with the money they inherited from their father, and want nothing to do with the responsibilities a peerage brings. Neither would so much take a seat in the House of Lords as fall off it stone drunk."

"Perhaps, but the Breckenridge title has lands and much wealth, does it not? Which is why our blackmailer accuses me of forging my credentials to get my hands on it."

"Well, you cannot, can you? The money is managed by a trustee, who I assure you, as the name implies, is trustworthy. My father also keeps an eye on all Peter will inherit at his majority. My father has no flies on him—he'd never let you coerce a farthing out of me or Peter."

"Comforting," I said. "However, the wealth might be attractive even if having a title tacked to it is not. What is the Breckenridge estate worth?"

"Much," Donata said. "The Breckenridge seat is in Hampshire, among rich farmland. The income from it is vast. Breckenridge's father also purchased a home in Kent, and my husband bought another in Brighton, so he could chase the fashionable set. Breckenridge's father purchased this house outright as well."

Property, especially entailed property, could ensure that Peter lived well all his life, if he did not get into reckless habits. "Those houses and lands are all Peter's now?"

"All. Managed for him, as I say, by a trustee, until his majority. My widow's portion is quite large, and I have use of this house plus the dower house on the main estate, for my lifetime, even if I remarry. My father made bloody certain Breckenridge signed such agreements, so that I would not be left destitute, or ruined by a bad second marriage, and thrust back into my father's house as a poor relation."

Hardly poor. Donata's father, a wealthy peer

himself, would keep his daughter well, if it came to pass that she needed his charity. Her mother, a formidable woman in her own way, would also see to this.

"Which is why I thank God I didn't elope with the man I was potty about when I was seventeen," Donata went on. "I know you believe Aline and I are too exacting about Gabriella's come-out, but both of us know that a woman's fate depends on the negotiations between her father and her husband, not the wishes of her heart."

"As I made a foolish first marriage myself," I said, "I cannot argue with you."

"My man of business will be at your elbow when you negotiate with Gabriella's intended, whoever he may be. Aline and I are vetting every single young man invited to her ball as to suitability of temperament, income, background, and level in society. We are leaving nothing to chance."

And yet, I thought of Gabriella's irritation at being managed, her wistfulness that romance would have no part of it. I also understood Donata's point of view and agreed with her. I could see no other solution.

"You took a chance on your second husband," I observed. "But I understand that for a widow, such things are different."

"There was no chance about it," Donata said briskly. "I told you at the time that I looked into your background and learned all about you. I hardly ran away with the second footman."

I pulled her closer. "And if I had been a second footman?"

"Then we'd have had a shocking, and very discreet, *affaire*. I determined to have you one way or another, Gabriel."

I remembered finding her in my bed the evening after I'd met her, and her sharp look at me when I'd visited this house for the first time, investigating the death of her husband. She'd brought me here again when I was hurt, and joined me in the night. She had certainly shown persistence.

"You snared me in the end," I pointed out.

"No, I did not. You chose, and you know it."

"That is true." I pressed a kiss to her hair. "Shall we rise from this very hard floor? I've had a melancholy afternoon and feel a need for softness."

Donata rose with a limberness which put me to shame. A woman who was belly-full should not have showed more athleticism than me, a hardened cavalryman.

She helped me to my feet, led me to her chamber, and showed me, over the next hour, just how pleasing softness could be.

***

Now that I knew the deceased girl had been a young woman called Judith Hartman, I had to decide how to discover who had murdered her and left her to dissolve into a collection of bones.

I lay in bed after I woke later that evening, and contemplated the pseudo-Grecian plaster frieze that marched around Donata's bedchamber's ceiling. She was gone—she was taking Gabriella for another fitting, then she must dress to move on to her evening's entertainments. Donata had breezed away, leaving her indolent husband lounging in her bed.

Judith could have been the victim of a robbery, hit hard when she struggled. I would think a thief would have yanked the gold locket free of its chain or stripped her of any valuable clothing, but perhaps he—or she—had been unnerved at finding they'd killed her, and fled.

If so, I might never discover who'd done this. Or, the person could have been caught in another robbery and been long since hanged or transported. Or died naturally, never having confessed to the crime.

The blow had caught Judith across the face, from the top of her head to her mouth. She'd been facing her killer.

I thought about the bones of her hands, intact. The fingers had lain straight, relaxed, not curled into claws as though she defended herself. I had no idea whether the position of the hand would endure through the years. Denis's surgeon might, but I was not optimistic about being able to speak to him again. Coombs might know, however.

I could question Coombs about Hartman as well, see what he remembered about him, and about Judith.

I ground the heels of my hands into my eyes. I'd promised to discover who'd murdered Judith, accidentally or otherwise, and I would. The length of time between the death and today daunted me somewhat, but I was determined. I'd found a young woman called Sarah Oswold when she'd gone missing in London, and I'd discovered who'd stolen the church plate in Norfolk years after it had been taken. The passage of time had not stopped me in either case.

Still, the task seemed impossible, and this thought tempted me to remain still and do nothing. But I would certainly fail if I didn't begin.

By the time I heaved my sore body out of bed, Donata and Gabriella had returned from their shopping. Donata disappeared into her dressing room with her abigail, ready to transform herself for another night at soirees, supper parties, and the theatre.

Gabriella would stay in, and I decided I would too. No reason to go dashing about London when I was ill-tempered and hurt.

In light of what had happened with Peter in the park, and recalling my awful fears of last night, I sent word to Grenville via Bartholomew to please look after my wife this evening and escort her everywhere.

Bartholomew charged back not fifteen minutes later with Grenville's reply that he'd be delighted. I had a quiet word with Brewster outside to also not let Donata out of his sight.

Grenville's coach stopped in front of the house not long later, and Donata emerged, resplendent in a garnet-colored gown trimmed with gold, gloves covering her arms, and diamonds glittering in her hair and on her bosom. A flimsy shawl was all the protection she had against the night, but I had to admit she would turn the heads of all she passed.

I kissed her cheek, promising not to smear her rouge, and she gave me a warm look. Bartholomew and another footman held a canopy over her head between the door and Grenville's carriage, keeping the mist from her.

Grenville did not descend, but held his hands out to Donata to help her into the coach. He nodded at me, his expression grave—he'd heard the tale of the attack. He would take good care of her, I knew.

"Pray do not worry so, Gabriel," Donata said before she sat down opposite Grenville. "I will scuttle home like a *virtuous* wife before dawn."

Grenville looked mystified, I only smiled, and Bartholomew stepped between us to shut the door.

The carriage was gone, leaving me on my own with my daughter.

Gabriella came down for supper. She and I ate in the dining room, candlelight throwing a golden glow over us as the footmen served, and Barnstable hovered to watch that all went smoothly.

I still was not used to the luxury of having light whenever I wanted—Donata's staff saw that a supply of beeswax candles were available every day. In June, light lasted well into the night, but the dining room, in the back of the house, never saw much sun.

Gabriella had heard all about the incident with Peter. "How awful," she said. "He is not afraid, though, brave lad. He says he intends to ride out again with you as usual."

"Mmm." I'd decide whether we should or not. "I am pleased you are in tonight, Gabriella. I knew I'd never confine Donata to the house, but I confess relief you are here where I can see you."

"I have learned to take care in London," Gabriella said, her eyes darkening. She'd been abducted while running alone through Covent Garden, and the harrowing incident still weighed upon her mind. "I am not so foolish as to dash about by myself, on foot. The innocent country girl has been erased from me."

I smiled. "I hope not entirely."

"That is what the young woman you are investigating did, I presume," Gabriella went on, dragging her fork across her fish in buttery sauce. "Walked alone, and came to grief."

"She did." I told her what Grenville and I had discovered today, not flinching about giving

Gabriella the details. I would not hide the dangers of the world from her, never again.

"Perhaps you can help me," I said. "What reasons would a daughter of a protective father have for leaving the house by herself? I assume if she'd had a maid with her, the maid would have at least run for help, or been able to tell the family what happened."

Gabriella took a thoughtful bite of fish. "If she had a protective father, and she went alone, I would say she was meeting a young man."

"Yes." I swallowed uneasiness that such a solution would spring at once to her mind. "Eloping with him? Or simply meeting him?"

"That is more difficult to say." Gabriella's face creased as she thought. "If no valise was found with her things, it might have been stolen, or she might have run out of the house simply to speak to the young man, intending to go back home after the tryst. Lady Aline, however, told me the tale of a young lady who walked out of her father's house with nothing and climbed into a carriage her young man sent to meet her. She ran off with a dragoon officer and married him."

A romantic tale. "We have no way of knowing whether a conveyance met Miss Hartman, or she walked to her destination. Did this young man hit her? And why, if she'd come to meet him clandestinely? I would assume him a lover or secret affianced. Or was it a robber? Or someone she quarreled with who struck her in a moment of anger? The blow was certainly hard."

Gabriella shuddered. "Poor girl."

I reached for her hand. "I beg your pardon. I did not mean to distress you."

"I am not distressed." Gabriella slid her hand

from mine and drank from her goblet of watered wine. "I feel sorry for her, only. She must have been eager, running to meet him. I hope her death was quick."

"She died at once it seems." Both surgeons had said that, and those men had seen death. "I am trying to decide what to do next."

"Her father or family would know — or could guess — what man she went to meet. Or, at least tell you about the men Miss Hartman knew."

Or women, I added silently. A strong woman, with the right weapon, could strike a blow like that.

"The trouble is, Mr. Hartman will not speak," I said. "He has made it clear he wants no one investigating his daughter's death."

Gabriella flashed me a smile. "Dear Father, I doubt you will let that stop you."

"No, indeed," I said with conviction.

"Mr. Hartman must have brothers, friends, or other children, who might be more forthcoming," Gabriella suggested.

"Precisely my thoughts," I said, thinking of the assistant Hartman had identified as his nephew. "You are certainly my daughter."

Gabriella flushed. "I am proud to be."

The women in my family were busy melting my heart today. When Gabriella had first discovered, a year ago, that I was her true father, not Major Auberge, she'd been furious and grief-stricken. She'd hated me on sight, and I could not blame her.

By the time I'd married Donata, she'd accepted me. This was the first time I'd heard Gabriella say she was pleased.

I gave her hand another squeeze, uncertain how to respond. I was saved from breaking down and weeping by Barnstable signaling the footmen to remove the fish plates and begin serving the meat.

***

True to her word, Donata returned home, in Grenville's carriage, by three in the morning.

"I had a lovely time," Donata said, kissing my cheek where I stood at the bottom of the stairs, clad in a loose dressing gown over my shirtsleeves and trousers. "Grenville is a fine dancer and stood up with me most of the night. We had marvelous fun daring the *ton* to believe we were having a love affair. Do not be alarmed if you hear it put about."

I pictured Grenville and Donata, who'd become very good friends, whispering like schoolchildren as they planned their ruse.

"Why on earth should you want such a story put about?" I asked, unoffended.

"Because it is in bad taste for a woman to be in love with her own husband. I'd be ridiculed everywhere." She patted my cheek, bathing me in lemony perfume. "Do not worry, Gabriel. Everyone knows how fond you are of Grenville and he of you. They will no doubt believe we are in a ménage a trois. Good night."

My wife's idea of humor was sometimes lost on me. I imagined Grenville laughing even now.

I spent a fairly restless night, mostly because of soreness from my fall. My dreams spun endlessly. I saw a young woman who looked much like Gabriella but my fancy painted her as Judith Hartman — young, dark-haired, vibrant. She came at me along the crowds of the Strand, waving to me, calling.

But when she reached me, the skin of her face fell away, and she was nothing more than bones at my feet, her empty eye sockets turned up to me in pleading, one of them smashed.

I jerked awake early, my head aching, my limbs stiff.

I rose, trying to swallow enough coffee to banish the visions, and put forth plans to find out about Mr. Hartman. I went through the cards I collected and pulled out the one handed to me by Mr. Molodzinski, when he'd come to thank me for defending him against Mr. Denis.

I dressed, hired a hackney, collected Brewster, who'd returned to the house, looking half asleep, and journeyed to the City.

We traveled eastward via the wide stretch of Holborn, where molly houses nestled into the back lanes and barristers' inns and solicitors' offices faced the street.

The road sloped down to become Newgate Street, the grim prison walls enclosing those awaiting trial and execution, the dome of Saint Paul's rising beyond it. After that, Cheapside led us to a six-way junction and Mansion House, where the Lord Mayor of London presided. Beyond that, Threadneedle Street held the Bank of England; Cornhill, the Royal Exchange; and Lombard Street, moneylenders and the Post Office.

Molodzinski's house was in between these streets of great wealth. As a man of business, advising his clients on their personal financial affairs, I imagined him opening his window to hear how best to invest the fortunes of those he represented.

Molodzinski's abode was a modest one, in a modest court between Cornhill and Lombard Street. His card was of cheap paper, and so I concluded that his clients were middle class, and not those middle class who'd amassed great fortunes. Ordinary folk, I surmised as his young clerk admitted me to ordinary rooms in an ordinary house.

"Captain Lacey." Molodzinski came from his office at the top of the stairs as I made my stiff way up them. He gazed down at me, the relief on his still-bruised face puzzling. "How delightful. Please, do come in."

He sounded extremely nervous. He waited for me to reach the landing, then he took my elbow with the pretense of assisting me, and nearly dragged me into his office.

I understood Molodzinski's anxiousness as soon as I walked inside. James Denis turned from the window, where he'd been gazing down at the street.

He looked me over in his cold way and gave me a slight nod. "Captain."

Chapter Fourteen

I nodded in return. "Mr. Denis."

Molodzinski hovered just inside the door, clasping his hands. Any moment, he'd bolt. "You have come to discuss business, Captain? Perhaps, you would like to speak privately?"

His eyes begged me to agree. "Of course," I said. I bowed to Denis. "Will you excuse us?"

Denis didn't move. "Whatever business you have, you may discuss before me. I am discreet."

Molodzinski began, "Perhaps the captain would be more comfortable …"

"He means it's none of your affair," I said bluntly to Denis. "Which it is not."

Denis gave me a weary look. "Captain, I will not allow you to spirit Mr. Molodzinski away in hopes he can elude me. He cannot. State your business—it is bound to be of interest to me as well."

I did not want Denis in this. I hoped to give Hartman peace now that he knew his daughter was dead. Denis was excellent at bringing wrongdoers to justice—when he wished—but Hartman hardly needed Denis in his affairs.

"Perhaps I will call on you another time," I said to Molodzinski. "Or, you are welcome in South Audley Street."

"No." Molodzinski gazed at me in desperation. "Please, do not go."

"He fears I will strike him dead the moment your back is turned," Denis said. "And I might. You should stay, Captain, and prevent the tragedy."

Denis's sense of humor was even more obscure than my wife's.

"Very well," I said, losing my patience. I thumped myself onto a hard wooden chair, one of the few in the rather barren, high-ceiling room. The windows were open, early summer warmth and the stench of the city floating in. "Mr. Molodzinski, I would like to know all you can tell me about a shopkeeper called Joseph Hartman and his family. His daughter has been killed, and I am seeking information about her and her last days."

Molodzinski blinked. "His daughter was killed? Dear, dear. Poor man."

"Do you know him?"

Molodzinski, despite his nervousness, looked amused. "Because he is a Jew, as am I? I do not believe I've even heard of him."

I suppressed an impatient noise. "No, I mean because you are a man of business to shopkeepers like him, and you might know who handles his affairs. I cannot ask Hartman himself, because he has warned me off."

"Ah." Molodzinski looked a bit more interested. "Perhaps I could make inquiries."

Denis broke in. "This is the same dead woman you came to me about? Or have you found another unfortunate in the meantime?"

"The same," I said tightly. "I have managed to discover her identity without you, thank you."

Denis's eyes went colder still. "I know what Mr. Brewster did. I am not happy with him, as I have explained to him."

I thought of Brewster's exhausted look this morning and wondered now whether he'd been able to go home at all. Had he spent the hours between seeing Donata safely to our house and my leaving the next morning being berated by Denis? Denis did not seem particularly fatigued, but then, he never did.

"Mr. Brewster, in his own way, has honor," I said. "Allow him to rest from time to time, and see his wife."

"Mr. Brewster's loyalties have become a bit fluid," Denis said. "Please remember that I pay his wages."

"Yes, you are the master of us all," I said, my hot temper bubbling high. Molodzinski gave me a fearful look, but I could not cease. I pointed at him. "Whatever this man has done cannot be worth you coming here yourself to reprimand him. I do my best to vex you all the time, but *he* is rather harmless."

"He is a murderer, Lacey," Denis said.

I stopped. I'd been drawing a breath to contradict him, and I nearly choked on it.

I swung back to Molodzinski. His face was red, his dark eyes full of shame. His voice dropped to a near whisper. "Not on purpose."

My words halted again. Manslaughter then? And why, if he'd killed a person, intentionally or no, was he free to go about his business?

"If you were acquitted," I said slowly, "then Mr. Denis should have no hold on you."

"He has never been arrested," Denis said. "The only one who knows he killed this man is myself. And now, you."

Molodzinski took a step toward Denis. "You promised your silence, that you would not betray me to the magistrates. Gave your word."

Denis transferred his frosty look to Molodzinski. "In return for your services when I wished them, yes. Which you have been reluctant to furnish. But Captain Lacey is not a magistrate. If he decides to keep your secret, it will be safer with him than anyone in London."

I tried to ignore Denis while I faced Molodzinski. "Will you tell me what happened?" This man did not look like a killer, not even an accidental one.

Molodzinski let out a sigh that came from the bottom of his boots. "I was approached by some … men. Four of them. One was a client. They wanted me to embezzle from two other of my clients, to ruin the gentlemen, and of course pass on their money to them. When I continually refused, they sent a ruffian to persuade me. I fought with him, and he fell down the stairs. Broke his neck."

Molodzinski snapped his mouth shut, as though reminding himself to say nothing further. A plausible tale, but I wondered whether there was more to it.

"These men who'd asked you to embezzle must have noticed that the ruffian they sent to you had died," I said.

Molodzinski shuddered. "I'd had some dealings with Mr. Denis in the past—the money I told you I borrowed from him. I asked for his help."

Denis finished. "I made certain that the ruffian's

death was not connected to Mr. Molodzinski, and that the consortium took their business elsewhere."

I imagine Denis willingly performing these tasks in order to have a man of business in his pocket. Though Molodzinski was not wealthy, he'd have access to information, could pry information out of other men of business, and would know of dealings on the exchanges, perhaps before others became aware of them.

What Denis prized above all else was knowledge.

The fact that Denis was here now told me that perhaps Molodzinski was reluctant to give Denis this information.

"I understand your quandary," I said to Molodzinski. "I will keep your confidence."

Molodzinski looked surprised but grateful. "Thank you, sir. Thank you. I am in your debt."

"It seems your debt is extending to many," Denis said in a dry voice. "But please, do what Captain Lacey asks of you. His intentions are usually benign, even if he is insistent."

My annoyance returned. "He is obviously an honorable man," I said, pointing my walking stick in Molodzinski's direction. "He defended himself against a pack of criminals — very different from him striking down an innocent. You would do a kindness to leave him be."

Denis regarded me stonily. "My business would be in pieces if I followed your precepts. Forgive me if I do not rush to obey you. Please, continue your errand here. I will deal with Mr. Molodzinski later. I cannot hope to prevail against your tenacity when you wish to discover answers."

I was not flattered, but glad he would not hinder Molodzinski in responding to my questions.

Denis made no move to leave, however. He stood like a monolith while I turned back to Molodzinski and explained the circumstances with Hartman and his daughter.

Molodzinski lost his fearfulness of me as he listened, and his expression changed to one of sympathy.

"I can inquire, Captain. I laughed at you when I accused you of coming to me, one Jew to track down another, but it is true that our community in London is rather small. I do not know this man personally, but I know how to find others who will. I must warn you, not everyone will welcome an outsider asking questions. I am pleased I live in this country in this time, when we are not being expelled or imprisoned simply for being Jewish, but insults come readily to Gentiles, and we are not wholly embraced."

"I do understand," I said. "Though you might not think it. I have knowledge of what it is to be on the outside looking in. Lack of funds has a way of separating a man, even when others pretend it does not."

Molodzinski looked surprised. "You live in a sumptuous enough house." He hesitated. "Though so does the Prince of Wales, and he is up to his ears in debt."

"I married well," I said, my smile wry. "But my station in life is below my wife's, so I am looked at askance."

"True, wealth will ingratiate a man when all other factors about him would normally repulse." Molodzinski shook his head. "That is the way of the world."

He reiterated that he'd ask about Hartman for me, and send word to my rooms in Grimpen Lane. The interview was at an end.

I was reluctant to leave him alone with Denis, at Denis's mercy. Though I did not believe Denis would allow my presence to stop him meting out punishment as he thought fit, he might at least hesitate.

Denis, however, took up the hat he'd left on a table and motioned me to leave with him. I thanked Molodzinski again, shook his hand, and left the office.

My hackney waited, with Brewster lounging against it, talking with the coachman. Brewster went at once to Denis when he stepped outside — they exchanged a few words I could not hear, then Brewster came back to the hackney, handed up coin, and dismissed the coach.

The hackney drove on, leaving me with Denis, as Denis's coach pulled forward to retrieve him.

In a few minutes, I once more found myself inside Denis's austere but elegant carriage, facing the man who controlled most of the criminal element in London.

"I will not apologize for defending Mr. Molodzinski," I said before Denis could speak. "He was in an unfortunate situation, and you took advantage of him."

"I did indeed," Denis said without changing expression. "But I did not bring you with me to rebuke you. I want you to tell me about the attack on your son in the park."

I started. "Why? Brewster must have reported it to you."

"He did. He was quite angry about it. But I would like the matter described from your point of view."

"I saw the man coming and thought nothing of

it." I related what had happened, ending with Peter's assessment that the horseflesh was costly.

Denis tapped one finger to the gold head of his walking stick. "A member of the *haut ton* attempting to knock small boys from horses? This is a strange occurrence."

"Hardly one for humor. If his sack had hit Peter, Peter might have been seriously hurt."

"I was not laughing. I was remarking on the incongruity. Oddities interest me. You are correct that the place to start looking for the culprit is the horse. Even if the man did not own the horse, a groom or stable lad will remember him hiring it."

"Possibly. I have already sent Bartholomew to the stables in and about Hyde Park to make inquiries. I have no doubt that he and his brother will quickly find something for me. It was a fine hunter, and fresh—the rider could not have ridden it far that day. Likely it was cared for nearby."

Denis gave me a nod. "I agree with your logic."

"May I ask why you are interested? Why should an attack on my stepson distress you?"

Denis moved his hand on the walking stick, his fingers caressed by his skin-tight kid gloves. "I have become quite protective of you. A blow to your beloved family would cripple you. That would lose me a valuable asset. Also, my enemies might attempt to reach me by using you."

My heart beat thick and hard. "Cease requesting my help, and your enemies will have nothing to hold over you. I refuse to let any of my family come to harm because of you."

Denis flicked his fingers. "I would have considered your debt to me paid had you not sought my assistance so many times in these past few years.

And I do like to keep an eye on you. However, I do not truly believe this is the work of my enemies. They are not so crude."

"Not a thought that comforts me," I said. "I agree, it was clumsy. Which is why I suspect one of small Peter's relations is at the heart of it. Someone suddenly wants to be Viscount Breckenridge."

"A comfortable and lucrative peerage," Denis agreed. "I will assist you in unraveling that problem, but I advise you drop investigating the shopkeeper's dead daughter."

"No," I said. "Her killer should not go free."

"You are willing to let Molodzinski go free. Even when he admitted himself he'd taken a life."

"Entirely different. I've done battle. I know the fear, the desperation of fighting for one's life. In my case I was commended for my bravery. Whoever killed Miss Hartman was a coward. What could she have done to warrant such a thing?"

"Not all ladies are kind, gentle creatures," Denis said. "Perhaps she angered her killer, threatened him in some way, with words alone. Made him fear *her*."

"Why he did it is immaterial," I said in a hard voice. "He should have found another way to resolve his quarrel with her. The blow was hard, and not accidental."

"How can you be certain?" Denis asked, eyeing me. "Something might have fallen on her, or she hit her head as she went down."

"Your surgeon says no. He said that her falling would have crushed her more, looked different—how, I do not know. He said it was a strike, swift and hard, with a thin, blunt weapon, like a poker or crowbar."

Denis nodded. "He is likely correct. He is an

expert on wounds."

I studied Denis in curiosity. "And you will tell me no more about him?"

"No." Denis lifted his walking stick, a heavy thing, its shaft of polished mahogany, and tapped the roof of the coach.

Immediately we halted. I glanced out and saw we'd reached the end of Fleet Street, at Temple Bar, the gate to the city designed by Sir Christopher Wren to replace the more ancient gate destroyed in the Great Fire.

"Good day to you, Captain," Denis said.

There were shouts behind and around us as the coach blocked traffic. Brewster wrenched open the door, reaching in big hands to pull me out, not bothering to bring down the steps.

The snarls quieted a little when Brewster glared, but whether the passers-by understood who was in the coach or not, I could not be certain. The carters and draymen of London cared little who got in their way—they were evil-tempered to one and all.

Brewster slammed the door, half dragged me aside, and Denis's coach moved on.

***

Because I was relatively close to Covent Garden, I decided to walk to my rooms, on the off chance that Hartman himself had sent word to me there.

When I reached it by way of Drury Lane and Russel Street, Mrs. Beltan, who kept my mail in my absence, handed me letters, but told me no shopkeeper had come to call. Nor had she received any message from one, written or otherwise.

I was about to leave the warm, bread-scented shop when she stopped me. "There was a young lady, however. I say *young*—perhaps getting on for middle age."

"A lady?" I lifted my brows. "Did she leave a name?"

"She did not," Mrs. Beltan said. "Refused to. But she said she'd try again today. I offered to send for you, but oddly, she did not wish me to do that either." She shook her head, turning back to the line of women purchasing bread for the day's meals.

Mrs. Beltan was too busy to give me the particulars of the lady, so I ascended to my rooms to see if she'd left me some message.

She had. I found scrawled on a scrap of paper, set in the center of my writing table, *Will return at 11* AM.

It was ten of the clock now. I crumpled the paper, thrust it into my pocket, and sat down to read the rest of my letters and wait.

Chapter Fifteen

I heard Brewster haul himself up the steps. He entered without knocking, balancing two mugs of coffee in one great hand.

"So you're waiting, then." He thunked a mug to my writing table, the hot coffee splashing droplets to the letters.

"Go if you like," I said. "She left a note that she'd return at eleven. Time for you to do your morning shopping."

Brewster gave me an evil look. He moved to the door and leaned against the doorframe, sipping the hot brew.

"She might be someone come to do you 'arm," he said.

"I will attempt to defend myself." I began opening the letters and sifting through them.

"She might bring help to best you. I was watching the rider yesterday, Captain. It could have been a woman."

I thought of the lithe and athletic way the fellow had ridden, light in the saddle, agile with the reins, moving as one with the horse. "One hell of a good rider," I said. "Perhaps, in addition to finding the horse, I should inquire about the reputation of skilled horsemen. Even the best might have found those moves difficult."

"His nibs has it aright. You are too trusting of the fairer sex." Brewster made the pronouncement decidedly. "I've seen women vaulting onto and off horses like nothing, hanging upside down from their bellies even. Acrobats and traveling performers can do it. I've seen women dressed as men do all sorts of riding feats, and then reveal themselves to be ladies to the astonishment of the crowd."

I believed him. Brewster and his wife highly enjoyed entertainments, whether inside theatres or on the streets, or performed by strolling players at outlying inns.

"I hadn't thought of it that way." I gave him a nod. "Thank you."

"So this lady what ran down your son might be coming here to shoot you." Brewster dug his shoulder into the doorframe. "I'll stay."

"Why did you tell Denis you'd found the surgeon for me?" I asked curiously. "I did not plan to mention it to him."

"He'd have found out, one way or another. He always does, don't he? Best it came from me, straight up, than he visits my house and asks why I lied to him." Brewster gave a slight shiver. "Facing him down and confessing is much better."

"My apologies. I know he was angry with you. I'll speak to him."

Brewster barked a laugh. "Won't do no good. The

deed is done, he is angry, he'll punish the both of us, and we'll not do it again. That is the way of him. Straightforward."

"Unreasonable. Even I see that the world is not black and white. Some things must be done, whether we, or Denis, like it or not. A man's actions do not always reflect his motives, or what is in his heart."

"He's always had to see it, though, as you say, black and white, hasn't he? Or he'd have been dead a long time ago."

I agreed that Denis's early life had been difficult, and he'd been saved only by his quick mind and complete ruthlessness.

"He and I will always disagree about many things," I concluded. "Still, I will speak to him about you. You've been of great help to me."

"I wish you wouldn't," Brewster said darkly. "The point is, he pays a good wage. I'd rather not lose my post, if it's all the same to you."

"Very well." I returned to my letters. "See that you don't pocket anything priceless while you're here, won't you?"

I heard the grin in his voice. "You ain't got much, I have to tell you, Captain."

He knew exactly what incident I referred to. A glance at him showed he'd folded his arms tightly, as though ready to prove he wasn't touching anything.

My first few letters were nothing remarkable—a bill for meals at a nearby public house, a note from my father's man of business answering a question I'd asked him about my property in Norfolk—namely, how much land around the house was actually still mine.

I also had a breezy but polite letter from one Frederick Hilliard, an actor and famous *travesti* from

Drury Lane theatre. He thanked me for my introduction to Leland Derwent, and told me they'd become good friends.

Leland still grieves, and always will, I am afraid. I have taken it upon myself to cheer him, but not to chivvy him, if you understand. He can speak to me of the one he loved, as he can speak to no other. He regards you fondly, sweet lad.

Freddie Hilliard was a tall, solid-bodied, deep-voiced man who could transform himself into a woman onstage with amazing verisimilitude. He had his audiences roaring with laughter, or weeping when he portrayed a woman of deep sorrow. I admired his talent, and he'd been of great help during Leland's tragedy earlier this year. I agreed Leland would find comfort in him.

I pocketed the missive to share with Donata, broke the seal on the last letter, and froze.

You fought well in the park, proved yourself to be a fine cavalryman. But this does not mean the man who came back from the dead is the true Gabriel Lacey. The price of my silence has increased.

I could not stop a sharp intake of breath. Brewster was at my side in an instant, his large fingers pulling the letter from my grasp.

"Ye see?" He said, reading the words. "It *was* a woman in the park, and she slipped in this letter when she was up here."

"It came by post." I indicated the mark that the letter had been pre-paid.

"Hmm," Brewster said, unconvinced. "What does it mean, *the man who came back from the dead*? When did you die?"

I shrugged. "On the Peninsula. Captured and dragged off by French soldiers and made sport of. It's when I got this." I tapped my ruined left knee.

"But I assure you, it was I who made it back to camp, after a long struggle. Part of me did die on that journey, but not in the way the writer implies."

Brewster peered from the letter to my leg and back again. "Why does he—or she—want you not to be *you*?"

"Who can say? To discredit Donata? To have me arrested for fraud? Me defrauding the new Viscount Breckenridge would be a great scandal. I was present at the former Viscount Breckenridge's death after all, which has been pointed out in the letters." I let out a sigh. "I believe, though, that this blackguard simply wants money."

Brewster dropped the letter back to the writing table. "I suppose you could have murdered Breckenridge, then taken up with his wife—not much grieving on her part from what I heard. You started squiring her about not long after, you know. You have been uncommon clever, Captain."

I looked up to rebuke his teasing, and realized we were not alone.

I had not heard anyone enter over Brewster's rumbling voice, but I now saw a woman standing in the doorway to the stairwell, her quiet presence unassuming.

I rose quickly to my feet, stepped too hard on my bad leg, and bit back a grunt as I reached for my walking stick. Brewster swung around, and in one step, had himself between me and the woman.

She looked nothing like an adept rider who could hang underneath a horse. The lady was past her first youth but still relatively young, in her thirties, I'd judge. She was plump, gently so. The sleeves of her morning gown clung to her round arms then tapered to strong wrists and fleshy hands in gloves.

The hair under her small-brimmed bonnet was dark brown, the green ribbon of the hat matching the dark green of her simple but becoming gown. Having grown used to Donata and her exacting taste, I recognized that this woman had learned how to dress the very best for her means.

She had dark eyes, a pale face, a wide mouth, and a severe look. She was quite attractive, or would be but for the bleak anger and sorrow in her eyes.

"Captain Lacey?"

I bowed. "I am he. You are the lady who wishes to speak to me?"

The clock on my mantel began striking eleven, the bells of St. Paul's, Covent Garden, taking up its tune. She was exactly on time.

"Might I ask your name?" I went on.

The lady looked me over, as though trying to make up her mind about me, then Brewster. Her glance dismissed him as the hired help.

Not a lady of timid deference, I was understanding. She'd learned to face down the world without trembling.

"I am Miss Hartman," she said. "I understand you revealed to my father that my sister, Judith, is dead."

I straightened in astonishment. "Yes," I said, finding the word hardly adequate.

"I also know my father bade you not to pursue the matter further." Miss Hartman's voice was hard. "I am here, contrary to my father's wishes, to ask you to do just that." She lifted her chin. "I know who killed my sister, and I want you to prove it."

Chapter Sixteen

Brewster and I both remained fixed in stunned silence. Miss Hartman's green bodice rose with her breath, but her face was as chill as marble.

"Miss Hartman," I finally managed. "Please, sit. Tell me all."

She studied me a few moments longer, then she moved to a straight-backed chair at my table and lowered herself into it. She was so stiff that her own back barely touched that of the chair.

I signaled for Brewster to leave us. He did not look happy, but he walked out to the landing and closed the door behind him. He'd listen through it; I knew that.

I always found it interesting to observe which of my chairs my visitors selected. Those who had no shame in seeking out comfort chose the upholstered wing chair at the fireplace. Those who were more about business sat in one of the hard, wooden chairs from the seventeenth century. Those who were particularly nervous would remain standing altogether.

Miss Hartman gave me a chilly look as I sat down in the other hard, spindled chair and faced her.

"If you know who killed her," I began, "why not go to the magistrates?"

"One must have evidence," Miss Hartman answered crisply. "Or money to bring suit. I have neither. I only *know*. But I have heard through others that sometimes you, Captain, find ways to uncover proofs that the Runners can not."

"Others have flattered me," I said. "In this case, however, your determination and mine match. Who is this person you suspect?"

"Her husband." The words came readily. "I see from your surprise that my father did not tell you she was married. But she was. Legitimately. In the eyes of the laws of England, I mean—not in the eyes of my father. Judith married a Gentile. She converted to become a member of the Church of England, and married him with banns read and the entire rigmarole. My father turned his back on her."

My heartbeat quickened. "And the name of this husband?"

"Mr. Andrew Bennett. Oh, so very respectable. He married again, not two years after Judith disappeared. And then a third time. His second wife died as well."

"I see." I tried to stem my rising excitement. A man with too many wives in quick succession could be suspicious, or he could simply be unfortunate. Life was dangerous, illness happened all too often, as did accidents. A thrice-widowed man—or woman— was not uncommon. However, my interest perked at this gentleman who seemed to find wives so readily.

"You are skeptical," Miss Hartman said. "But I know him. I could not say that his second wife died in unusual circumstances — she was very ill in the end — but I have my doubts. He certainly was quick to consider Judith dead and himself free to marry again."

"A judge would have to agree that a missing woman was deceased," I observed. "Time passing is only part of it."

"I know." Miss Hartman's eyes snapped. "When Judith could not be found, Mr. Bennett concluded very quickly that she'd died — insisted within months that we give up hope. He lived with the woman who would be his second wife for two years before Judith was declared officially deceased and he could marry again."

"Your sister's marriage — this was the shame your father referred to?"

"The marriage, certainly. And the fact that Judith turned her back on her family. She had no use for us. She tried to convince my father to convert, to become more English, to shave his beard and be more ambitious. The ghettos of the Continent were of the past; the traditional ways were of the past. One must live in the present."

Her anger was evident. "You do not share this view?" I asked gently.

"There is a saying — that one must not *das Kind mit dem Bad ausschütten* — throw the baby out with the bath. One can live well in London without ignoring one's past."

I preferred to ignore mine, but I knew what she meant. "Judith could not find the balance between two worlds?" When Miss Hartman's eyes flickered, I stopped. "I beg your pardon. I did not mean to use her given name." It was not done unless a gentleman was a close friend of the family, and even then, only in proper circumstances.

"You mistake me, sir," Miss Hartman said. "It is good to hear her name again. My father will not speak it. My mother would not before her death."

"And your name?" I asked. "If I may be so bold as to inquire."

For answer, she opened a small reticule that matched her gown and handed me a card. *Miss Devorah Hartman.*

Miss, I noted. Never married. I laid the card carefully on my writing table.

"Where might I find this Andrew Bennett?" I asked. "What is his profession?"

"He claimed to be a lecturer in Greek." Miss Hartman's voice was thick with cynicism. "He also said he knew Hebrew, which is how he came to be acquainted with my father. A scholar, he styled himself, though I've never seen him look at a book." Her lip curled. "Mr. Bennett now lives in some leisure in Cavendish Square, in the house of his third wife. He acquired much money from his second wife, who'd inherited several thousand pounds before she died. His third wife must also have inherited something from a generous parent. I imagine you will find Mr. Bennett at home."

The man sounded a bounder, if nothing else.

Then again, I, a penniless gentleman, had just married a widow of considerable fortune. *I* knew my reasons had nothing to do with her money, but those outside my circle of acquaintance — and a few within it — no doubt suspected me of financial ambition. Indeed, I was now receiving nasty letters about it.

"I will speak to him," I said. "Be assured I do

want to find your sister's killer."

"Well, you need look no further than Mr. Bennett."

That remained to be seen. "What else can you tell me about your sister?" I asked.

Devorah's eyes widened slightly. "Is there any reason to know? I care only for catching the man who ended her life."

"Yes," I said, trying not to let my impatience show, "but I might be able to snare him more readily if I know something about Judith. Mr. Bennett could have made certain to give himself an unbreakable alibi, or to destroy all evidence. I can't bring him to trial without proof of a crime. Knowing more about your sister will help me question him."

Devorah let out a sigh, though her sour look did not leave her. "Very well. Judith was a bit frivolous, as you no doubt guessed. She saw that becoming more Anglo would give her a wider circle of friends, more acceptance, more opportunity to enter the society she craved.

"She was not wrong. Though she had to endure cuts about being a Jewess, she happily put up with it to wear lovely ensembles, ride in Hyde Park, and be invited to soirees. We hadn't the money to be accepted in aristocratic circles, but she reached as high as she could. Mr. Bennett being a gentleman and a scholar from a prestigious college helped."

Devorah shook her head. "Besides this obstinacy, Judith was sweet-natured. She'd never hurt anyone on purpose. She cried when my father did not understand her wish to marry Bennett, but she was in love. She believed he'd come around when she had her first son."

I remembered what the surgeon had said about

Judith, that she'd borne no children. But she might have started one, the tiny thing washed away when she'd become bones.

"Was she increasing?" I asked, making my voice gentle.

"No." Devorah was resolute. "Never. She and Bennett were married two years, but Judith never conceived. He blamed her, but ... Bennett has never sired a child, to my knowledge, even after three marriages. I'm sure his seed is the culprit."

Her cheeks burned red as she pronounced this, but she folded her lips, as though daring me to remark upon her impropriety.

A picture of Judith Hartman began to weave in my mind. Sweet-natured, wanting to move beyond what she saw as the confines of her life, and too trusting.

My own daughter was as sunny and trusting as I imagined Judith to be. I felt disquiet.

I comforted myself by reflecting that Gabriella was different in one respect—she'd told me she preferred her quiet country life to that of high society.

But then, I, her father, had been born to the correct religion in a country in which it was a great asset to belong to the national church. Judith had converted to the C of E in order for her marriage to be accepted in her husband's world.

I knew full well that plenty of people declared they were "married" without the bother of the formalities. They lived in a semblance of wedlock without it being legally acknowledged, though no one said much.

Judith had not been willing to do this. She'd wanted to become Anglo and Mrs. Andrew Bennett, leaving her Jewish life behind.

"Thank you, Miss Hartman," I said. "I will visit Mr. Bennett and see what I can do."

She did not express gratitude or rhapsodize about my kindness. Devorah simply rose, clutched her reticule, gave me a polite nod, and made for the door.

Brewster opened it for her from the other side with the attentiveness of a well-trained footman. He stepped back as she walked out, me stumping after her.

"How may I send word to you?" I asked as she descended the stairs. "I assume you do not wish your father to know of this visit."

Devorah paused halfway down. "Indeed, no. Write any message for me and leave it with the bakeshop woman below. I beg you not to call upon my father, or attempt to visit him in his home, or even to walk into our neighborhood." She gave me another stiff bow. "Good day, Captain."

She continued down the stairs, her heels clicking on the bare, polished wood. A draft blew upward as she opened the door below, then cut off when she slammed it.

"Whew," Brewster said. "A cold fish."

"I imagine life has not been easy for her." I ascended the few steps I'd gone down, reentered my rooms, and moved to the window. Miss Hartman marched down the narrow cul-de-sac of Grimpen Lane for Russell Street, her bonnet moving neither left nor right as she went.

"Life ain't easy for most," Brewster said. "You either learn to live in spite of it, or become so brittle it breaks you."

"Her parents likely expected her to fill the role of

the lost sister," I said. "To become her, perhaps. And were disappointed when she could not."

The low crown of Miss Hartman's bonnet bobbed slightly, then was lost as she turned to the more crowded street.

"Jews are hard on their women," Brewster said with an air of one who knew the way of the world. "Expect them to be pillars of virtue. Then more or less bargain away their daughters to their friends when it's time for them to marry. They hide their wives—they can't even sit with the men in their house of worship. It's men in one world, women in another."

"The *haut ton* is not much different," I felt obliged to point out, though I had no idea whether his assessment of a Hebrew woman's life was correct. "Men have their clubs; women organize fetes."

"Ye live separate lives, that is true, but ye don't sequester your wives. Your lady gads about as she pleases, without you putting the shackles on her." His lips twitched. "'Tis more the other way 'round."

I gave him a severe look. "I will thank you to keep your opinions on my marriage to yourself. Not all of us can be as idyllically happy as you."

Brewster looked pleased. "My Em's a rare one, that's for certain. Now, are you about to rush to Cavendish Square and look up this Mr. Bennett?"

"Not immediately," I said. "I'd like to ask Pomeroy's opinion of all this. If Mr. Bennett is careless enough to lose two wives, one completely disappearing, the magistrates might have taken notice. Not necessarily, but I'd like to find out."

"Well." Brewster ran his hand through his hair and replaced his hat. "If you're going to Bow Street, then I'll bugger off home for a few minutes. I haven't seen me wife for a time. Mr. Denis kept me with him all night."

"Sleep as much as you like," I said. "You have no need to accompany me. Cavendish Square is not Seven Dials."

Brewster snorted. "Captain, you could find trouble inside St. James's Palace. Likely more than you could in Seven Dials. I'll be going with you."

With that, he settled his hat more firmly on his head, marched down the stairs, and out.

He could have napped in my bedchamber or upstairs in the attics, but I knew the real reason for his going. I didn't blame him. Emily Brewster was a fine woman, indeed.

***

Milton Pomeroy, my sergeant until 1814, now a famed Bow Street Runner, was not in the magistrate's house when I entered it. Timothy Spendlove, unfortunately, was.

I was glad Brewster had gone. Spendlove might have come up with an excuse to arrest him, knowing he was a hired ruffian for Denis. I knew he always looked for an excuse to arrest me.

"Captain." His hail stopped me as I was leaving, having ascertained that Pomeroy was not in.

Spendlove's hair and long side whiskers were a dark red, his face completely covered with freckles, his eyes light blue. Spendlove was a big man, of my height and build, and had a voice as strong as Pomeroy's, though he liked to lower it to intimidating tones.

"What brings you to the magistrate's house?" Spendlove asked. "Come to give yourself up?"

Chapter Seventeen

I did not necessarily wish to reveal to Spendlove all that I was doing. On the other hand, I could not think of a man who would be more dogged in bringing Mr. Bennett to justice, if Bennett had indeed killed Judith.

Then again, Spendlove was ruthless. He might go to Hartman and threaten him until he agreed to prosecute Bennett. Spendlove would reap a reward if he got Bennett convicted. Pomeroy, then, would never forgive me for bringing a good case to any Runner but him.

But overall, the case was Thompson's, and his decision. I had no patience with the ambitions of Spendlove and the Runners. Nor did I want them to make Hartman any more miserable than I'd already done.

I lifted my walking stick in a half salute. "I will call on Pomeroy later," I said and turned to leave.

"I heard of the attack on young Lord

Breckenridge," Spendlove called after me. His voice was loud enough to attract the attention of every patroller and criminal in the hall and on the staircase. "Bad business, young lordships run down in full daylight, in public. That what you came to talk to Pomeroy about? Any idea who did it?"

"Not as yet," I said, my words clipped.

"I'd take care, were I you." Spendlove's eyes glittered with something I couldn't decipher. "You never know when a villain like that might strike again."

I frowned at him, but Spendlove only gave me a nod and spun away to move deeper into the house.

Outside the sun was warm but not hot, the sky full of soft white clouds, the day cheerful. I would not let an encounter with Spendlove ruin it.

The letter in my pocket, which I'd planned to show to Pomeroy after I asked him about Bennett, had already ruined it. Threats to my family incensed me.

I did not care so much for a madman going about proclaiming I was not Gabriel Lacey—I had witnesses, including Pomeroy himself, to counter the claim—but I did care for one coming at Peter, and talking about *the price of my silence.* Bloody hell.

I'd given instructions to Barnstable to keep my family home when they woke. After I spoke to Mr. Bennett in Cavendish Square, I would make certain we all spent a day indoors. Donata would chafe, but this newest letter increased my alarm.

I hired a hackney, not bothering to wait for Brewster's return, and took myself to Cavendish Square.

Cavendish Square held a length of large, old, colonnaded houses surrounding an oval green, which was fenced off from the traffic around it. The place had been highly fashionable in the last century, housing such people as George Romney and Horatio Nelson and his wife. Bennett had done well for himself indeed.

The house in which Mr. Bennett dwelled with his third wife had an ostentatious facade with many windows, ionic columns flanking the door, and a pediment capping the first floor. Very Greek, very austere.

I wondered who the house belonged to. Women rarely owned property outright—they could inherit a trust that kept property for them, usually set up by fathers or grandfathers to ensure the females of the family weren't preyed upon by unscrupulous fortune-hunters. When a woman married, all her property went to her husband. In my case, Donata's money and anywhere she lived was controlled by several trusts, so I couldn't touch any of it.

I had an allowance from one of these trusts, which was all I needed. Donata's father and his man of business had hammered out the agreements with me before our marriage, and I'd readily signed.

My man of business had been unhappy with me for not fighting for more money, but at my stage of life, I wanted only enough to not have to scrabble for my supper. Any grandiose ideas of amassing a fortune had died into flickers long ago.

Mr. Bennett's wife had either inherited this house in a trust, or, like Donata's, it had been set up for her to live in for her lifetime. I hoped so, for her sake. Mr. Bennett's wives had the habit of dying—if she had a lifetime lease, when she was gone, Mr. Bennett would be out.

A correct footman answered the door, took my

card, showed no interest in it, and ushered me to a reception room.

The house reminded me of a museum. The wide front hall led to a grand staircase of polished dark wood, leading up into dark reaches. The hall itself, and the reception room, were silent, dimly lit, and held a jumble of treasures from the past.

Heavy cabinets with glass doors lined the hall, and treated me to a display of ancient maritime instruments — an astrolabe, a sextant, a primitive compass, a telescope. More nautical trinkets filled other cabinets — carvings from shark's teeth, stones from distant shores, a pressed exotic flower, which was tall, orange, and spikelike.

Wooden carvings done by the natives of some South Sea land were on display next to lacquer pitchers and bowls, along with porcelain that looked distinctly Chinese. Grenville could likely have identified the countries and time periods of all the objects.

The reception room contained India. My time in that area had been mostly on the battlefields, marching and fighting in perpetual heat and constant rain. But I remembered the strings of bells adorning elephants — bells everywhere, in fact — woven wicker baskets and furniture, peacock feathers, silken carpets, bright silks draped over the furniture and hanging from the walls.

This collection had been here for some time. The silks were beginning to fade and the bells were dusty, as though the current inhabitants of the house did not treasure them as had their original owners.

The footman returned to retrieve me, and I followed him upstairs to a parlor in the front of the house.

China and other countries of mainland Asia prevailed here—porcelain bowls and vases, several tall screens inlaid with mother-of-pearl, bronzes of the round-bellied Buddha, and figures of many-armed gods, including a woman with two rows of breasts and flames coming from her mouth.

"Kali, goddess of destruction," a light voice said behind me.

I turned to find a woman in a long-sleeved gray gown, her chest and shoulders covered with a fichu. The fichu was a bit out of date, but this lady seemed somewhat old-fashioned herself.

She was perhaps in her mid-thirties, the same age as Devorah Hartman. She wore a soft cap over her hair, which was a rich chocolate brown, and her eyes were deep blue. She studied me with an air of quiet dignity, but not much curiosity.

I thought it odd that such a genteel woman would not object to the bronzes all over the room depicting nudity in male and female figures. I caught sight of a small figurine in a cabinet behind her depicting an erotic act—a man standing on his hands, his severely elongated penis reaching to the open mouth of a woman. The lady in front of me, proper, serene, and modestly covered, did not even notice it.

"Mrs. Bennett?" I asked.

"I am she." The lady had my card in her hand. "Captain Gabriel Lacey. You wished to speak to my husband?"

"Is he not at home?" I asked. She could have sent the footman with the message. Why receive me? Alone?

"No, he is out. On business." The last word was delivered defiantly, as though I had come to accuse Mr. Bennett of being on a frivolous errand.

"I can return later," I said. "I have no wish to disturb you."

"Or you can speak to me. I have Mr. Bennett's full confidence."

More defiance. I was interested.

I swept a glance around the room. "Is one of your family a world traveler?" I knew Bennett hadn't collected these things. They'd sat here for a long time, become so much a part of the fabric of this house they were passed by without attention.

"My father, my grandfather, and my great-grandfather." Mrs. Bennett's voice took on a touch of pride. "They were prominent in the East India Company. They took many voyages of both exploration and trade, and as you can see, returned with a multitude of treasures."

She opened her fingers to gesture to the room, like a guide in her personal museum.

"It is quite a collection," I said. "I have a friend who also acquires things on world travel. When I was a traveller, I hadn't the foresight to pick up anything at all."

"Mr. Grenville, you mean." A smile touched her mouth. "I have heard of you, his dearest friend. Also his famous collection, which, I can assure you does not match my family's in quantity. My great-grandfather was Captain Woolwich, my grandfather was also a ship's captain, and my father."

She was very proud, and I did not confess I'd never heard of the Woolwichs, great merchant captains of the East India Company. My life had been absorbed by the army, and many soldiers considered the merchantmen soft and self-indulgent. We were no doubt completely wrong, but all groups of men believe they are superior to others who are not fortunate enough to be among them.

"And Mr. Bennett?" I asked. "Is he a seafaring man?"

The woman sounded amused. "Indeed no. Mr. Bennett has his feet firmly on dry land, which I appreciate in him. The sea is romantic, I suppose, but one does not see one's husband much. I prefer a husband who remains in London."

She would have watched her mother say good-bye to her father often, and the man stay away for long stretches of time.

"I understand," I said. "Difficult for a wife to accompany her husband on long sea voyages. Your father left all this to you?" I looked around again. My impertinent question perhaps would be forgiven if I seemed sufficiently awed by the treasures, many of which could be bought cheaply in crowded Asian bazaars.

"Left to me?" Mrs. Bennett looked puzzled, then she laughed. Her plainness vanished as her face lit. Perhaps I wronged Bennett—he might have fallen in love with her laughter instead of her obvious fortune.

"My father is not deceased, Captain," she said. "He is upstairs, in his rooms. He would like to meet you, a friend of the famous Mr. Grenville. Will you come up?"

Chapter Eighteen

I did not mask my astonishment well, and she laughed at me again.

I agreed to meet her so-famous father—my curiosity getting the better of me—and she took me up another flight of stairs to a bedchamber in the rear of the vast house.

This chamber was enormous. I remembered the first time I'd awakened in a bed in Grenville's home, thinking of myself as a tiny speck in the middle of the ocean of the room. That bedchamber could easily fit into this one.

I'd expected the nautical and Far Eastern themes in the lower parts of the house to carry on here, but that was not the case. The bedroom had been furnished with fairly modern pieces—Sheraton and Hepplewhite predominated here. Unlike the walls in Donata's house, which were pure Adam, a wallpaper from the eighteenth century, fading now, depicted ladies and gentlemen in powdered wigs and pointed shoes, taking their leisure in the country.

In the middle of this huge chamber, pulled from the wall, was a bed with heavy curtains around it. The curtains on the side facing away from the window were drawn back, while all the others were closed, presumably to keep away drafts.

Mrs. Bennett led me, without hesitation, to the bed.

Lying propped on pillows in the middle of it was an elderly man. He was a bit shrunken, but I could tell he'd once been tall and strong. The strength was evident in the hard blue eyes in his very wrinkled face. There I read anger that his body had weakened without his permission.

"Captain Lacey?" His voice was quiet, raspy, but I could hear that it once had boomed out down a long deck filled with scrambling sailors. "I am Captain Woolwich. Pleased to make your acquaintance."

He held out a hand. I shook it, finding his bare fingers smooth and nearly hairless, but his grip powerful.

Woolwich looked behind me at his daughter. "Run away, Margaret. We men wish to speak alone."

Margaret, instead of being either offended or subdued, gave her father a sunny smile and left the room. The heels of her soft shoes kicked up the back hem of her dull gray gown as she went.

She closed the door carefully, as though not wishing to disturb her father with the click of the latch, and we heard her footfalls on the landing. Woolwich waited until her footsteps faded down the stairs before he waved me to sit in a chair drawn up to the bed.

"She's a good girl, but a featherhead," he growled. "Her mother was a spirited, intelligent creature, but

Margaret has none of that in her. I would suspect my lady of a dalliance when I was away, but Margaret looks too much like my family. And I have no brothers my wife could have substituted for my attentions." He gave a cough and cleared his throat. "Now then, Captain, why are you here? Please tell me you are after my worthless son-in-law."

"I did come to speak to him, yes," I began cautiously. "I take it he is out?"

"Yes, he goes to the Stock Exchange and pretends to understand all that goes on. Really, he is making certain my shares in all my investments have not lost any value. What has he done, Captain? Committed a crime? Have you come to take him to the magistrate?"

His blue eyes were bright with both cynicism and hope.

"What can you tell me about Mr. Bennett?" I asked.

"Ha, so you will not give me your purpose. All the same, I have read of you, and heard how you and Mr. Grenville work with the Runners to reveal blackguards and evil men. Now, here you are asking about Bennett. High time, too. He is the worst of blackguards, Captain. An oily rakehell, I'd judge him, though he goes to church of a Sunday and is a pious prig."

"Where does he come from?" I settled in, happy to have my suspicions confirmed.

"Heaven knows. Oh, he speaks well enough— claims he went to a fine school and is now a scholar, and that is easily ascertained. But though he has the voice of a gentleman, there's something wrong with him."

"What about his family? Has no one inquired

about them?"

"To be sure, I have. Mr. Bennett's father was a respectable gentleman of Derbyshire, and none have anything bad to say about him. He died when his son — Andrew — was about sixteen. Andrew had a guardian then, an uncle, but the uncle more or less ignored him, and Andrew continued his schooling at Balliol, so he claims. Again, easily found out, so I believe him. When he came into his majority, Andrew took the money he inherited from his father, cut ties with his uncle — whom he claims was a cruel man — and set up on his own."

"He married," I said. "Twice before."

"Oh, yes, he told us all about it. The tragic life of Andrew Bennett."

"His first wife …" I prompted.

"Miss Judith Hartman. Lovely girl, he says. Father unreasonable." Woolwich coughed into his leathery fist. "Father not a fool, I'd say. Poor Judith lost, never to be found again. Oh, well, there's Miss Watson, with her large dowry. Father a nabob. Made Bennett several thousand pounds richer, then she took ill and died, ever so convenient, poor thing. Never knew what became of Miss Hartman. Either she came to her senses and fled far from his reach, or he killed her and buried her in the cellar."

I flinched. Too close to the mark. "Miss Hartman has been found," I said quietly. "I should say — she was found long ago, but no one knew who she was. I have brought to light that the body was that of Miss Judith Hartman. She was struck on the head and dropped into the river."

Woolwich ceased moving. Breathing. He stared at me, his eyes burning in his wan face, his body motionless.

He didn't breathe for so long that I became alarmed. I rose from my seat, took a silver flask from the bedside table and opened it. As I'd suspected, the scent of good brandy wafted out.

I held it to Woolwich's nose. He gasped and began to cough.

The coughing wracked him, shook his body. His eyes watered. I decided I'd better fetch his daughter, but when I started for the bell, the old man wheezed, "No!"

I turned back. Woolwich grabbed the flask from me, upended it, and poured a quantity of brandy down his throat. He coughed for a few more seconds, then settled down and breathed easier.

"I knew it," he whispered. "He's a bloody murderer."

"I unfortunately cannot swear to that," I said. "There is nothing to say his was the hand that struck down Miss Hartman. That is why I came here — to speak to him, to find out all about him."

"You doubt me?" Woolwich glared imperiously. Onboard ship, his word would have been law. He must have great difficulty ordering about a daughter who only gave him a fond look and obeyed because it suited her.

"I cannot in all good conscience send a man to the gallows if he is not guilty of murder," I said. "Even if he is a reprobate. I must be certain."

"Be certain of this, Captain. That man is wrong. He has turned my daughter's head. She was very much what the dandy set called an *ape-leader* or *on the shelf* — so many terms for a useless spinster. Mr. Bennett courted her ardently and led her up the aisle two months after he met her. Long enough for the banns, but not much beyond. He insisted it be done properly. They did not have my blessing, but Margaret was of age, and so was he. Can a father stop two people in their thirties marrying when there is no impediment? *He'll come 'round,* I hear her say often enough to Bennett. He is unctuous to me, never says a bad word around me. But what you tell me makes me greatly fear for my daughter."

I shared his worry. I pictured Gabriella as Judith—romantic, swept off her feet, then beaten down and discarded when the hoped-for wealth from the marriage did not come. The icy dread in my heart matched what must have been in Hartman's, and now Woolwich's.

"I understand," I said. "I have a daughter myself."

Woolwich heaved himself from his pillows, still clutching the brandy. He seized my hand with his empty one. "Then please, Captain, I beg of you. Do whatever you can to remove that man from my house, and my daughter's life."

His clasp held the fierce strength that had once pervaded his body. He must have led his men by force of personality alone.

"I will do what I can," I said.

Woolwich's fingers bit down. "No. You rid me of Bennett, or do not come back. I don't have the luxury of hope."

He was compelling. Ship's captains, at least in the Royal Navy, could be horrible martinets who let their crews and all aboard starve while they feasted, or they were forceful men who ensured that anyone under their command was well looked after. Woolwich struck me as the second sort, but one who brooked no fools.

I needed to speak to Bennett, assess for myself what sort of man he was and whether he'd killed

Judith, but I found myself making a rash promise.

"I will ensure that he leaves you and your daughter alone," I told him. "You have my word on it."

Woolwich continued to grip my hand as he looked into my eyes. He seemed to be satisfied by what he saw, because he finally released me and sank back, relieved.

"I have heard you are a man of honor," he said, his voice weakening. "I have little to do these days but read every newspaper that comes my way, so do not be surprised that I know exactly who you are. I know that you cut the face of a man in Brooks's — you claim for cheating, but I have other ideas. You also lit into a gentleman of the *ton* with your fists for abducting young women, and left him bleeding. I hope you are of the same mettle and haven't become soft through your marriage. The gentleman I've read about is the one who needs to help me."

"I am that gentleman," I said with conviction. "As much as my friends despair of me."

"Good." Woolwich took another long drink of brandy, then his hand moved fretfully on the covers. "Send my daughter back to me. She is not astute, but she is kindly. Even pretends to like the tales of my voyages."

"I believe she is quite proud of you," I said. "Good day to you, sir, and I thank you for your candor."

"Just take that libertine out of my house," Woolwich said. "Before he murders me and then Margaret. Viper to my bosom."

He trailed off into mutters, finished with me. I took my leave, descending the stairs and instructing the footman at the bottom to send Margaret up to the old man.

I also gave the footman my card. "Please tell Mr. Bennett to call upon me at seven this evening," I said. "In Grosvenor Street. The home of Mr. Grenville."

The footman looked suitably impressed, as he did with the coins I pressed into his hand. "Yes, sir," he babbled. "Thank you, sir. I'll fetch you a hackney, sir."

***

I'd decided to invite Bennett to Grenville's for several reasons.

First, I did not want him in South Audley Street anywhere near Gabriella. He might see the obvious wealth of the house and get ideas.

I also did not want him in Grimpen Lane, because I had the feeling that Bennett was a snob. He'd be more likely to rush to speak to me if I gave him Grenville's address.

I would have to warn Grenville, of course.

Brewster turned up when the hackney did. Before Brewster could climb onto it for our ride through the streets, I pulled him aside.

"Can you arrange to have this house watched?" I asked. "I fear for the inhabitants inside."

Brewster glanced at the columned façade and gave me a doubtful look. "As I have told you, Captain, I don't work for you. I can't tell my colleagues who to watch and where to go. His nibs wouldn't stand for it."

"No," I said. "But you can hire others, whom you trust. Paid for by me." My allowance should be put to some good.

Brewster had to think about this. "I'd still want to ask Mr. Denis. He's already put out with me."

"He is more put out with *me*, but I am used to it.

Even better would be to slip someone into the house, to pretend to be a footman or some such, tell me what happens, and guard the elderly man and his daughter. From everyone, including the daughter's husband."

Brewster rubbed his upper lip. "Happens I might know a lad. He's a real footman, haughty and all. Bit of a thief, though."

"I will make it worth his while to keep his hands off the silver," I said testily. "Have your footman tell Captain Woolwich I sent him. I imagine Woolwich still controls who works for the household and who does not."

"All right, then." Brewster nodded, a little more at ease. "Where are you off to?"

"To find a horse," I said.

I'd love to have swung myself up into the carriage on that note and left in dramatic exit, but my knee chose to collapse. Brewster got me inside, conveyed the direction I wanted to the coachman, and slammed the door, looking amused.

***

When I arrived at the South Audley Street house, Bartholomew was waiting for me outside. He had news.

"One Irish hunter, red, with two white stockings and a star," he said triumphantly as he helped me from the carriage. Then he calmed. "Two, actually. Very well matched, but in different stables from different sires and dams. Fancy that."

"Never mind their history," I said, somewhat waspishly. "Where did you find them?"

My leg hurt, and I was ready to consign Bennett to the mercy of Brewster and his fists.

Brewster could persuade the man to move on if

anyone could. I'd be no better than Denis if I employed him so, but at the moment, I did not care.

"One in Hyde Park, for hire," Bartholomew said, ignoring my bad mood. "The other in Grosvenor Mews. Matthias thought it sounded familiar. It's a gelding what belongs to one of Mr. Grenville's neighbors."

Chapter Nineteen

"What neighbor?" I asked, nonplussed.

"Viscount Compton, an elderly gentleman. He loves this horse. Calls it Irish Red. Very original."

I'd met Compton a time or two at Grenville's clubs. "It was not an elderly viscount galloping toward us in the Row," I said.

"No, indeed. Which is why I believe that it was the one for hire in Hyde Park. Stands to reason."

"All right, then. Who hired it?"

"Well." Bartholomew rubbed his chin. Behind him, the hackney driver jolted his coach back into the stream of carts, carriages, and people. "The head groom there, he wouldn't say." Bartholomew spoke over the noise of the street. "Says a man should be able to take a horse out without everyone asking about it. I told him what had happened, and he told me that there was no possibility any gent what hired this horse tried to knock young Peter to the ground. That we were mistaken in the mount."

I trusted Peter's description. He was in love with all things equine, and noticed everything about them.

"I will have a chat with the head groom," I said. "Try to loosen his tongue a bit." I was feeling murderous today.

"However," Bartholomew said firmly. "I did hang about and talked with the lads who do the mucking. Two of them told me what head groom didn't want them to, that this precise horse had gone missing for a couple of days, and then turned up, sweet as you please, this morning."

"Damnation."

My enemy then, had planned well. He'd know I'd try to discover the identity of the rider. What better way to cover it up than to steal the horse? He risked being caught or seen, of course, but apparently, he hadn't been. If he were not associated with the horse in any way, how would I ever discover who he was?

He'd either sneaked the horse back early this morning, or the horse had gotten away from him and found its way home.

"I will speak to the groom anyway," I said. "He might know more than he is letting on."

"True," Bartholomew said. "If he were paid well, he might lend out the horse and stay silent."

"Gabriella's come-out is in a few days," I said. "I want to ensure no mischief is done to her by this person who wishes to harm *me*."

Bartholomew looked worried. "We'll all keep an eye out, Captain. And I know you'll solve it by then."

I could not share his confidence. I entered the house, which was flowing with its usual efficiency, now that Donata was awake and directing things.

I sought Donata in her dressing room as she readied to make calls. Jacinthe scowled as she tugged Donata's bodice straight, her lip curled, which meant she'd lost an argument with my wife.

"Stay in," I told Donata. "I had another letter from our anonymous friend." I took it from my pocket and handed it to her.

"Dear me," Donata said after she read it. "What on earth can he hope to gain by pretending you are a fraud? Colonel Brandon has known you all these years. All he has to do is proclaim you are who you are, and the rumor will die. Brandon is a respectable colonel, from an old family, well connected, much admired, never mind his bad temper and slow thinking. There is no threat."

"I have reasoned this, which only makes me more fearful," I answered. "If this is a madman, to what lengths might he go? And so I repeat, stay in this afternoon."

"Nonsense. I have many visits to make, more ladies to butter up, so that they will praise Gabriella to the skies and make her a success."

"About that," I began. "We should put off the ball as well."

Donata jerked out of Jacinthe's hold to round on me. "Now you *have* run mad. We cannot possibly put it off. I cannot imagine a greater difficulty than canceling every plan Aline and I have made for the last sixmonth. I can imagine her colorful language on the subject. Not that I would dare tell her—I would send *you* into that lion's den. I assure you *no one* will be at the ball that has not been scrutinized a hundred times by the pair of us. Invitations are extremely limited. Those eliminated because their sons are libertines are in an uproar. Those who are invited are preening themselves that they were selected. The lady patronesses at Almack's are not as rigid in their criteria as we have been."

"I believe you," I said. "But, you recall that last

year, a man abducted my daughter and hid her in a ruined cellar in order to enjoy her when he was ready. He was part of your precious *haut ton*, and no one knew. How many highly selective come-outs had he been to? A good many, I'd think. You cannot ensure Gabriella's safety. The ball won't even be held here, so I can't simply lock her into her bedchamber if things begin to go wrong."

"You know why we chose Aline's house. Much larger and finer than this one."

"Pare down your guest list even further, and have it here if you will not cancel."

"Gabriel." Donata put her hand on my arm. "What is the matter with you? Shall we bolt the doors and cower inside because a fool writes ridiculous letters? Yes, I was upset that Peter was attacked, which is why he stays in the nursery until you catch who is doing this. But he is a little boy. Shall the rest of us quiver in terror every time we put our nose out of the door? Do not let this man determine your life, Gabriel. Not that I noticed *you* staying home this morning yourself. Off you went, as soon as it was light. This, after railing at me for sleeping — safely — in your rooms in Grimpen Lane."

"Bloody hell, Donata."

"Back to swearing. You enjoy that."

"It is one thing to never go out for fear of what *might* happen," I said, trying to rein in my temper. "But this man has threatened us directly, tried violence against your son. I must ask — what is the matter with *you*?"

"My dear Gabriel, I have received more threats against me than I can count. From ladies certain I am carrying on affairs with their husbands. From gentlemen incensed I will *not* carry on affairs with them. From ladies angry at me for not inviting them or their daughters to important musicales. From musicians and poets not talented enough to merit my sponsorship. I could write out a long list. Angry and threatening letters, anonymous and signed, are a part of life in the Upper Ten Thousand. One does not let the writers know that they are in any way successful, or one will never have peace."

"Have any of them sent riders to knock your son to the ground?" I demanded.

"Lady Mary Trent tried to set my gown on fire once—I was wearing it at the time. So yes, violence abounds in the English upper classes. All these silly rules we follow are attempts to contain it."

"All the same," I said in a hard voice. "I do not wish you to go out today."

"You are uncommonly stubborn, Gabriel."

"When it comes to you, yes, I am. Have you ever done as you are told?"

"On rare occasion. Very well, I will submit to your wishes, and Jacinthe's, that I stay meekly at home and embroider. But we cannot cancel Gabriella's ball. That will hang on her for the rest of her life."

"Not if she goes back to France and quietly marries a French gentleman farmer," I said. "She knows that life. Is used to it." My heart wrenched even as I said the words. An English husband would have Gabriella stay in England, with me.

"You have no appreciation for my efforts, or Aline's. Gentlemen gad about all day with no idea how hard the delicate and weaker sex works. You would be exhausted in a half hour."

"I have no doubt," I said. "Very well—you and Aline will win with the come-out ball. But I will make sure that Gabriella is very well guarded. By me, and men more able-bodied than me. Tell Aline to expect extra footmen in her ranks."

Donata tossed down the reticule she'd snatched up. It clattered among her combs and brushes. "Do not tell me you will insinuate that awful Brewster into Aline's house. Will Mr. Denis provide the rest?"

"That awful Brewster has saved my skin more than once. He and his cohorts are handy with their fists, and not worried about from what walk of life the men they pummel come. They go, or Gabriella does not."

"You are very aggravating, my husband. I think you do not believe I am worried for her. Aline knows to take every precaution, as do I. We have managed to throw dozens of balls over the years without violence at any of them."

"Even so," I said. "Those are my conditions."

Donata made a noise of exasperation. "Very well. I will tell Aline to expect ruffians to invade her house but not to be alarmed. Any anger she has about it, I shall direct to you."

"I will be honored," I said, with a small bow.

"Then please go away, Gabriel. I must change my clothes again, and sulk."

As long as she stayed in the house, she could do as she pleased. I caught her hand, drew her to me, and kissed her cheek. "Thank you."

"Yes, all right." Donata frowned at me, but I saw the softening in her eyes.

I left her and went to my study to write letters— one to Denis and another to Grenville.

***

Donata, true to her word, forwent her calls to stay in and write her own letters. She could be as persuasive on paper, she claimed, as she could in person. Having received letters from her myself, I believed her.

She was adamant about going out later that evening, however, as she had invitations she could not possibly turn down without awkwardness, she claimed. After another heated discussion, I told her I'd accompany her. While supper balls did not move me to paroxysms of joy, I would tolerate one to keep my eye on her.

At seven, however, I had an appointment to keep with Grenville.

To preserve peace in my marriage, I asked Donata to accompany me. I rather think she'd have come anyway, had I not.

Donata dressed herself in a subdued gown of fawn sprigged with red flowers, covering her shoulders with a light shawl. Hagen drove us in the carriage the short distance to Grosvenor Street.

I gazed at number 12, three doors down from Grenville. This was the house of Viscount Compton, who owned the Irish hunter Bartholomew had found.

Though I was certain the horse stolen from Hyde Park had been the one the culprit rode, I couldn't help looking the house over. Viscount Compton's abode was no different on the outside than Grenville's, even more plain, I'd say. And why the man or anyone in his household would have a grudge against me, I could not tell.

We arrived at Grenville's punctually at seven. Mr. Bennett must have been very eager to meet the famous Lucius Grenville, because he was already there.

Matthias shot me a long look as he led us up the stairs to Grenville's front sitting room—the one

Grenville used for the unwashed masses, not his very private sanctum higher up in the house.

Matthias drew himself up to his full height as he opened the door to the sitting room. He became the haughtiest of haughty footmen as he announced:

"Captain and Mrs. Gabriel Lacey."

Grenville, dressed in his most severe black frock coat and trousers, and his most achingly white waistcoat and cravat, came forward to greet us.

"Lady Donata, how lovely you are." He took her hands and kissed her cheek. "And Lacey. Well met." He formally shook my hand.

A far cry from the Grenville in a dressing gown over shirtsleeves at the breakfast table. I concluded from his crisp suit and precise formality that he sincerely disliked Mr. Andrew Bennett.

That gentleman came forward, an eager smile on his face.

He was not what I expected. Devorah Hartman and Captain Woolwich had painted a picture of a groveling, crafty young rake who won the hearts of ladies and killed them for their money. I'd imagined handsomeness in a too-fulsome way, perhaps with the dark eyes and knowing look of a stage villain.

What I found was a young man heading for middle age, a little bit portly but still straight-backed and tall, with a soft, innocuous face and friendly brown eyes. He looked less the wily villain and more the hero's best friend. He'd be Horatio, not Hamlet.

He bowed to Donata, suitably awed by her lofty status, then to me. "Well met, Captain," he said, holding out his hand. "My father-in-law told me you had some news for me."

Mr. Bennett's handshake was firm, but not too much so, and not too soft either. I wondered if he practiced it.

Mr. Bennett withdrew, retaining the look of an interested puppy. "Mr. Grenville would not impart it," he said. "He insisted you tell me yourself."

"I thought it best," Grenville said smoothly.

I understood. Though Grenville would be curious to know Mr. Bennett's reaction, he did not want to be alone with him when the reaction occurred.

Grenville motioned for us to take a seat. With careful politeness, he led Donata to a chair and settled her, then sat in the one next to her. I preferred to remain standing, so Bennett did as well.

"What is it, Captain?" Bennett asked. "You are alarming me."

"I am afraid," I began, "that I have discovered what happened to your first wife, Judith Hartman."

Bennett stopped. The soft-eyed look deserted him for a second, his face losing color. "What?" he asked. "Tell me the worst."

I wondered a moment if *the worst* would mean her being found alive.

"She was discovered in the River Thames," I said. "Had been killed and discarded there perhaps fifteen years gone now. What is left of her was fished out ten years ago and stored in a cellar. Mr. Grenville, once we discovered her identity, arranged to have her sent back to her father, for burial."

As I spoke, Bennett had grown more and more pale. At last, his face resembled nothing less than the white of ghostly fog, his cheeks taking on a sheen of perspiration.

Bennett drew a quick, short breath as my speech ended, then his eyes rolled back into his head and he dropped to a heap on the floor.

Chapter Twenty

Grenville was on his feet. "Good Lord."

I reached down to heave Bennett to the nearest sofa. He was heavy for his size, and my leg hurt me. Grenville, after a stunned second, leapt to help.

Together, we got him stretched across a scroll-backed, silk-upholstered divan. I patted his cold cheek.

"Bennett."

"Did you kill him?" Donata leaned in. "No, I see his chest moving." She swung away, her skirts brushing my leg, and snatched up her reticule. She removed a small silver box, opened it on its hinge, and thrust it under Bennett's nose.

The acrid odor of vinegar came to me. Bennett's face screwed up, his eyes popped open, and he coughed.

Donata, satisfied, snapped the case shut.

Grenville returned with brandy. His absolute best was kept upstairs in reserve for him and very special guests. Even so, what was in the cup he offered Bennett now I considered much too good for the wretch.

Bennett drank, then coughed up most of the liquid, which Grenville caught on a handkerchief.

Bennett grabbed the linen cloth and applied it to his lips. "What … happened?" he asked around it.

Grenville gave his shoulder a pat. "You took a tumble to my sitting room floor. Are you hurt?"

"No." Bennett blinked as he thought about it. "I do not believe so." His gaze went to me. "Sir, did you say …"

"That Judith Hartman is dead, yes." I had stepped back from the tableau and folded my arms. "Shall I go through it again for you?"

"No … no." Bennett held up his hand. "Oh, my poor Judith. This is terrible. I assumed she had met an unfortunate end, but I did not dream …"

I watched him carefully. The flick of his eyes told me he lied.

"You knew," I said, already tired of him. "That is why you married again so quickly, how you convinced the magistrates you should be allowed to wed. You *knew* she was dead."

"No." The word was sharp, full of shock, bordering on anger. "No, Captain, you misunderstand. I perjured myself, it is true. I never believed she was dead at all."

It was Donata who interrupted the amazed silence that followed. She fixed Bennett with cold hauteur. "If you believed her alive, then why were you in such a hurry to marry the next lady?"

Bennett flushed. "I must confess to you. I am a warmhearted man." He pressed his hand to his chest. "When Judith walked away and did not return, I was hurt, unhappy, grieved. I put it about that she must have died so no one would know she deserted me. Her father, you see, was very unhappy about her marrying me, and she began to feel that she wronged him. She wished to reconcile. I believed, when she did not come home that day, that she had returned to her family."

"You would have soon learned otherwise," I said sternly.

"I did. I missed her so much." Bennett dabbed his cheeks with the brandy-stained handkerchief. "I finally went to the heart of the Hebrew area, and demanded to speak to Judith. Her father told me he hadn't seen her. I did not believe him, of course."

"So you went to court to have her declared dead?" He was not winning my respect with this story.

"I asked her neighbors, those who would speak to me. Her father did not allow her mother and sister to come down and listen to me — they might have told me the truth. But the Hebrews, they band together, and I was an outsider, the Englishman who'd stolen one of their own. The entire street more or less shoved me out and slammed the door, so to speak."

"Her father told you the truth. She hadn't come home."

"I concluded that after a time," Bennett admitted. "Judith was a sweet thing. She would have found some way to talk to me if she could, would have written at least. What I believed, gentlemen, your ladyship, was that her father had spirited her off somewhere — back to the Continent, out to the countryside to some other enclave of Hebrews, and she would never come back."

He sighed. "When I met my Seraphina, we came to love each other deeply, and it broke my heart that

I could not marry her. Hartman had metaphorically buried Judith—it hurt me to imagine what life she had—and so I hired a solicitor to help me declare Judith dead so that I could marry Seraphina. I wish you could have met *her*, Captain. You'd understand. A finer woman did not walk the world."

"You were living with her," I pointed out. "For a few years, I understand. Why the sudden need to have the banns read?"

Bennett blushed like a schoolboy. "We believed she was increasing. I did not want a child of mine to be born on the wrong side of the blanket. And so, I obtained a declaration that Judith was dead, and I married Seraphina. The banns were posted. It was in the newspapers. Hartman could have come forward, told the truth, stopped the marriage. He did not. I concluded he wanted nothing more to do with me— with me married again, Judith would be safe." His face fell. "Only now you tell me ..."

Tears trickled from his eyes, and he sniffled into the handkerchief.

"Mr. Bennett."

At my tone, Bennett looked up, eyes puffy and red. "Sir?"

"I do not understand you. You loved Judith, and yet you quickly married another. And since have married a third woman."

Bennett nodded. "Yes. My Maggie. The best woman in the world. You met her, Captain."

"So why this outpouring of grief for Judith?" I asked him severely. "You had finished with her years ago. Fifteen years, to be precise."

The handkerchief came up again. "Because all this time, I thought she was still alive. I had a notion that perhaps someday, we would meet once more. Spend our dotage together. Foolish, perhaps, but she was still in my heart."

"What of your current wife? Your dear Maggie?"

Bennett went redder still. "You can scarce understand, Captain. I loved Judith. I love Maggie. My heart does not shirk from both." He shook his head, eyes screwing up. "That scarce matters now. You've revealed that my poor, my dearest, sweetest Judith is ..."

Grenville and I exchanged a glance. He expressed in one flick of his brows that he had no idea what to make of the man.

Bennett's tears seemed real enough. He did everything to put forth a picture of a hapless gentleman caught in his own deeper feelings. Loved too much, grieved too hard. *Pity me.*

And yet, I understood why Woolwich did not like him. There was something wrong with the way Bennett spoke, begged us to understand him.

I felt as though I watched a play. The description of Bennett wandering into a Hebrew neighborhood and having every single one of them driving him, the Gentile, away, protecting their own, had the ring of the theatre to it. I knew that Londoners as a whole put the Hebrews into a box, and many men, as Brewster did, considered them "other" and disdained them collectively. Even so, I felt that Shakespeare or Sheridan could have written the scene.

I thought of Margaret Woolwich, good-natured but, as her father had claimed, not very intelligent. She'd have seen Bennett's surface and been satisfied with it. I wondered if Judith had been satisfied, or come to her senses — too late.

Donata, Grenville, and I were too worldly, had

known too many, to take Bennett's character as absolute.

Donata, in particular, regarded him with blatant cynicism. "You see, Mr. Bennett," she said, leaning down a little to pin him with her sharp stare. "We were of the mind that *you* had killed Judith. Struck her down with a poker or some such, so that you could marry your dear Seraphina."

Bennett came off the sofa. I was in his way, but his bulk shoved me aside.

"I?" Again the drama, his hand pressed to his heart, his eyes wide with horror. "Dear lady, Judith was to me as the most precious jewel in all the world. I would never hurt her. Not one hair on her head."

"Her hair was not in jeopardy," Donata said in her acerbic way. "Her head was bashed in, rather, and she was pushed into the river."

The slight widening of his eyes in shock was not feigned, I thought. "Please. How horrible. I cannot bear to think of it."

Donata was remorseless. "It was a bit worse for Judith."

"*Please.*" The handkerchief went to Bennett's mouth again, and he shuddered.

I broke in. "If not you—can you think of anyone who would want to hurt Judith?"

Bennett lowered his hand. He was white about the mouth. "No, indeed. Everyone loved her."

"Apparently not everyone," I said dryly. "If her death distresses you so, please help us find her killer."

"Oh. Ah, I see what you mean." Bennett's brows lowered as he thought. "She truly was well liked."

"Yet, she angered her family and her friends by becoming a *converso* and marrying you."

"That is true." Bennett pondered again, the very image of a concerned gentleman trying to help. "Very true. I do hate to speak ill of any lady, but her sister, Devorah—she is a bitter woman."

I gave him a neutral nod, not wanting to convey my own opinion of her. Devorah was indeed bitter.

"Her father and mother were quite angry as well," Bennett said. "And of course, the young man who had hopes of becoming her husband."

I hid my start. Neither Hartman nor Devorah had mentioned another suitor. "His name?" I asked.

"Let me think. I scarce remember. He was a Hebrew, of course, with one of their outlandish names. No, I have it—Stein. Yes. Itzak was his given name. I remember, because I told Judith I thought it a damned odd way to say *Isaac*."

Bennett regarded us as though we should be amused with him, but we remained stone-faced.

"Anyone else?" I asked.

Bennett shrugged. "I have little idea, Captain. I am not good at this sort of thing. Her father would know."

I would get her father to speak to me somehow. "If you happen to remember any more," I said, "you will send word, won't you?"

"Of course. Of course." Bennett flashed me an appealing look. "Please discover who killed my Judith. I beg of you, Captain, bring this man to justice. If I can be of further help, I will, I assure you."

Sincerity oozed from him. Grenville, who'd silently let Donata and me get on with interrogating him, finally spoke. "We shall do our best. Perhaps you should go home, Mr. Bennett. You have had a shock."

"Yes, indeed," Bennett said breathily. "I will return to my Margaret." Another glance at us, another flush. "I assure you, gentlemen, your ladyship, that Margaret knows about Judith. And Seraphina. I keep nothing from her. She knows all of my unhappy past."

During this speech, Grenville had moved for the bell, and Matthias opened the door after he'd let enough time lapse. No need to confirm that he'd indeed been listening.

Bennett, touching his breastbone again, prepared to make his exit.

"Seraphina," I said.

Bennett stopped short, turning in confusion. "Pardon?"

I leaned on my walking stick. "You told us that you married Seraphina because you believed she was increasing. Is that how she passed away, if I might inquire? In childbed?"

Anger flashed in Bennett's eyes—anger at me. "No, indeed. She was not increasing at all. It was a cancer." He shrugged helplessly. "Nothing we could do."

"I see." I felt a pang of pity for Seraphina. "I am sorry."

"Thank you." Bennett took my sorrow to be for him, when in fact, I was only sorry for his wife. All of his wives. "Good evening, your ladyship. Mr. Grenville. Captain."

Bennett's tone when he said *Captain* betrayed his irritation with me. Robbed of his exit as the forlorn hero, he simply walked out of the room.

Matthias, retaining his icy hauteur, said, "This way, sir," and led him down the stairs.

I moved to the window to watch Bennett emerge.

A hackney waited, the driver lounging apathetically on the box.

Bennett snapped something to him, the driver gave him a weary look, then started the horses before Bennett was all the way inside the coach. Bennett fell the rest of the way to his seat, his curse audible, then Matthias's gloved hand caught the door and slammed it shut.

I turned away to find my wife collapsed on another sofa, a goblet of brandy to her lips. She downed it in a practiced way and clicked the glass to the table.

"That was distasteful," she said, and I knew she did not mean the drink.

"Indeed," Grenville answered. He doctored himself with brandy as well, and poured a goblet for me. "Not a man who endears himself to other gentlemen."

"Only to ladies, it seems," Donata observed.

She sent a glance at me, knowing my own propensity for preferring the company of the fairer sex. I prayed I was not so horrible about it as Andrew Bennett.

"Do you think he killed her?" Grenville asked me.

I took the brandy he offered, poured it down my throat, and answered once the liquid had warmed me. "I know this—if my beloved wife had left the house one afternoon and did not return, I would shift heaven and earth to discover what had become of her."

Donata's wry expression faded. I'd begun to do just that the other night, when my dread that I'd lost her had overwhelmed me.

I held Donata's gaze with mine as I continued. "Even if she did not wish to come home with me again, I would not rest until I determined that she was safe and well."

"Yes," Donata said. "You would do just that."

Grenville sat down heavily next to Donata. "As would I," he said. "As would most gentlemen who love and esteem their wives. Not be quick to dismiss her so I could marry another."

"And yet." I sank to a chair, cradling my empty glass. "People do go missing, meet with an accident, are never seen again. He assumed she'd been taken in by her family, locked away from him. He could not fight her entire clan to wrest her out again."

"By law, he could," Donata pointed out, with another glance at me. "A wife belongs to the husband entirely. She ceases to be."

"Exactly," Grenville said. "So why did he not use the full force of the law to march to her father's house and drag her away? They married legally … we assume. I will check into that. But if all were aboveboard, and Bennett had the law on his side, why not use that?"

"Because Judith had no money," I suggested. "Her father made clear she'd get nothing from him, no help, nothing in a will or trust. Dear Seraphina brought him several thousand pounds."

"The question remains," Donata said. "Did he kill her?"

Chapter Twenty-One

I wanted to shout a definite, *Yes!*

"He was genuinely surprised when he heard Judith was dead," I said, unhappy. "The swoon was not false, nor was his shock."

"He might have bashed her over the head and walked away," Donata suggested in a calm voice. "And not realized he'd killed her. Struck out in anger when she refused to come home with him."

"Possibly," I said. "But the surgeon was fairly certain she'd died instantly, or nearly so, from the blow. I hesitate to conclude his innocence, but I am afraid he might be."

"He is a bad lot," Grenville said. "I cannot put my finger on why, but I know he is."

Donata said, "He tries too hard to be ingratiating. What was it you said Woolwich called him? Unctuous. He is certainly that."

"He is," I agreed. "I also believe he knew bloody well that his second wife was dying. Perhaps a doctor had told him of the cancer. He suddenly made plenty of effort to have Judith declared dead so he could marry Seraphina. Just in time to take control of her money."

Grenville tapped his goblet. "Why did Mr. Hartman not fight him? When the courts officially said Judith was deceased? Surely he'd have an opinion."

"Unless he already knew she was dead," Donata said coolly.

"I have a different theory," Grenville said. "To Mr. Hartman, she was already dead in his mind. Judith had abandoned him, her family, her religion, to take up with this knave. If Bennett had her made officially dead, that would enable Hartman to be finished with her."

I shook my head slowly. "You are not a father, Grenville. If my daughter ran away with a rogue, even if I disowned her in my anger, if she wanted to leave said rogue, I'd welcome her back with open arms. I would not let the world think her dead, but do all in my power to get her free of him."

"But Hartman perhaps did not have the power to free her from Bennett," Donata suggested. "If he were insanely wealthy, he'd not have as much trouble, but he is a modest shopkeeper. If Judith were declared dead, he would no longer have to worry about convincing Bennett to give her a divorce, and funding said divorce, and could keep her home with him."

"Our speculation becomes meaningless," I pointed out. "Judith did die, Hartman did not know; Bennett did not know, or so he claims. I was not present when Devorah found out about her sister's death, so I cannot say whether she knew. She was very angry when she came to see me—at her father, at Bennett. At me."

"Perhaps *she* met Judith," Donata said. "Quarreled with her, struck her. Not meaning to, possibly. Panics, pushes her into the water, runs home. Keeps the secret all these years."

"Can someone keep a secret that long?" I wondered.

Grenville said dryly, "If one is to be hanged for that secret, certainly." He rose. "The fact remains that someone killed her, and we are no closer to finding out who. We agree we do not like Mr. Bennett, but that does not mean he is a murderer."

"A careful man, that is a certainty," Donata said. She too got to her feet. "We shall have to find out more about him—which Gabriel is excellent at doing. He shakes people until they tell him what he wishes to know."

I had risen when she did, and I went to her, arranging her shawl around her shoulders. I liked that I now had the privilege of doing so. "Then I will shake them," I said.

***

I accompanied Donata to the supper ball later that evening as we had agreed. I wore my regimentals, as other military men did, though I was seeing fewer and fewer as the years went on. I felt at home, however, in the familiar dark blue coat with white facings, silver braid on my chest and shoulders, and my deep blue breeches and high boots.

The ball was held in a house in Mount Street, home to one of Donata's many friends, Lady Courtland, wife of an earl.

A card room had been set up for gentlemen who had no interest in dancing. I usually made for these first thing, now that I had a little more in my pockets to cover the wagers. Tonight, however, I felt the need to stay by Donata's side.

She did not appear to mind. As a couple, we wandered through the crowd, greeting acquaintances and friends. Donata liked being unconventional, though I knew we'd be laughed at for clinging so close to each other.

"I'm happy you've come tonight," Donata said to me, giving my arm a squeeze. "Not only does it clear my mind from that horrible interview with Mr. Bennett, but you can meet the young men who will be at Gabriella's come-out next week."

I had already met a few, and I thoroughly disapproved of them, for no reason at all.

They were paraded before me now, one by one. Not so blatantly—Donata knew how to handle people.

They were Edward Clayton, Emmett Garfield, Geoffrey Kent, and Daniel Marsden.

All four were sons of gentlemen with respectable estates and enough means to stay the Season in London without ruination. Geoffrey Kent was looking to begin a political career, and all four were primed to take over their father's estates when the time came, and in fact, helped run them now.

They were not aristocrats, though Clayton was distantly connected to an earl's family, but landed gentlemen, whose fathers owned lucrative estates.

They were, in fact, of the exact means and station in life that I was and my father had been. The difference was that my father had squandered all the income and let the house fall to ruin while these gentlemen's parents were more responsible.

I'd met Kent and Clayton before. They dressed

well but not flashily, were respectful to me and attentive to the ladies, and did not play for exorbitant stakes in the card room. I was trying very hard to find fault with them. Clayton, for instance, spoke with a nasally tone.

David Marsden had even fewer faults that I could discern, much to my irritation. He reminded me a bit of Leland Derwent—very polite, deferential to me and Donata without fawning. He was well educated and seemed to have actually studied something at university—he was interested in science and mathematics as well as ancient texts.

I was happy to meet Emmett Garfield, because here was a man I could actively dislike.

First, he was too handsome. The other three looked like what they were—sprigs of old English families, stretching into the distant past. They had fair hair, pudgy faces, and chins that spoke of too much inbreeding. Garfield had dark hair, a hint of the Continent about him, and was broad of shoulder and taut from riding and boxing. He enjoyed sport, he confessed, more than indoor activities.

He was also cocky. Garfield bowed courteously to me but his look was sly, I thought—he was assessing me as a potential father-in-law.

If he married Gabriella, he'd be connected to a wealthy viscount through me, and no doubt would try to use his charms to have young Peter doing whatever he wanted. The sparkle in his eyes told me Garfield knew exactly what I thought.

"Captain," he said, with the right amount of deference.

I shook his hand as politely as I could. "Mr. Garfield."

Donata had moved from my side to speak to

friends, the feathers in her headdress swaying, so I could not count upon her to warm the air with conversation.

"You are from Norfolk," Garfield observed, as I groped for something to say. "Lovely country. I have visited its lanes on an idle day after Newmarket. The draining projects have made the farms there quite rich."

"Not always," I answered. "There was a terrible yield a few years ago, when the summer never warmed."

"Yes, I remember. It affected us all, but it was particularly bad there, I heard. But I understand *your* farm does not produce at all?"

"Not at the moment," I said. "I will return there this year and begin improvements."

"Very wise." The young man had the audacity to wink. Mr. Garfield leaned closer to me. "I have heard it remarked upon, sir, that you came from nowhere, and now nearly are lord of somewhere — such was your skill."

"If you have heard such a thing," I snapped, "the speaker is very impertinent."

"I know, and I told him so." Garfield's smile was warm and engaging, which made me dislike him more. "But you must admit, you were uncommon clever. No one had ever heard of you, and now, here you are, the constant companion of Mr. Grenville, and married to one of the most prominent ladies of the *ton*."

So also had the anonymous letter-writer indicated.

My eyes narrowed as I wondered whether this young idiot was the letter-writer himself. He liked to ride, was athletic, and similar sentiments were coming from his mouth.

"Do not worry, Captain," Mr. Garfield went on. "I defend you to all comers."

"See that you do," I answered, my lips stiff.

I turned away from him—politely; I would not embarrass Donata by punching him outright—and walked toward the card room, not happy.

I could not speak to Donata again until we were on our way home. At supper we'd been seated far from each other—I had been conversing with another lady when the bell for supper rang, and as politeness dictated, I escorted her into the dining room and attended her for the meal.

The food was quite good, but my appetite was taken away by imagining the four young gentlemen dancing with my daughter at her come-out ball on Tuesday next. After that, they'd be welcomed to our house to court her.

Then marrying her, being responsible for her happiness. Food turned to dust in my mouth.

After supper, dancing had recommenced. Forced to be a wallflower by my injury, I watched Donata join sets and enjoy herself. She loved dancing, and was partnered by many old friends.

I watched my wife laughing, her hair shining as she turned under the candlelight of the chandeliers, her green velvet gown hugging her shoulders. She was a beautiful woman, full of grace.

Most of our acquaintance had been very surprised that Donata and I had made a match. I knew they assumed I'd want a plump, sweet-tempered homebody, whose chatelaine clanked with keys as she looked after me and her house, always ready with a soothing pat and a remedy to fix any ill.

However, I found in Donata not a wife to wait upon me, but a companion. I could speak to her on any topic, and she had the wit and interest to respond. She understood me as no other woman had — even more deeply sometimes than I wanted her to.

By the time we reached our carriage to return us to South Audley Street, I was tired, disgruntled, and ready to lay my head on her bosom.

I sat rigidly upright, however, on the journey home, anger in my heart.

"Emmett Garfield," I said when Donata had settled in beside me with a happy but weary sigh. "Why was *he* chosen as a potential husband for Gabriella?"

"Mr. Garfield?" Donata looked at me in surprise, then she groaned softly and stretched one foot in the leather shoe she wore to move between engagements. Her maid carried her satin, beaded dancing slippers in a special box. "He comes from one of the best families and has a sensible business head. He would never bankrupt Gabriella, and will run his estate well."

"I do not like him," I said. "He is supercilious." *Arrogant, high-handed, cocksure* ... I could continue for some time.

Donata waved her hand, and a drooping feather brushed her cheek. "He is harmless. A bit full of himself, yes, but that will ease as he becomes older and more jaded by life. His father was the same way, Aline tells me, but is now the wisest of gentlemen."

"A son does not always become the twin of his father," I said — in my case, thank God. "I would like you to cross Mr. Garfield from your guest list."

Her eyes widened. "Indeed, I will not. To do so would be to enrage his family, who are old friends of Aline's. I agree — Mr. Garfield grated upon me when

I first met him, but when you get past his feeble attempts at wit, he is quite personable."

"If you will forgive me, he is also good looking," I said coldly. "Which does nothing for *me*, but might cause you and Aline, and Gabriella, to overlook his defects."

Donata sent me a pitying look. "Absolute nonsense. I do not judge a man's character on his looks. How foolish."

"You might not, but Gabriella? She is young, naive, has rusticated in France …"

"Yes, the French are known for their celibate ways." Donata put her hand on my chest. "Do not worry so, Gabriel. If I thought him a bad sort, I would never have invited him, old friends of Aline's or no. He is nothing like Mr. Bennett, trust me."

"But he might have written the letters." I poured out my worry, describing the conversation I'd had with him.

"Hmm." Donata's brows drew together. "I will have to think about that. But admit, Gabriel, that what the letter-writer claims is nothing more than what ill-willed members of my set have said. Or what journalists have speculated. All are baffled that I esteem you so much, and conclude that I must be a halfwit, bedazzled by a fraud. But as we are not Margaret Woolwich and Mr. Bennett, I refuse to be angered by such things. Mr. Garfield is only repeating what he has heard."

"That may be," I conceded, though I would take it upon myself to find out. "But I still don't like him."

Donata smoothed my cheek, and rested her head on my shoulder as the carriage swayed slowly home. "My dear, you will not like any gentleman who looks at Gabriella. Even when she is in her dotage."

I had to agree that this was true.

***

I dreamed of Judith again that night, even though Donata slept beside me. In this dream, she looked like her sister, Devorah, prim, cool, unforgiving. Again I saw her coming toward me on a street, again, when she reached me, she deteriorated into bones.

I tossed, woke sweating, and left Donata's bed so I would not wake her. I spent the rest of the night alone in my bedchamber, staring at the canopy, until exhaustion overcame me, and I slept, this time without dreams.

In the morning I journeyed in a hackney to Bow Street and once again looked for Pomeroy. Today, I found him in.

"Pleasant to see ye, Captain!" he boomed down the stairs as a patroller motioned me to go up. "Hear Thompson has you poring over a bag of bones. I'll wager you know who they belong to, how he died, who killed him, and what he had for breakfast that morning."

"Not quite," I said as I reached him.

I glanced around for Spendlove, certain that Pomeroy's bellowing would tell the man all he needed to know.

"You've come to ask for my help, have you?" Pomeroy continued at the top of his voice. "What can I do that the great Captain Lacey cannot?"

His blue eyes twinkled, and his grin was wide.

"You can keep my inquiries to yourself for one. May we speak in private?"

"Of course!" Pomeroy gestured me into a small room at the top of the stairs, one I'd been in before. Here was a table and a few chairs, shelves of ledgers and papers, a place to write up reports.

"The dead woman's name is Judith Hartman," I said, seeing no reason to keep it secret anymore. Thompson would tell Pomeroy that if he asked— indeed would have written it into an official record. "This is Thompson's case, so please respect that."

"Now, what sort of Runner would I be if I pinched convictions off others?" The glint in Pomeroy's eye told me he'd do just that whenever he could. He liked Thompson, however. Respected him.

"I want to know two things," I said. "One, if there have been any complaints made about Mr. Andrew Bennett—who seems to lose wives in convenient fashion. Two, if Miss Hartman's disappearance was reported at the time she went missing—about fifteen years ago—how would I find out? I want to paint a picture of her last days, but the people in her life are being singularly uncooperative."

"Couldn't be you're putting their backs up, could it?" Pomeroy's good humor returned. "Haven't heard a word, to my knowledge, about this Bennett chap, or Miss Hartman. Fifteen years, eh? Before my time. Fifteen years ago, I was rushing around following your orders."

This was so. By then we'd left France, the Peace of Amiens evaporating, and gone back to England for training. Long days reviewing troops, drilling, solving petty problems of soldiers weary of waiting for things to happen. I'd tried to bury myself in routine to take away the fiery pain of losing my wife and daughter.

"There would be records," I said.

"Aye, that there would. Do you mean you want to root around in papers fifteen years old? If I can even put my hands on them?"

"Yes," I answered. "Unless someone here

remembers the exact case."

"London is a busy place," Pomeroy said. "I imagine many things happened here in 1803."

"Where would I find these records?" I persisted.

Pomeroy let out a sigh. "Follow me, Captain. I don't know if you'll find what you need, but if anyone can, it will be you."

When I saw the room where the records were kept, however, I nearly gave up the slender hope of my idea.

The chamber below street level to which Pomeroy led me was crammed with shelves, tables, boxes, desks, cabinets—all of them full of papers, ledgers, books, and sheets filled with fine-lined writing.

"Good Lord," I said.

"Records kept since 1724." Pomeroy proudly waved a hand at them. "Clerk's records, warrants, court records, every decision by the magistrate, accounts … if someone thought it worth writing down, they wrote it down. Me, I've never had to look for anything beyond a few years ago."

"I see." My mouth was dry. "Is there some sort of organization?"

Pomeroy shrugged. "I usually have a clerk fetch information for me. But fifteen years ago … Well, poke around as you like, Captain. If anyone objects, tell them to come find me."

He left me to it. Glumly, I pulled a ledger from the first shelf. There wasn't much light down here, and I peered at the crowded page until I realized it was records for this house's poor box.

There was a reason I'd taken well to fighting but never aspired to an administrative post. Brandon had always thought I should be groomed to be an aide-de-camp, but I was not one for records, papers, and the tedious details of army life.

I was much better at yelling at men and keeping them safe. Reading, in my opinion, should be confined to entertaining histories, scientific discoveries, and well-told stories.

I'd brought Bartholomew with me today. I sent for him now, and he looked around with the same dismay.

"Bleedin' hell, sir. Why would people want to write so much down?"

"Court records are important," I said. "A way to ensure that judges and magistrates remain honest."

"Does it work?" Bartholomew asked, his tone dubious.

"Who knows? Fortunately for me, I have become acquainted with a gentleman who might be able to unravel the puzzle for me. Will you go to Cornhill in the City and ask Mr. Molodzinski to join me here?"

Chapter Twenty-Two

By the time Molodzinski arrived, I had at least found a section of the chamber containing records near a year I was looking for.

I had told myself that a report of Judith's disappearance might not exist at all, or be buried in a cubbyhole in another magistrate's house, such as the one at Whitechapel. But Bow Street was sort of a collective whirlpool, since it was the first house to put together the Runners. If a report had been made, I guessed I'd find a copy of it here.

Molodzinski looked around at the chaos, his dark eyes shining.

"Ah," he said. "I can see why you sent for an expert."

"I'm looking for any record of Judith Hartman's disappearance being reported. Any mention of her at all, actually. Or any information about her husband, Andrew Bennett. I would like to see a record of Miss Hartman's marriage to Bennett as well—I'll have to visit the vicar who married them."

So muttering to myself, I picked over another ledger. Molodzinski said nothing at all but quietly went to work, and soon assessed what was what.

We never found anything about Bennett—no mention of him at all. However, after another hour, Molodzinski ferreted out a note in a book, written in the cramped hand of a long-since-gone patroller.

The pages recorded his reports of 19 May, 1803. I read through it, picturing the man's face screwing up as he struggled with spelling.

Reported missing, Miss Hartman, daughter of a Hebrew. Last seen in Aldgate High Street, not far from the great sinigog, according to Miss Devra Hartman, sister. Both are daughters of Mr. Joseph Hartman of the Strand.

"The significant thing," I said, peering at the note, "besides his misspellings, is that there is no mention of Mr. Andrew Bennett. She's styled as *Miss Hartman*. A spinster, not a wife."

"Perhaps the elder Miss Hartman did not consider her sister married," Molodzinski speculated. "Miss Hartman and her father strike me as those clinging to traditional ways." He pressed his hands to his chest. "I consider myself very modern, very free thinking, though I have no intention of converting to the Anglo religion, thank you very much. But Hartman, though he wears the clothes of an Englishman, he keeps his beard and is a traditionalist at heart, especially when it comes to his daughters."

"It seems Devorah agrees with him," I said. "So she noticed Judith gone. How, I wonder, if they were estranged? Had she planned to meet with her?"

"For that, you'll have to ask her. But wait, I have found another mention."

A similar report, in another hand, had been

written five days later. *Missing, Mrs. Andrew Bennett. Last seen, Aldgate High Street Wednesday, 16 May. Told to me by Mr. Itzak Stein, a Hebrew.*

"Mr. Stein again," I said, excitement stirring. "The man who hoped to be Judith's husband." I copied out the reports into my silver-cased notebook then snapped the case shut. "I believe I will pay a visit to Mr. Stein." I paused. "As soon as I have an address."

"Not today, you won't," Molodzinski said. "It's Saturday. If he's anything like Hartman and his elder daughter, he will be at the Great Synagogue, muttering and praying."

Saturday was considered the Sabbath among the Hebrews. This fact had come up a time or two in the army, but then, most of us had not stopped battles or marches for any sort of holy day. Hebrews had to pretend at least to belong to the official church to take the oath to join the army, but there had been ways around that.

I looked Molodzinski up and down. "You do not seem to be there with him."

Molodzinski shook his head, self-deprecating. "Me, I am a sinner and not so pious. My mother is no longer alive to scold me, and so I rush to help you in your investigations instead of spending my day in contemplation and study."

I slid my notebook into my pocket and took up my hat. "If Mr. Stein is at the synagogue, then I will take myself there and wait for him to come out."

"Will you? Do you know what he looks like?"

I deflated. "No, I don't. But perhaps Hartman will point him out to me."

"Hartman might shoot you on the spot. Never mind." Molodzinski pulled on his gloves. "I will go with you, ask about Mr. Stein for you, and prevent you having Hartman's fist up your nose. Or his eldest daughter's — she sounds formidable."

"She is," I agreed.

"Then it is settled. I will protect you from the wrath of Miss Hartman."

Chuckling, Molodzinski led the way from the cellar back to the main floor of the Bow Street house.

Outside, the clouds had gathered to threaten more rain, but it was still dry, warm, and a bit sticky.

Later this summer, once the Season was officially over, we would repair first to Norfolk to see the ongoing work on my ancestral home, then visit Donata's family in Oxfordshire. We'd journey from there to Hampshire to the Breckenridge estate, which I'd never seen. I looked forward to cool country breezes and long rides on horseback, taking my ease from the crowded city.

The crowded city now pressed upon us. On Saturday, those of the Christian faith were working, hurrying, shopping, readying themselves for their one day of rest a week.

I could not censure Molodzinski for not attending his house of worship today, because I, cradle-born to the C of E, spent my Sundays with my feet up at home, not racing to the nearest church to listen to the vicar's hour-long sermon.

The airless hackney lurched through streets at a slow pace, taking us too near the river for my taste. Molodzinski pointedly drew a handkerchief from his pocket and flapped it in front of his nose. That appendage was less swollen now, as was his eye, though his bruises from Denis's men were still dark.

We emerged into the City and made for Cornhill, passing Molodzinski's place of work, and through Leadenhall into Aldgate, east of Aldgate High Street, where Judith had last been seen.

A turning from Aldgate, called Duke's Place, housed what was known as the Great Synagogue. Another synagogue stood further up the road — Bevis Marks — but Molodzinski confidently steered me into Duke's Place. What the difference was between the two I did not wish to profess my ignorance and ask.

I had passed this synagogue whenever I had dealings in this part of London, but aside from a few curious glances, I'd never given it much thought. The building was quietly unpretentious in the Adam style, with flights of steps leading to an arched portico, above which were many-paned windows.

Apparently I could enter as a visitor, and as I moved into the interior, I removed my hat.

"Heads remained covered, Captain," Molodzinski said in a quiet voice. Startled, I replaced my hat on my head, feeling odd to do so, and followed him in.

The service had already begun. Molodzinski slipped us to a bench in the back, and we sat quietly.

I looked around in wonder. We were in a lofty room that rose three stories above us, many arched windows letting in soft daylight. As was the outside, the inside was subdued yet beautifully elegant. The walls were pale, the flat corbeled ceiling softly arched around its edges. Enormous chandeliers hung from this ceiling, and I amused myself trying to count the candles in their many tiers.

In the center of the house was a sort of platform, under another chandelier, enclosed by a railing, where men stood to read or chant. Beyond them, on the far end of the room was an arched recess, flanked by columns and encircled by a low gold screen. No one went near this place, which had been treated with the reverence of an altar, but I knew it was not one. Perhaps it was the place where they kept the holy books, but I wasn't certain.

Brewster had been correct when he'd said that the men and women were separated for the service. On the ground floor, where Molodzinski and I sat, were only men. I looked up at the gallery that encircled the first floor to see the ladies sitting behind a railing, their colorful gowns welcome hues in this place of white.

A few of the women peered curiously down at me, likely wondering who was this stiff Anglo in their midst. I spied Devorah Hartman among them, but she did not look at me—I could not tell whether she'd noticed me at all. She had her head bowed, her gaze downward, her eyes possibly closed.

I looked for Mr. Hartman among the men, but there were too many here today for me to distinguish him.

In the middle platform, a man—a cantor, I supposed—began to sing.

A curious thing happened. I could not understand one word of his chant, sung in a clear, beautiful tenor, but I felt peace steal over me. Around me, heads were bowed, men studying books in their hands or with eyes closed in prayer.

In the light, the calm, the air, cooled by the openness of the space, the thick walls protectively between me and the noise and stink of the city, I slipped into a state of great ease. My limbs relaxed; the nagging pain that was my constant companion, fell away.

I floated on the music, lifted by a service I could not begin to follow.

My understanding mattered little, I realized. I'd watched natives of India kneel in reverence before gleaming statues of ancient gods, offering food that could ill be spared, or flowers, or simply pressing their hands together and bowing in prayer. I'd seen Mohammedans in the north of India likewise lost in blissful prayer, bent to the floor on their carpets.

It didn't matter, I'd realized then, that the precepts of our religions were different. These men around me believed in the same God I did, even if they did not believe the Lord Jesus Christ to be the son of that God. We were lifted together by the beauty of the voice that sang the words, the sweet air that floated around us, and the light of the many candles.

Or perhaps I was simply swept up in the beauty and serenity of it all. I understood why men became religious—if I could feel this ease, this sensation of being cradled in gentle warmth all the time, I would abandon my life and become a hermit and a mystic.

I could imagine what Donata would have to say about that. The image of her made me smile, and give up my sudden inclination to monkhood. I settled in and simply enjoyed the service.

I did not want this tranquility to come to an end, but finally, Molodzinski indicated it was time to leave. I rose with the others and filed out of the lovely hall into daylight.

The sounds of the City came back to me, and unfortunately, the smell. I again thought of country breezes with regret.

Molodzinski was speaking to a knot of men, greeting them, laughing when they expressed surprise to see him there. He introduced me, and I shook hands with several gentlemen, who welcomed me politely. As we exchanged pleasantries, one of the men gestured to another walking out into the courtyard.

"There's Mr. Stein," he said, and beckoned him over.

Stein was of an age with Andrew Bennett and Devorah. They would have all been very young when Judith died, in their early twenties. Though some men did make their careers and fortunes by the time they were twenty-two, looking back from my decrepit age of forty, I knew how stupidly childish one who'd just come into his majority could be.

Itzak Stein had hair a few shades lighter than Devorah Hartman's, wide brown eyes, and a soft face. His firm mouth, though, showed me he was not weak of character, even if he looked a bit like a calf. He was clean-shaven and wore a suit whose modest cut even Grenville would approve.

"Captain Lacey," Mr. Stein said, taking my hand in a firm grip. "Miss Hartman told me she'd come to visit you."

I raised my brows as I shook his hand. "She did not mention you, I feel I should tell you."

"I am not surprised." Stein gave me a thin smile. "She never considered me good enough for her younger sister." He hesitated. "When Devorah told me she'd gone to you, I'd planned to visit you myself, but my wife convinced me not to. Water under the bridge, she said. All in the past, not our business. I agreed with her, but I am glad you sought me out."

Chapter Twenty-Three

So, I reflected, Mr. Stein was another man who'd moved on after Judith's death.

Had she been so forgettable? It had been many years after my wife left me before I'd even contemplated marrying again, though I admit to several love affairs. But marriage—I'd not wanted to take the step of declaring my wife gone, abandoning me, perhaps lying dead. That would have made it too final.

"You reported her missing," I said to Stein. "To Bow Street."

"To the Whitechapel magistrate's house," Stein corrected me. "It was the nearest."

I knew the magistrate there—Sir Montague Harris. I would have to find out if he'd been there at the relevant time.

"Why did you?" I asked. "The note in the records said you waited nearly a week before you sought the magistrate."

Stein let out a sigh. "Judith no longer wanted anything to do with me—I was not certain she'd welcome me looking for her. She'd made it clear she despised her family, her faith, her friends ... me. We were backward to her—never mind we live elbow-to-elbow with Anglos and share almost all aspects of their lives. No, because we still attend the synagogue and observe *kiddush*, we are medieval and slow. She was impatient for life, was Judith."

Around us men flowed back into London, heading home for meals and the end of their Sabbath day. Molodzinski had discreetly moved from us and was engaged in conversation with his acquaintance.

"She presumably found this new life with Mr. Bennett," I said.

A flash of anger lit Mr. Stein's affable face. Anything soft in him fled, and his eyes hardened.

"Bennett flattered her, cajoled her, turned her from her family. My father and hers had agreed upon our marriage, and Judith had been all for it. I loved her, pure and simple. I am not a traditionalist—I did not expect her to cover herself from all eyes and hide at home. When I escorted her out, with her father, we were lively and happy. But Bennett—he convinced Judith that what she had was wrong and dull. She'd only see life if she fled the confines of her father's house and moved with him to Oxford Street."

"That is where they lived?" I asked.

"He'd bought a house there with money his father left him, or so he claimed. Judith at first told Devorah—with whom she still corresponded—that she was happy there. But later ... I don't know what transpired. She disliked the house, she wanted to move to a better ..."

Had Judith been of a character that needed constant novelty? Or had she discovered that Bennett had, in truth, little to give her? Perhaps the house had been only leased, perhaps he'd counted on Judith's family to provide her with money. I would seek Bennett again and throttle answers from him.

"If she lived at Oxford Street," I began. "Why had she gone to Aldgate High Street? Where both you and Devorah reported her last seen?"

Stein shook his head. "I could not say. Judith occasionally met Devorah, though not often, because Devorah liked to scold her. Devorah told me she saw Judith by chance at Aldgate High Street. Judith glanced her way then hurried off, gone. When letters to Judith went unanswered in the next few days, Devorah went to the house in Oxford Street to find Judith and Bennett both gone. Moved out a few days before, the neighbors said. After a tremendous row."

My brows rose. "Indeed?" Bennett had omitted *this* fact. "That is when Devorah reported her missing?"

"She did. I had not known Devorah had gone to the magistrate until later. I myself approached the Oxford Street house — in case the neighbors were mistaken — but no. They were gone. I saw Bennett on that street, or supposed I did, a few days later, without Judith. I followed him. He went to another house, and I glimpsed, while the door was open, a woman who welcomed him in, but she was not Judith."

Very interesting, indeed. "Where was this house?"

Stein blinked his large eyes at me. "This was years ago, Captain. I no longer remember the number of Bennett's house, though I think it was near Swallow Street. This house was further along, around Soho

Square."

"Did you inquire further?" I asked.

"No—I was angry, and alarmed. But I had no wish to confront Bennett so I went to the magistrate." He let out another defeated breath. "All for nothing. Devorah and I searched, but we never found Judith. Bennett came to me looking for her as well, convinced I and her family had taken her back. He left after calling me some appalling names, and I never saw him again. Neither Mr. Hartman nor I had the money at the time to offer sufficient reward or hire someone to help us. After a time, we assumed her dead. And now it appears we were correct."

His sorrow was genuine, I thought, but faded now. He remembered Judith with regret, but I did not read in him a lingering rage at Bennett or grief at Judith's death. She was gone, had been for a long time, and he had a new family, a new life.

Had *this* man struck her down? Had Stein, with his calf eyes, been unforgiving when Judith eloped? Perhaps Judith had come to meet him somewhere near Aldgate High Street—she might have been unhappy with Bennett and thought she could speak to Stein about it. Maybe she hoped Stein might forgive her and help her get free of Bennett. Or simply came at his summons. Stein might have walked her nearer the river, argued with her, struck her, pushed her in.

Devorah had caught sight of her by chance, and Stein had become worried when she reported Judith missing. He'd reported her missing as well, because that is what a man who'd cared about a woman would do, jilted by her or not.

For whatever reason those reports and Judith's bones found five years later had not been connected.

Remembering the sea of papers under the Bow Street house, I was not terribly surprised.

Stein had strong hands and a solid build. He'd have been even more strong and agile in his twenties. A quarrel gone wrong? Or had he planned to kill Judith for disgracing him?

Proof. I needed proof. A confession would be fine as well.

Stein regarded me calmly. I read in him no urge to confess his great sin to me. I would have to trick or frighten it out of him.

Or, Stein might have had nothing to do with it, had only made the best of his life after his disappointment. I hoped, for his wife's sake, that he'd found a friend and helpmeet in the current Mrs. Stein, and appreciated it.

Stein tipped his hat. "If that is all, Captain, my wife expects me home."

"Of course," I said. "May I call upon you if I need to speak to you again?"

"Send word," Stein said quickly. "I will meet you."

He did not want me at his house, speaking to him of the past. If he were innocent, I could understand. If guilty — well, I'd make certain he paid.

Judith might have been like a butterfly, flitting after happiness as she saw it, hurting those she left behind, but she shouldn't have been killed. Her family had known her as the young, rather silly thing who wrestled herself from the perceived confinement of her life.

I'd seen her as a collection of bones, lost, forgotten, an object of pity. I'd pot who killed her, never mind the trouble I'd cause.

"I will send word," I responded. "Good day, Mr.

Stein."

We shook hands again, and parted.

"You never said you were coming to dwell among the Hebrews," a voice at my back remarked.

I turned without much surprise to find Brewster. Likely, he'd seen me leave Bow Street and followed. Bartholomew lounged near the hackney I'd hired for the day, waiting for me.

"Are you converting?" Brewster asked when I turned to him.

"Trying to solve a crime," I countered. "Tell me, did you ask your footman friend to infiltrate the house in Cavendish Square?"

"I did. And he did. He's chuffed at the job. Says they took him on at once. Pay is decent, though the others there warned him servants don't stick it long. They can't stand that Bennett chap."

I imagined I wouldn't stick it long either.

I sought Molodzinski and thanked him for his trouble.

"Glad to help," Molodzinski said. "I have been asking about Hartman and his family, but I haven't learned much more than you have. Hartman is one whose father, and his father before him, embraced Englishness only reluctantly. Hartman is happy to live and work without impediment, but he yearns for the old ways. Me, I like the new days."

"The new days are dangerous," I pointed out, with a glance at his bruises.

"Ha. So were the old, Captain. At one point in history, and not so long ago as all that, it was a crime to be a Jew. I like the new, enlightened days."

I agreed he had the right of it, and took my leave of him.

"Bartholomew," I said as Brewster and I

approached the hackney. "Would you like to do some covert investigation for me?"

Bartholomew brightened. "Of course I would, Captain. As I said, I'm your man."

"Good. Then take yourself to Cavendish Square and become acquainted with the servants below stairs in Captain Woolwich's house. Any time Mr. Bennett leaves that house, follow him and report to me what he does. I'll give you some money so you can stay at a public house—I want you to observe him for some days."

Bartholomew's eyes lit, then he frowned. "If I'm following this gent about, who will look after you at home?"

I waved that away. "I will manage—as I did for many years." I took coins from my pocket and dropped them into his hand. "Do not let Bennett see you. He has met Matthias, and you two are much alike."

"He'll never know I'm there," Bartholomew promised. He touched his forehead in salute and jogged away.

"You know, my bloke Jack will find anything wrong going on in that house," Brewster said, sounding the slightest bit hurt.

"*Inside,*" I said. "Your man won't be able to invent enough excuses to leave the house to follow Bennett every day. Believe me, I will be agog to hear Jack's reports."

Brewster looked mollified. "Where to now, Captain?"

"Home," I said. "I have promised my wife to take great care when I am out. Although I need to look into two houses in Oxford Street, exact addresses vague. Damn it all, I wish my information wasn't from so many years ago—if Bennett had been visiting a mistress, I might never find her. He might have long ago finished with her, or she has left London, or died, or she was not his mistress at all."

"Tall order," Brewster agreed.

"Hence, I asked Bartholomew to watch him. I am interested in what Mr. Bennett does with his day."

Brewster grunted. "I understand. I might not be able to help you with this much longer, I have to warn you. Mr. Denis has suggested that, as he puts it, my talents be employed elsewhere, and another of his men set to watch you."

My brows rose. "Truly? But you are excellent at it. I never know when you are going to pop up."

Brewster's cheekbones stained red. "Happarently, I am looking after you too well. His nibs wants no harm to come to you, but he's not happy that you talk to me, like, and stand me drinks. Or that I took you to visit my missus for tea. Says I can't intimidate you if I let you speak with me."

"In other words, he wishes to protect me but also keep me in my place."

"Somefink like that."

I hid my annoyance. "Would it be helpful if I had you knock me about a time or two? I could show him my injuries as proof you are sufficiently intimidating."

Brewster grinned. "Then *your* missus would light into me. Think I'll risk the displeasure of his nibs, instead. But I'd be sorry to lose the post," he said. "It's not dull, following you about."

He closed his mouth over this declaration and shoved me up into the hackney. Declaring it was overly hot inside, Brewster elected to ride on the box with the coachman.

I reflected, as the hackney pulled away and headed for Leadenhall, that with Brewster I'd begun to forge an unlikely, but not unwelcome, friendship.

***

I could do little myself to investigate Judith's murder over the next few days, much as I longed to drag Bennett from his home and beat answers from him.

When I returned home Saturday afternoon, I found Lady Aline closeted with Donata. Both ladies pounced on me and recruited me to do errands that had left them in despair.

The come-out was to be held at Lady Aline's very large house in Berkeley Square. When I'd asked, in all innocence, when that decision had been made, why it could not be held in Donata's house, I was given stares that told me I was a blithering fool. Not enough room, Donata had said crisply. And this house was pokey, not like Aline's lofty grandeur.

I could not agree, but I decided not to argue.

The hired musicians and music master had apparently had a falling out. I was sent 'round to reconcile them and make certain they would still come. The hired furniture — extra chairs, tables, and dressing tables for the withdrawing rooms — had to be directed into place with a firm hand, as did the many candles for the colossal chandeliers. I was also to ensure the temperamental pastry maker prepared exactly what was wished in the exact way Donata had instructed.

When I was not busy with these devastating tasks, I was writing letters to soothe the tempers of the gentlemen whose families had not been invited.

I drew the line, I said, at fighting duels over it.

I was glad I'd put Bartholomew and Brewster's

friend Jack in place to watch over Mr. Bennett. Bartholomew, true to his word, followed the man about but made certain to never be spotted. Bennett never noticed, Bartholomew said in his messages to me. The man never looked around.

Brewster reported to me what his friend discovered—Jack could not write a clear sentence, Brewster said, so had to convey the information through him.

Even so, between them, they learned nothing of great interest. Bennett had done nothing sinister, although both Bartholomew and Jack agreed the man was an ass.

I put forth one more inquiry. It occurred to me, as I sat in the elegant synagogue, having no idea as to the significance of the ceremony—would Judith likewise have had no sense of what was happening in an English church? Granted, our services were in English, but they were a bit archaic, and I imagine, somewhat byzantine to those not raised to them.

I wanted very much to know whether Bennett had tricked her into believing she'd married him. Why he should fool her, I didn't know, but I wanted to see a record of their marriage in black and white.

Grenville, after I'd told him about the reports I'd found at Bow Street and my talk with Stein, offered to track down the marriage record. He knew the curates or vicars of every church in London, since he'd gone to school with most of them, or at least members of their families.

He cheerfully left me to the sphere of my womenfolk, who were driving me mad with this approaching event, and headed off to investigate.

Dreams of Judith still came to me, always the same. She'd walk to me, sometimes looking like her sister, sometimes Gabriella. She'd hold out her hand, which would turn skeletal, and then she'd fall to the street, broken and dead.

Tuesday dawned, and so we came to Gabriella's come-out.

Chapter Twenty-Four

Lady Aline's Berkeley Square house glowed with light. The candles I'd wrangled glittered from every sconce and chandelier that filled the ballroom on the first floor.

The musicians, reconciled, played in a gallery above the ballroom, so that melodies trickled down like starlight.

Denis had agreed to supply extra guards, and some of the footmen rushing about with trays were large, hard-faced men, bulging in their livery. Guests threw them startled glances, but they did their tasks with cool efficiency.

Gabriella made no grand entrance. *Nothing vulgar,* Donata had said. *Simply a ball given by Aline, and Gabriella will be introduced.*

I'd had a vague notion that my daughter could not be "out" until she was presented to Queen Charlotte at one of her gatherings, as Donata had described happened to her. Donata had given me one of her looks that told me I was hopeless, then explained that Gabriella, if she married into the peerage, could wait to be presented after her wedding. Besides, Queen Charlotte, elderly and ill, rarely held Drawing Rooms these days. Gabriella was not the daughter of a peer, and Aline and Donata hosting her would be sufficient.

Donata also warned me that the lady patronesses of Almack's might never give Gabriella a voucher to attend an insipid ball at that bastion of respectability. She was confident, however, that Gabriella did not need to appear there to find a husband. Donata and Aline, I was assured, knew exactly what they were about.

I'd backed away and left them to it.

Gabriella was so beautiful tonight I stopped, my heart aching, when she entered, quietly and without fuss, at Lady Aline's side. She'd spent all day readying herself, and the result made my eyes sting.

Her dark hair was caught up from her neck by a thin bandeau that allowed several curls to cascade to her shoulders. Her gown was of a shimmering ivory satin, and her puffed sleeves were covered with silver netting that let the shine of the material below gleam through.

The gown was simple, almost unadorned. Three buttons decorated her short bodice. Then the high-waisted skirt flowed without hindrance to her slippered feet, where it was trimmed with one row of appliquéd cotton lace. Small diamond earrings, a present from Donata, dangled from Gabriella's ears, and a thin gold necklace—my gift—rested on her bosom.

I went directly to her, took her hands, and kissed her cheek.

The cheek flushed beneath my lips. "Do I not look

fine?" Gabriella asked me when I straightened. "I've never owned such a dress. I wish Mama and Papa could see me."

The wistfulness in her words smote me. I'd brought her here to this city, far from anything familiar, because I wanted to get to know her. Gabriella had good-naturedly gone along with Donata's plans, but the flash of homesickness in her eyes now tore at me.

"You must wear it for them, then, when you return to France," I said.

Aline, overhearing, let her brows rise on her rouged face. She said nothing, however, because others were approaching.

Gabriella brightened. "I will show it off for them, then. That is, if Lady Donata does not mind." She glanced around, her regret forgotten. "The room is so very beautiful, is it not?"

You are the most beautiful thing in it, I wanted to say. I held my tongue, not wanting to look a foolish, doting father.

It was time for introductions. Gabriella had met most of the people here before—ladies and gentlemen of Donata's and Aline's acquaintance, and their sons and daughters. She'd made friends with some of the girls, and was pronounced "a lovely thing, so unspoiled" by their mothers.

Now, Gabriella would be one of them, ready to be married. Only Donata and Aline, Grenville, and of course, Gabriella, knew that her mother was still alive—they thought me a widower, Gabriella raised in France by a relative.

Carlotta Lacey, my first wife, had ceased to exist long ago. Colette Auberge, whom she'd become, had now married her major, after I, with much underhanded assistance from James Denis, divorced her. Though it had to go through the courts, Denis's influence was such that the issue was never revealed to the public. I'd toady to Denis for a long time to ensure our disgrace never came to light, so Gabriella's chances would not be ruined by it.

Not that, among the *ton*, elopements with lovers and divorces never happened. My first marriage and its end was almost unremarkable among some of the more famous cases.

The gathering began in earnest, and Gabriella was whisked away from me to meet the masses.

The masses were small for a Mayfair ball, I was grateful to see, though the room did fill. Ladies in finery, gentlemen in severe black—all had come to greet my Gabriella.

I knew everyone here, including the Brandons. Aline greeted Louisa with delight, and then I kissed her cheek, murmuring my thanks to her for coming. Brandon had already slipped into the card room, so I felt free to give Louisa's hands a warm squeeze.

"You look well, Gabriel," Louisa said, returning my kiss. "If a trifle harassed."

"Worried father," I replied. "Louisa, how the devil will I rest until I know she's happy?"

Louisa Brandon, her blond hair having darkened in the twenty-odd years I'd known her, her face only now showing lines, smiled and reached up to pat my shoulder.

"Do not worry, you shall never rest. There will always be something in Gabriella's life to fret you. Rejoice that she is here to fret over."

I warmed. "That is true. I ought to have known you would show me the right of it."

"She is a lovely young woman, Gabriel. But not a

silly girl. I doubt she'll let a roué turn her head."

I saw the roué I most objected to sidle up to Aline and Gabriella across the room—with his mother, of course.

I bristled. "I do *not* like that young man."

"Emmett Garfield?" Louisa looked surprised. "Nothing wrong with Mr. Garfield. He acts a fool sometimes, but there is no badness in him."

I realized I'd needed a male opinion of Mr. Garfield. Ladies might not look further than his well-featured face and too-charming manner.

Gabriella was smiling at him, shaking his hand. Garfield bowed to her; she curtsied. Her face was flushed, her eyes sparkling.

"Curb yourself, Gabriel." Louisa sounded amused.

I realized I was growling. I halted the sound in my throat, but it continued inside my head. This would be a long evening.

***

As certain as I was that Mr. Garfield would pick up Gabriella and run off with her, no such frightening thing happened. The night, I almost hated to admit, came off without incident.

My daughter danced nearly every dance, leading out the first set, happy and eager. Her first partner, I was pleased to see, was the quiet Leland-like Mr. Marsden, not Mr. Garfield. Mr. Garfield was farther down the row in the dance, smiling and engaging his partner in conversation, as a gentleman should.

I still did not like him.

Leland Derwent himself was there, having come with his father, Sir Gideon, and cousin, Catherine Danbury. Leland did not dance, his subdued dress indicating he was still in mourning for his friend.

"It hurts," he confided in me when we had a moment together. "But my father has been very understanding, as has Catherine. I did not know how sympathetic they would be."

"They love you," I said. "Simple as that."

"Yes. I had not realized how much."

They would help him heal. My estimation of Sir Gideon's goodness rose higher still. "Mr. Hilliard has been a friend as well, I understand."

Leland flushed. "Freddie has been kind to me. But he is not Gareth."

And no one ever would be. I understood that. I had hope, though. Leland was young, with a large heart and a capacity for love.

Gabriella was never without a partner, or a group of young ladies to speak with. Donata and Aline had chosen the guests well, I had to admit. They'd invited kind people, those who would not sneer at Gabriella because her father was a penniless captain from Norfolk. They accepted her at the same time they looked upon her as a refreshing newcomer.

Donata gloated in her triumph, but I could not chide her. She had brought it off. A success.

Donata and Gabriella planned to spend the night at Aline's, and as things wound to a close in the wee hours, I considered returning home and collapsing into bed. The gentlemen had all gone by now, so I had no more need to stay and be a snarling guard dog.

Before I could depart, however, Grenville sought me. He'd stood up for two dances with Gabriella and put about that he thoroughly approved of her. This would guarantee her success far more than all the machinations Donata and Aline had gone through for this party.

When I'd gently teased Donata about this, she'd only stared at me and said, "Of course. Why do you think I invited him?"

Grenville's good humor had deserted him now, and his face had lost color. "Lacey, there you are. Come with me."

Without waiting to see whether I followed, he hurried down the stairs to the front door, where Bartholomew stood.

"Sir," Bartholomew called.

His voice echoed through Lady Aline's rotunda-like entrance hall. The cupola at the top of the staircase reflected the word back.

I pulled Bartholomew outside. His face too was pale, his agitation evident. "What is it?"

"Jack—the footman, Mr. Brewster's friend." Bartholomew's eyes were wide, his body trembling under my steadying hand. "He's dead, sir. Someone's killed him."

Chapter Twenty-Five

Grenville's carriage clattered to a halt next to us. Matthias, as worried as his brother, opened the door.

Grenville gestured at the pair of them. "Get in and tell us all about it."

Bartholomew waited to help me and Grenville in before he launched himself up, followed by Matthias. The carriage started off, I knew not where, but I did not care at the moment.

Bartholomew leaned toward us. "I've been following Mr. Bennett wherever I could, just as you told me, sir. Well, earlier this evening, I followed him to Oxford Street. You told me to watch him especially there. Usually when he goes, he's finding a hackney to take him to the City. Today, though, he walked on toward Soho, and he stopped at a house just off the square. Number 18. I made a note of it."

"Good lad," I said, impatient. "Did he kill this Jack?"

"I'm getting to that, sir. When Mr. Bennett came

out of the house in Oxford Street, I think he spied me. He turned his head at the wrong time, then went on as though thinking nothing of it, then he stopped and looked back. I'd hidden by that time, but he looked about very carefully. Then he returned to Cavendish Square. So—when he went out later, I asked Jack to follow. He was more or less finished with his duties for the night anyway, and crept out.

"Mr. Bennett came back around one of the clock, but Jack didn't. I thought maybe Jack had stopped at a public house to refresh himself, and I walked in the direction Bennett had gone to see if I could find him.

"I found him all right. There was a crowd mobbing about just beyond the turning to Soho Square, and there was Jack. Lying dead on the cobbles, his head bashed in. People were shouting for the Watch, for a doctor. I pushed through, telling them I was his friend, but I could see he was for it."

Bartholomew pushed his hand through his hair. "Bloody hell, sir. I sent him after Mr. Bennett, and I got him killed."

No, *I* had.

"Damn it," I said feelingly.

"Any indication that Bennett struck him down?" Grenville asked.

"Well, he must have done." Bartholomew's eyes widened. "He knew Jack was following him, he dragged him aside, and hit him over the head. Just like he did that poor Miss Hartman."

My heart was beating thick and hard, fingers tingling as I clutched my walking stick. "This time he will be arrested and made to pay. We must fetch Pomeroy."

Matthias nodded. Grenville broke in, his voice the only calm one inside the carriage.

"Lacey, we should not be precipitate. I hate to suggest it, but he might not have anything to do with this killing. Jack might have gotten into a fight in a public house where he stopped, as Bartholomew suggested, to wet his throat."

I glared at him. "Do you believe that?"

"I do not know what to believe," Grenville said. "But if we make accusations, and they are wrong, then Bennett might escape us for Miss Hartman's murder. He is the type of man to flee. We must go carefully."

I did not want to go carefully. I wanted to break Bennett's neck.

I balled one fist, controlling my temper with effort. Grenville was correct—if we spooked Bennett, he might run to the Continent or some such, where we would be hard-pressed to find him and bring him back.

If I went to Pomeroy and asked that Bennett be watched, Pomeroy would be ham-handed about it and spook him all the same. Spendlove, getting wind, would be even more ruthless.

"Matthias," I said. "Would you deliver a message to Mr. Denis for me? Or have Mr. Brewster do it, if you can find him first."

"No, no," Grenville said quickly. "I will go. I cannot ask Matthias to walk into a lion's den. We are near Curzon Street; why not visit him now? I take it you are going to ask him to watch Mr. Bennett."

I tapped on the roof and called for Jackson to stop. The carriage halted. "You go on to Curzon Street," I told Grenville. "I am off to Cavendish Square. When Bennett hears about his dead footman, he might flee. I will stay there until Brewster or whomever Denis sends arrives. Please impress upon Mr. Denis the importance of the situation."

Grenville looked doubtful. "I will try. But I cannot say he will listen to me."

"He'll send men to Cavendish Square if only to drag me out of Bennett's house to beat me for my impertinence. But that doesn't matter. I want them there. Bennett might escape the Watch, but he will not escape Denis."

I did not give Grenville time to argue. Jackson had thoughtfully pulled over to the side of the street so I did not have to land in the middle of traffic. I slammed the door and moved off, hobbling to the nearest hackney stand.

***

Bennett had already gone to bed, to sleep the sleep of the just when I arrived. The startled footman who answered the door told me this, then went pale with shock when I explained that Jack was dead.

I told the footman I would be sitting the rest of the night in the upstairs hall to prevent more murders in this household. "No, do not rouse Mr. Bennett," I finished. "Let him sleep. We will tell him in the morning."

The footman scuttled away. He hurried down the back stairs, his voice ringing out the news about Jack before the door shut behind him to muffle his frantic words.

I slid out the flask I'd brought with me tonight in case I needed to settle my stomach while watching the young men flutter around Gabriella. I took a fortifying sip of brandy then ascended the stairs to the second floor and planted myself on a cushioned bench in the hall.

It was warm, the house stuffy, which would ensure I didn't catch cold. It might send me to sleep though. I firmed my jaw, determined to be wakeful and not let Bennett slip away.

I did not have to wait long to discover what Denis would do. Within an hour, the footman who'd admitted me scurried up the stairs to say a man called Brewster was asking for me.

I went down. Brewster was in the street, the bulk of him tight with anger.

"His nibs says you should have asked him for his help in the first place," Brewster began. Any friendliness he'd showed me a few days ago was gone. "Not had me send in someone out of his depth."

Denis, I recalled, had warned me off the business entirely, thus forcing me to use the assistance of those I could. Perhaps Denis's anger hid remorse.

"Brewster, I am so very sorry. I never thought it would come to this."

Surprise flickered in his eyes. "You're not to blame, Captain. *I* am. I didn't take the danger seriously. Mr. Denis has sent six men. They've dispersed all around the house. This Bennett steps a foot out, they'll be on him. He'll not get away."

"I'll avenge your friend, Brewster. I promise you that."

"Jack were a bloody thief," Brewster said, scowling. "But a good lad for all that."

"Perhaps one of the men can be spared to accompany me to Soho," I said. "I want to know where Bennett went tonight."

"I'll spare me," Brewster returned. "I'm not letting you out of my sight. Not again, sir."

***

Brewster had a quick word with one of the ruffians I'd witnessed beating Molodzinski in Denis's staircase hall, then he trotted after me as I strode south to Oxford Street. I was too agitated and too cramped to wait for a hackney, so I simply walked.

Bartholomew had said Bennett visited number 18 in a lane off Soho Square. It stood to reason that Bennett had returned there again when Jack was following him—though I couldn't be certain. Regardless, I wanted to know what business he had at that address.

We headed from Oxford Street down into Soho Square. In the late part of the last century, a brothel patronized by the wealthy wanting novelty had stood in this square. From tales I'd heard, it had been part brothel, part stage set. A man would arrange to meet one of the courtesans of the house, and then upon entering a bedroom would find the lights going out and a specter or skeleton coming at him instead. Such were the entertainments of the rich and world-weary.

That house was gone now, but other brothels had sprung up. Soho Square spilled out its south side not far from Seven Dials, where life was dangerous.

The only number 18 was in a small lane on this south end. The house itself was solid and plain, nothing unusual.

In spite of the late hour, a light burned in the upper windows. Was this a discreet brothel? Or the home of Bennett's mistress? Or some other sort of house—a gaming hell, perhaps, where Bennett squandered away Captain Woolwich's money?

The only way to discover was to enter. I knocked.

The door was wrenched open by, of all things, a small urchin. He was about nine years old and had a belligerent face and brown eyes.

While brothels often had boys who ran errands

and were on hand for much more sordid requests, this boy did not have the look. He was a sturdy lad, and when I studied his face, a realization struck me and struck me hard.

"Well," the boy asked. "Whatcha want?"

I stood, dumbfounded, unable to speak. Before the lad could slam the door in my face, a woman came down the stairs. She was pretty, about thirty, with brown hair peeping from under a cap.

"Mark," she called. "Who is it?" She reached the bottom of the stairs, saw me, and stopped short. "If you've come from the beaks, you needn't bother me," she snapped. "He's paid the debt."

I finally swallowed the lump in my throat. "I am not a creditor, madam, nor from the magistrates." I drew a breath and took a chance. "Mrs. Andrew Bennett?"

She looked me up and down. "Yes, that's me. Who are you? What's happened?"

Behind me, Brewster made an amazed sound. "'Struth," he said.

I agreed with him wholeheartedly.

Chapter Twenty-Six

Mrs. Bennett—her Christian name was Ella—let us come in out of the night but no farther than the vestibule. Her son Mark hovered nearby as though ready to launch into us if we made any move toward his mother.

Two more children lingered upstairs, peering down through the railings. So much for the theory that Bennett was impotent.

"I would like to talk with Mr. Bennett," I said after I'd recovered my powers of speech. "Is he in?"

"He's not. His work took him off again. Ye still haven't told me what you want."

The woman was comely, and her eyes, though now full of anger, could be soft, I sensed. Bennett had set himself up a nice little nest here.

Was he married to her in truth? Or had he fooled her as I'd suspected he'd tricked Judith Hartman?

I cast around for some excuse to have called. "I need to pass on a message. About his work. Where would Mr. Bennett be tonight?"

Ella's brows remained lowered. "Well, I'm not certain. He travels about. Ye leave your message with me, and your name, and I'll see he gets it."

"Ah." No one had ever assumed me a quick thinker, and I found it difficult to be anything other than painfully honest. "Yes, well, please tell him that Mr. ... Ah ..." I floundered.

"Brewster," Brewster said quickly. He poked a thumb at me. "He's Mr. Brewster."

"Yes," I said. "My name should be enough. When do you expect him to return?"

"Couldn't say. Call back in a couple of days."

The dismissal was evident. I gave her a polite bow, and made for the door. "My apologies for disturbing you," I said. "Have a good night."

Ella looked slightly appeased at my courtesy, but she folded her arms and waited for me to leave.

We got ourselves outside into the lane, and I slapped on my hat. "Bloody hell," I muttered.

"Very cozy," Brewster said. "Not that I'd try it. My Em would find me out and come at me with a hatchet."

"That is a point." We headed into the busier realm of Soho Square, undiminished even at this late hour. "This house is not that far from Cavendish Square — a different world, but he ought to have put much more distance between them."

"Mayhap he likes to stay in an area what he's familiar with. Oi — Look sharp, Captain."

A small body darted in front of me, the boy who had Andrew Bennett's eyes. "Ye leave me mum alone."

I tipped my hat to him. "I do apologize, Mr. Bennett. I did not realize it was so late to call."

Young Mark kept his fists clenched, clearly not knowing what to make of me. "When ye see me dad, tell him to come home. Me mum is missing him."

"He stays away often does he?" I asked. "His work, no doubt."

The lad scoffed. "I know what his work is, don't I? He's a card sharp. Must be. He comes in, gives mum plenty of money, and he's off again. He has to spend days in the gambling dens, I warrant, to come with so much. So why do you really want to see him?"

"Not about anything to do with gambling," I said. "I promise you. Do you have any idea where he goes? I could find him and send him home."

Mark deflated. "Nah. I tried to follow him once, but got lost. He doesn't like us going very far from the house, so I don't know my way about. 'Tis dangerous 'round here, he says."

"He is right." I took a coin from my pocket and handed it to him. "I will look for him and send him home."

The coin was snatched from my hand and disappeared while my fingers still felt its imprint. "Thank ye, sir."

I touched my hat again. "Good night."

"Night." Mark skimmed around me and was gone, running hard back to the lane.

Brewster and I were left alone with the denizens of Soho.

"Well," I said, my spirits rising. "At last, I have something to arrest the bloody man for."

***

I returned home and slept, confident that Denis's men would not let Bennett out of their sight. Tomorrow, I would speak to Pomeroy and have Bennett charged with bigamy.

In the morning, after a refreshingly dreamless sleep, I ate breakfast with good appetite, refraining from whistling a sunny tune. I was closing in on Bennett, and would get him one way or another.

I penned a note to Grenville, telling him of the night's adventures and where I was off to, and sent one of the footmen running to his house with it. Bartholomew was up in the attics, snoring away, and I'd let him sleep. He'd had a bad night.

I found Brewster outside the front door when I emerged. He was taking his job as watchdog seriously.

The air inside the hackney we took to Bow Street was as stuffy as ever, but today it did not bother me. A breeze wafted outside, the sky was blue, roses bloomed in the public gardens, and all was right in my world. The nagging worries about Gabriella and the army of suitors that would descend upon our house I pushed firmly aside.

Pomeroy was in. In triumph, I presented my findings and suspicions about Bennett and said I wanted to bring suit against him for bigamy.

Pomeroy only looked at me and raised his large mug of coffee to his lips.

"He'll not be the first gentleman who has himself a second so-called wife tucked somewhere, sir."

"Using the same name as his first wife? I mean his legitimate wife?"

Pomeroy shrugged. "Happens. Mayhap he likes to pretend his mistress is his darling wife, especially when his legal darling wife is a shrew. Who knows? He might have these 'Mrs. Bennetts', all over London."

"He has children with her. I wager this Ella does not know she is not his wife."

"Possibly not," Pomeroy said. "Don't mean he's a bigamist. Just crafty. Bring me evidence he's married both these women in a church with a vicar, all laid out in the parish register, with banns or a special license—then I can take a case to the magistrate. Otherwise, he's no different from your gentlemen of the town what maintain houses for wives and however many mistresses they can afford."

"Bloody hell, Pomeroy."

"Captain, you cannot have a man arrested, tried, and hanged because you don't like him. Laws of England were made to keep that from happening—in theory. If not, every blessed one of us would be dead."

"I believe him a killer," I said in a hard voice. "Twice over now—who knows how many times? We must stop him."

"Aye—I don't much want a man who disposes of wives in such a cavalier manner running about the streets. But I need something more to arrest him on than you *think* he killed a woman fifteen years ago. I need a murder weapon with blood on it, blood on his clothes, a witness …"

"Any murder weapon and bloody clothes will have been destroyed years ago, and you know it. I wager the crowbar that struck her is at the bottom of the Thames, his clothes long since burned. What witness will remember exactly what he did or saw on an exact day fifteen years gone?"

Pomeroy shrugged again. "Until such a one comes forward, or this Mr. Bennett breaks down and confesses all, there's nothing to arrest him for."

"Very well then." I was angry, but I knew Pomeroy was correct on all counts.

I could not drag in a man on suspicion alone. Ella

might have taken Bennett's last name, but it did not mean he'd married her in truth. That he'd legally married Margaret, his current wife, I believed—I imagined Captain Woolwich had made damn certain of it.

"I also *think* he did another murder," I said. "Last night. Of a man employed as a footman in his house. Jack … I don't know his surname."

Pomeroy's brows rose. "Jack Tyler? Known as Jack the Fox? He was a thief. The Watch thinks he was struck down when he tried to rob someone in the street."

"It was Bennett," I said with conviction. "Jack was working more or less for me, keeping watch on Bennett and his house. He followed him last night, and then Jack was dead. Bennett must have found him out and killed him. I'm certain of it."

"Well," Pomeroy said cheerfully. "You find me a witness and a bloody murder weapon, and I'll happily arrest him. My patrollers are running around Oxford Street in quest of such things even now, so they might beat you to it. Meanwhile, don't let the man arrest you for having him followed about, all right, Captain?"

***

I did not believe Grenville would be awake so early, but when I returned to South Audley Street, I found him there, waiting for me in my study.

"Pomeroy is right, I'm afraid," Grenville said, after I told him what had transpired at Bow Street. "About the bigamy. I once knew a man who required each of his mistresses to call themselves Marie Antoinette. He went through a string of them, all Maries. Lavished such gifts and riches on them I'm certain they'd have called themselves

Nebuchadnezzar if he'd asked."

"You said you would question friends about parish registers to discover whether he legally married Judith Hartman," I reminded him. "I believe we should check *all* the parish registers, to find out if he's had any other marriages we don't know about."

"I don't know all the vicars in England," Grenville warned. "Though I know a good many. I have the feeling I will be swimming in punch before the week is out."

"Thank you," I said, pulling myself from my thoughts to fix my gaze on him. "Your help is invaluable."

Grenville waved that aside. "Do not make me blush, Lacey. You know I am happy to assist—I'd have fled London long ago in ennui if not for you and your nose for trouble. I look forward to seeing what you will dig up in Egypt, so to speak."

My heart beat faster. "You are putting the plans in place, then?"

"Of course. We will begin the New Year voyaging to the sands of the desert."

The prospect sent a pleasant sensation through me, though I was not certain now I wanted to leave my family, especially when Donata would have her child not long before that.

"What does Marianne say about you running away?"

"Quite a bit." Grenville sent me a wan smile across the desk. "But she also says that by then she will be happy to see the back of me. I assured her it is only for a few months—we do not want to stay longer than the first part of April, when the temperatures begin to climb, especially in the driest regions. I believe that will be enough time for us to explore the wonders and not become too used to them."

"I look forward to it," I said with all sincerity.

"As do I." Grenville rose. "Now I am off to speak to vicars. Imagine what rumors *that* will start." He sounded weary, but I saw a sparkle in his eyes. He enjoyed baffling the *ton*.

When he'd gone, I was restless. Donata and Gabriella were not home yet—I imagined they'd sleep well into the afternoon. Then they'd linger to have a good gossip about the events of the night before.

I longed to rush back to Cavendish Square and shake Bennett, but I stopped myself. I did not want to alert him that I was closing in on him. I trusted Denis's men to keep him pinned down, but Bennett was cunning. Grenville had the right of it—if he knew I was onto him, he might find a way to bolt past even Denis's diligent guards.

Meanwhile, I contained my restlessness with a ride in Hyde Park.

The day was truly delicious, the grass bright green, roses blooming, the Serpentine sparkling under the sunshine. The Rotten Row was nearly deserted, and I set my horse into a fast canter, letting his speed clear the fogged thoughts in my brain.

I saw as I neared the end of the Row, close to Hyde Park Corner, the red Irish hunter who had tried to run down Peter, being quietly ridden toward me. I halted in surprise.

On its back was none other than Emmett Garfield, my daughter's would-be suitor.

Chapter Twenty-Seven

I nudged my horse forward. The hunter coming toward me trotted evenly, Mr. Garfield rising and falling expertly with its pace.

I guided my mount directly into Mr. Garfield's path, halting and turning to put the breadth of my horse in front of his.

Garfield pulled up and blinked at me from under his tall hat. "Sir?" He remembered his manners and bowed in the saddle. "Good morning."

"Where did you get that horse?" I demanded.

Mr. Garfield cast a startled look at his mount as though for a moment, he couldn't remember. "From Lord Compton. I sometimes borrow him." He patted the horse's neck, its rich coat gleaming with care. "Lord Compton and my father are old friends."

"Did you borrow the horse on Thursday last?" I went on remorselessly.

Garfield looked puzzled. I noticed he was behaving less the conceited man-about-town as he had in the ballrooms, and more an ordinary young man confused by his elders.

"No, sir. Thursday last I was in Surrey. All day. I did not return until the next morning."

His answer displeased me. I could easily verify where he'd been by asking his friends and family — or having Grenville do it — so he had no reason to lie. I remembered now, that at the supper ball on Friday, when I'd met him, he'd spoken of an uncle in Surrey and his visit to him.

Logic told me that Mr. Garfield would not profit by hurting me or Peter. He might believe that laying me up or killing me would prevent me from objecting to his marrying Gabriella, but it would not benefit him to hurt Peter.

Nor would it help Mr. Garfield if I were ruined, as the blackmailing letters threatened. A disgrace to me and my family was a disgrace to Gabriella. I doubted Garfield's father would condone him bringing home a bride with scandal attached to her. If my antecedents were publicly called into question, so would hers be.

I let out a long sigh that stirred my now-nervous mount. I calmed him with a hand to his shoulder. "Does Viscount Compton lend his horse out often?"

Garfield considered. "I suppose so. He knows a great many people."

Bloody hell. And this might not even be the horse in question. The hunter housed at the park's stables, gone missing during the day of the attack, was the likelier culprit.

"I beg your pardon for my abruptness, Mr. Garfield. I am out of sorts today. A horse like that was ridden at my stepson last week, nearly knocking him to the ground."

"I heard about that, sir." Mr. Garfield looked appropriately indignant. "Miss Lacey told me. I understand your agitation then, upon seeing a similar horse."

I was not in a good enough temper to have a young man tell me of conversations with my daughter, but I supposed I would have to become used to it.

"When you return the horse today, will you ask Lord Compton who else he lent him to? Last Thursday to be precise."

"Of course, sir." Garfield saluted me with his crop, eager to help.

"A long shot, possibly," I said. "But I would be grateful of the information."

Garfield nodded, but he made no move to continue riding. "Now that I have met you by chance, sir … No, I confess, not by chance. I was told how often you ride early in the park. I want to tell you that I have every wish to —"

"Stop." I cut him off with a raised hand. "Not today, Mr. Garfield. I am in no mood."

"But, sir, I long to —"

"No." The word was sharp enough to make him draw back. "Not now. Call upon me … in a few years' time."

He looked startled. "Years …"

"Good day, Mr. Garfield."

I heard him draw breath to argue, but I swung my horse around and rode off before he could say another word.

***

By the time I returned to South Audley Street, Brewster, who had been following me doggedly, announced that Denis wanted to see me.

"How the devil do you know?" I asked crossly as I left the mews, where I'd handed the horse to

Donata's groom. "You have been standing at the edge of the Row, staring at me the last hour."

"Lad came with a message. I'm to bring you to him directly."

I did not always like to run to Denis when he beckoned, but he had been good to lend me the men to keep watch last night on Bennett and at Lady Aline's. "Very well," I said, swallowing my impatience.

Not long later, I entered Denis's house, which was quiet today, and pulled myself up the now familiar staircase to the austere study at the top of the landing.

Denis was at his desk, writing something, his pen scratching in the silence. He continued, ignoring me, while I was shown to my usual chair by the unyielding butler.

After a time, Denis laid down his pen, sanded the paper, and set it aside.

He folded his long hands on the desk's top and looked at me. "You travel to Egypt in the winter."

Not a question. I would not be surprised if Denis knew our complete itinerary before I did.

"That is so," I replied.

"There is an object, in Alexandria, that I would like you to acquire for me."

Ah. I realized the reason he'd so readily sent his men to help me with Gabriella's come-out and with Bennett. Denis's services were never without cost.

"Acquire," I repeated. "How?"

Denis gave a small shrug. "Bargain for it. Purchase it. I will send a sum of money with you. *You*, I trust with such an amount. If the price is higher, you or Mr. Grenville will have to furnish the difference. But I want the object."

"What is it? Something important, if you are willing to send *me* for it. It must be an object I'd not throw away to spite you."

"That would be foolish indeed. I will keep a description of it to myself until you are ready to leave. I would not want others to know of my interest and acquire it before I can."

"I am not a teller of tales," I said stiffly.

"You would remark upon it to Mr. Grenville, who might let it slip to his paramour, who might let it slip to a friend ... The best way to keep a secret, Lacey, is to tell it to no one."

"I concede your point," I said dryly. "Shall you convey your instructions to me in a sealed letter, warning me not to open it until I am in Egypt?"

Denis gave me a thin smile. "By the time you board your ship, I will tell you. Then no word of it will be able to reach Alexandria before you do."

I nodded in surrender, and changed the subject. "Have you had any report from your men about Bennett? Is he staying at home?"

"He has not left his house since last night. His servants are talking of the death of Jack the footman, but Mr. Bennett had seemingly not noticed his absence. Mrs. Bennett is much distressed, but apparently Mr. Bennett is not one who pays servants much mind."

"No, he is focused very much on himself," I agreed. "Which is why I'm investigating his marriages." I told him of the "Mrs. Bennett" I'd found off Soho Square.

A flicker of interest lit Denis's eyes. "Remarkable. Wise to have Mr. Grenville check the parish records. I might be able to expedite the process. I am able to quickly lay my hands on information of all sorts."

I frowned. "You are being extraordinarily helpful against this nobody, Bennett."

Another slight lift of his shoulders. "I very much want the object from Alexandria. And a man who would kill his wife and toss her into the river to become a pile of bones puts a bad taste in my mouth. Killer or bigamist, you will have your conviction."

***

I resisted the temptation to rush from there to Cavendish Square and see for myself what was transpiring. I chafed, but I decided to let Grenville and Denis perform their respective tasks. I wanted to be home when Gabriella returned, in any case.

She arrived, with Donata, at three that afternoon. Donata declared herself exhausted and she retired, but Gabriella was bubbling with good spirits.

"I enjoyed myself immensely," Gabriella said after embracing me, and we sat down with tea in my study. "I never knew how much I enjoyed dancing, and the company was fine."

It had been. I had to admit that Lady Aline and Donata knew how to plan an event.

"They invited the most agreeable people they knew," I said warningly. "Not all *ton* gatherings are the same."

"Yes, but I know the agreeable people now," Gabriella said, brimming with confidence. "I will seek them at whatever outing I attend, and we shall be friends together."

I cleared my throat. "Do you include young gentlemen in the agreeable company?"

"Of course." Gabriella blushed. "I will admit, Father, that it was pleasant to be the focus of all attention. But I know that this will not be commonplace. Last night was my hour to shine. I am also quite relieved it is over."

I relaxed but not entirely. "They will come to court you now," I said. "The gentlemen."

"Yes, indeed." Gabriella made a wry face. "Lady Donata and Lady Aline have quite drilled that idea into me. But I am eighteen. Not yet ready to plunge into running a household. I have much to learn yet."

I wanted to collapse in relief at the statement, but I was no fool. Gabriella could declare such things only because she had not yet met the gentleman she'd run to when he called.

"In any case," I said. "I am happy you enjoyed it so. I did too, in spite of my misgivings. I must tell you, however, that when these gentlemen visit, I shall hover."

Gabriella laughed. "Lady Donata said you would. It is a fine thing to have so many to look after me."

I warmed under her praise. Every father wanted to be first in his daughter's eyes, I supposed.

"I must change," Gabriella said, jumping to her feet. "I will begin wearing the ensembles Lady Donata chivvied me into. She has been very kind, though I am not certain how I will find use for that many gowns. She says that I will begin having callers today, so I must be ready."

So soon. But, yes, the flowers had already begun to arrive, prim posies that honored my daughter.

I was descending into hell.

I took myself to Donata's chamber, knocked softly, and was admitted. She lay on her chaise, in a peignoir, her hair tucked under a cap, a cup of strong tea at her lips. "There you are, Gabriel," she said tiredly.

I drew a chair to her and sat on its edge. "Are you all right?"

"No, I feel unwell." She glanced up from her tea. "Do not look alarmed; it is nothing. I have carried a child before, and I know what happens. I stayed on my feet too long last night, is all. I will take a rest. I was far more ill when I carried Peter, believe me. And then I had no come-out to orchestrate, only servants to order about."

"Gabriella's suitors will soon come calling, she says. This afternoon."

"Aline is journeying here to sit as chaperone. You need not worry that Gabriella will run off into the mist."

"But she might accept a proposal," I pointed out glumly. "This very day."

Donata sent me a wan smile. "Gabriella is the most sensible young woman I've ever met. Astonishingly so, considering she is your daughter, and that her mother is insipid. The phlegmatic French major must be responsible for her steadiness."

"She had a happy home." I was grateful to Auberge for providing that, at least, even as I seethed at him for taking her away.

But would I have preferred Gabriella to be alone and miserable? No, indeed. The situation would ever be complicated.

I leaned forward and kissed Donata. "Thank you for all you've done for her."

"She is a sweet girl, and I like her." Donata finished this statement with a flush. "And truth to tell, I want to show I can be a much better mother than that milk-and-water miss you married."

"You have surpassed all women, in my eyes, in many ways," I said. "For one thing, I never will have to guess your opinions."

Donata's blush deepened. "Perhaps I am too candid at times. Admit, Gabriel, that if I were sweet and simpering, you would not like me."

I thought of Margaret Bennett with her smiles and confidence in her fool of a husband.

"No, I would not," I declared, and kissed her again.

***

Lady Aline had arrived and was in place by the time I descended. The callers had begun, ladies of Donata's acquaintance, understanding but distressed that Donata was ill today.

Gabriella, in a day gown of long-sleeved light muslin, the white material embroidered over with ivory thread, sat daintily, conversed with the older ladies, and was kind and friendly to the younger.

And the gentlemen came. The drawing room was ever full, no matter how many callers arrived and went, so that I ceased worrying that Gabriella would be caught alone with a suitor. The lads were polite, correct, and kept a requisite distance, even if they were obviously eager and a bit fawning.

Mr. Garfield arrived in the company of another of the young men, Mr. Kent. Mr. Garfield even allowed Mr. Kent to take a chair close to Gabriella, in order to turn aside and greet me.

"Good afternoon, sir." Garfield bowed, the sweep of it holding arrogance. I suppose he'd donned his self-satisfaction along with his very fashionable suit, a near copy of one Grenville owned.

"Mr. Garfield," I said politely. "Good afternoon."

Garfield bent to put his head nearer to mine. "May we speak privately?"

"Only if it is about the horse," I answered, my look stern.

"To be sure. To be sure." Garfield's eyes glinted, as though he were trying to think of a jest that included both horses and women entering the marriage mart, such as I'd heard gentlemen at Grenville's clubs do. I was either mistaken, or he thought better of it, because he simply walked with me to the back sitting room in silence.

When we reached the deserted room—though the doors were open, all comers clustered around Gabriella—Garfield faced me.

"I asked Lord Compton who'd taken out the horse, just as you requested. He doesn't ride much anymore, but likes the hunter to be exercised by his friends. His reply will astonish you."

He was brimming with excitement, anticipating my reaction.

Mr. Garfield was not endearing himself to me in any way. "What is it?" I demanded.

Garfield's animation did not dim. "Lord Compton proclaimed that on Thursday last, he did lend out his hunter—to *you*."

Chapter Twenty-Eight

My reaction must have been all Garfield had hoped for. He grinned in triumph.

"I knew you'd be surprised, sir."

"Quite," I said, frowning at him. "He is certain? Although, obviously, mistaken."

"I agree. How could you have ridden his borrowed horse and your own at the same time at the same moment? But he was adamant, sir. *That friend of Grenville's, that captain who married Breckenridge's widow. Lacey, that's his name.*"

Garfield gave a fair imitation of the elderly viscount. I clenched my hand on my walking stick.

"Accompany me to Compton's," I said.

Garfield's smirk vanished. He gave an anguished look to Gabriella, who was laughing with Mr. Kent. "But, sir."

"You may throw yourself at Gabriella's feet another time. I will make your apologies. She will understand."

Garfield had deflated so rapidly it was comical.

"Lord Compton won't be home now. He'll be at his club."

"Then we shall go to his club."

I guided Mr. Garfield out through the door that led to the hall. No need to parade through the front drawing room again.

Garfield was angry and disappointed, but then he brightened. No doubt he surmised that assisting the father would pave his way more smoothly to the daughter. He should not let himself be read so easily.

Viscount Compton's club was Brooks's, in St. James's Street. The viscount was in the dining room, but seated in a corner on a sofa rather than at one of the large tables. The remains of coffee lay before him on a stand.

He set aside a newspaper and peered up at us nearsightedly. "Who is that? Oh, Garfield's boy. Back to speak to me again? I am popular with the younger set today."

"This is Captain Lacey, sir," Garfield said, deferential. He gestured to me and raised his voice. "You said you lent him your hunter."

"I can hear you—my trouble is with my eyes, not my ears." Compton, with a shock of gray hair and very blue eyes, squinted at me. "How are you, Captain?"

"A bit puzzled, sir," I said. "You told Mr. Garfield you let me borrow your hunter, but you did no such thing."

"Nonsense. You came to me, gave me Grenville's card, and asked. I know you were a cavalryman. I'm happy to have the beast ridden by those who know how, and Grenville says good things about you. That you're a man of honor and all."

"You spoke to me personally?" I asked. I did not

like this. "Or did you only receive my message?"

"You stood in my sitting room. I admit, Captain, that my eyesight is not very good, and I don't keep my house light, but you look the same. And sound the same. I sent you out to my groom. Now, either you have forgotten already, which means something wrong with your mind, or someone impersonated you."

"Since I clearly remember the day," I said, "then it is the latter. Why, I have no idea. But this person tried to run down young Lord Breckenridge with your horse."

Compton's rheumy eyes widened. "Dear me. I knew nothing of this."

"Perhaps I can speak with your stablemen," I said.

"You may, of course. But if they did not know you on sight either, they might be of no help. Damn it all—you have my abject apologies. I saw nothing wrong in it."

"Not your fault." My disquiet grew. "If this gentleman tries to see you again, please send word. To Mr. Grenville if you cannot trust whether it is me or the gentleman purporting to be me."

"How very confusing," Compton said. "Rest assured, I will have my household be on the alert. One gentleman should not go around impersonating another, blast him."

"I quite agree. Thank you, sir."

"I do hope you find him," Compton said. "The blackguard."

So did I. I left Brooks's with Garfield, most uneasy.

***

When we returned to the South Audley Street house, the callers had gone, and Gabriella and Aline were readying themselves for their evening, shut away upstairs.

Garfield was disappointed to have missed her, but he was polite with his leave-taking, and promised that, if he heard anything of my double, he would tell me immediately.

Barnstable handed me a note from Grenville, asking me to call. I looked in on Donata, found her sleeping, and walked from South Audley Street to Grosvenor Street, too impatient to wait for a vehicle.

As I walked along Mount Street, followed by the faithful Brewster, I could not stop myself ducking through the passage to Grosvenor Mews, and found Lord Compton's stables and groom.

"He was like you, sir," the groom said, looking me up and down after my question. "But not you, I see now. I've noted you on the street, visiting Mr. Grenville. I thought him you."

The groom was distressed, no doubt fearing he'd lose his place, since the horse and rider in question had caused such mischief.

I assured him that in a situation so bizarre, it was not his fault, and left him.

"Do you have a brother, Captain?" Brewster asked as we tramped on to Grosvenor Street. "Or a cousin?"

"No," I said shortly. "No brother. Any cousins would have to be very distant. Would the resemblance hold up?"

Brewster shrugged. "I'd have to see the two of you together. Mr. Denis won't like this — two Captain Laceys to deal with."

"Not amusing, Brewster."

"I know," Brewster said, then was silent as we trudged on.

As soon as the footman let me into the house, Grenville called down over the banisters. "Lacey. I have much news."

He did not rush down the stairs but bounced on his toes in his soft, indoor shoes as I climbed the staircase.

"As do I," I said.

"Excellent. Gautier has brought up a bottle of port, and we will dissect this case over it."

Not long later, we were ensconced in his private study, the silken tent he'd brought back from the Arab lands hanging over us and casting a red glow over all. The port, a darker red, filled the glasses with rich liquid.

"I've discovered much, Lacey," Grenville said. "And Mr. Denis's letter this afternoon filled in the rest."

I took a sip of port, savoring it, even in my restiveness. "Regale me."

"I've looked at six parish registers in total," Grenville said. "Three today. That was all I could manage before I had to return home and recover. My old cronies can talk for a long time about nothing. It was easy to discover that Bennett married Margaret Woolwich at St. Marylebone. Bennett's servants provided me that gossip through Bartholomew. I began there and then went to St. Giles and St. Martin in the Fields. Today, St. Paul's Covent Garden, then on to St. Mary le Strand, and finally St. Clement Danes. London has so very many churches—I never appreciated the fact. Rather took them all for granted."

My interest piqued. "You would not look so pleased with yourself if you had found nothing."

Grenville's eyes sparkled. "I was a bit hampered

by not knowing from which parish Mr. Bennett hailed. But it turns out, it does not matter. The man is a thorough fraud. At St. Clement Danes, he married the woman you met, Ella Bennett. Ten years ago. All registered and aboveboard. He married Margaret eight years ago, and so that marriage must be a false one."

I clenched my goblet of port so hard a bit splashed to my hand. "Got him," I said. "The proof Pomeroy needs."

Grenville smiled at me. "I have more to report. When I returned home, flushed with triumph, I read Mr. Denis's letter. The man is thorough. He found where Bennett had married Judith Hartman. Very much legally—in Christ Church, Spitalfields. He claimed to be a member of that parish."

"So he did not perpetrate fraud on Judith. That is good."

"Who knows?" Grenville said. "Mr. Denis went on to say that Mr. Bennett is recorded as having married two more women, one in Surrey, and one in Southwark. The lady in Surrey believes she is a widow—I suppose he grew tired of traveling so far. These are all within the last ten years, and all of them, with the exception of Ella in Soho and Judith, had a fair-sized dowry."

"Good Lord."

I sank back in my chair. Ella's son had assumed his father a gambler because he came and gave Ella large handfuls of cash.

"He is robbing Peter to pay Paul," I realized. "Or at least, Margaret and his other wives to pay Ella. Perhaps he gave up the lady in Surrey after he spent all her money."

"That can be ascertained. Shall we turn all this

over to Mr. Pomeroy, so that he can find out?"

"Yes." I stood up, setting the excellent port aside without reluctance. "Let us at once to Cavendish Square, truss up Bennett, and drag him off. What a scoundrel."

Grenville rose quickly to his feet. "Indeed. Poor Margaret. And what will become of this Ella?"

"He will pay back every penny he took from these ladies," I said firmly. "He's robbed them and their families of money under false pretenses. He likely killed Judith because he could get no money out of her — or perhaps he was already married to yet another, and she discovered it. She tries to return home, he finds her and quarrels with her, then murders her."

"That could be," Grenville said. "But again, we have no proof."

"Pomeroy or Thompson can wrangle a confession from him. He will hang — after he makes restitution to his wronged wives."

I could see Grenville thought me too optimistic, but I was happy to be able to apprehend the man at last. Judith's bones could be laid to rest, where she might cease haunting my dreams.

***

We rode to Cavendish Square in Grenville's luxurious carriage. Along the way, I read Denis's succinct, precise letter, which was mostly a list of Bennett's current and previous marriages.

My contempt for Bennett increased the closer we drew to him. Had Judith confronted him? Her dark hair falling about her face as she shouted at him, demanding to know what he had done to her?

Had Bennett himself broken her arm some time before her death, and Hartman had sent her to the surgeon, Coombs, hiding her identity to hide that she was married to a fraud? Had that been what Hartman meant by *her shame?*

Denis's list went back only ten years, aside from the evidence of marriage to Judith, but when he dug deeper, what would we find?

By the time we reached Cavendish Square, I was worked up into one of my fine tempers. I saw Denis's men discreetly and not so discreetly on the lookout as I lifted the door knocker and let it fall.

I asked to speak, not to Mr. Bennett, but to Captain Woolwich.

The captain was in his bed still, his wasted body a far cry from the strength in his eyes. He received me politely, but I read his simmering anger, which matched mine.

I introduced Grenville as politeness dictated, but neither Woolwich nor I had patience for any niceties.

"You told me to come back when I could rid you of Andrew Bennett," I said to Woolwich. "I can." I handed him Denis's letter and Grenville's notes.

Woolwich read them in silence. The color drained from his face, then he dropped the papers and began to cough.

I sprang forward. "Grenville. Brandy."

Grenville already had taken out his flask. He held it to Woolwich's mouth, and Woolwich calmed enough to drink.

Woolwich took a long breath then another sip of brandy. Finally, he nodded to Grenville that he was all right, though his face remained gray.

"At last," he said hoarsely. "I knew he was a wrong 'un."

"He is a fraud, a bigamist, and a crook," I said. "Will you prosecute?"

"Oh, yes." Red crept back into Woolwich's cheeks. "Even if it takes the rest of my fortune to do it. Did he kill his first wife? If she *was* his first."

"I believe he did kill her," I said. "I will certainly try to have him prosecuted for it."

"Good." Woolwich gave me an approving nod. "Thank you, Captain."

I sobered. "What about your daughter? Would you like me to break the news to her?"

"No." Woolwich coughed again, but gently this time. He lifted a handkerchief from the covers and patted his mouth. "She is my daughter. I will tell her. He has ruined her, poor child."

"Yes." Margaret's marriage was false, which meant she was the same as a mistress. The world would hold this against her, through no fault of her own. "I am sorry to have to reveal such a thing."

"I'd rather she lose her character than remain living with that charlatan," Woolwich said. "So would you. I will make sure she's looked after all her days."

There remained little more to say. I took the papers back from Woolwich, and Grenville and I left the room.

Bennett himself waited for us on the first-floor landing. "Mr. Grenville," he said, staring. "An honor to have you in my house. Captain ... What is this all about?"

He gave us an affable look, innocent, as though nothing were wrong. I wanted to push him down the stairs.

Grenville stepped between us. "Mr. Bennett, I would like you to ride with me in my carriage."

"Oh?" Bennett brightened. "Where are we going?"

"To visit a friend," Grenville said. "I would like him to meet you."

Grenville's cool self-assurance moved Bennett as all my raging likely never would. I barely contained myself as we went down the stairs and out into the street.

In spite of the wheeled vehicles, horses, and foot traffic surging around the square, Jackson had kept Grenville's team quiet, the coach waiting a foot from the door. Grenville himself opened the carriage door, though the footman from the house darted forward to assist us in.

Bennett suspected nothing at first. I sat myself across from him, laying my stick across my knees. Grenville settled beside me, but before the carriage could move forward, Brewster opened the other door and scrambled in, landing next to Bennett. Jackson started the horses, and off we went.

"What is happening?" Bennett asked nervously.

Brewster hemmed him in, his bulk filling most of the seat. "We're off to Bow Street," he said.

Bennett shifted his worried look to Grenville, who nodded. "It's a bad show, Bennett," Grenville said, at his most haughty. "You've hurt a good many people, and now you have no friends left."

"I do not … I do not understand, gentlemen."

He would protest to the last. I leaned forward, my walking stick between my hands. "We've found you out. All your wives of your so-called marriages. We have found four—perhaps there are more?"

Bennett's breath stopped. Then it began again, his face going a peculiar shade of yellow. "You mistake me, sir. I told you, I am warm-hearted. I play at making them my wives—a pleasant fiction."

"Not at all," Grenville said. "You tried hard to

make them appear legal, at least to satisfy the ladies and their families. They were respectable women, not the sort to readily become your mistresses. And if you could convince their families that the marriages were legal, you swept in the dowry and any property."

Bennett went even more pale. "You will not be able to verify this."

"Of course we will," Grenville said. "We have the records, possibly the testimony of the ladies themselves. I imagine none of them would be happy to hear of the others."

Bennett stared a while longer, realizing that he was at the end of his games. He shot Grenville a look of appeal. "Gentlemen, can you blame me? A man can fall in love more than once in his life. In this country, divorce or annulment is nearly impossible. One can not end a marriage when one falls in love again."

"Indeed," Grenville said. "And a good thing — where would we all be if we picked up and discarded wives at will? You did the thing very thoroughly, Bennett. And that will convict you."

"But surely." His smile incensed me. "We can come to some arrangement."

I pressed the end of my walking stick to his thigh. "That is not all of it. Why did you murder Judith? Did she discover your cavalier approach to marriage, after you convinced her to leave her family, her friends, her entire religion behind for you? She sacrificed everything, and then no doubt discovered what sort of man you were. Is that why you killed her?"

"No!" Bennett's voice rose in pitch. "I'd never hurt Judith. Never!" Tears welled in his eyes. "My poor, sweet Judith."

"Enough." Grenville's smooth word cut through Bennett's rising hysterics. "Do not weep — I might be ill. You broke her arm ..."

"No!" Another wail, and Bennett began shaking his head. "I never hurt her. That was an accident. She fell. Slipped. Truly. I swear. I am not a murderer."

I kept my voice quiet as I pressed harder with the stick. "And yet, she died. I will watch you hang for it, Bennett. I vow this."

"I never killed her." Bennett's tears overflowed. "I grieved when she disappeared. I admit to marrying when perhaps I should not, but only because I love too much. I *love*. I would never hurt any of them."

His words rang with sincerity. My hope for a frantic confession evaporated. "What about Jack?" I asked. "I'm certain you had no love for *him*."

Bennett snuffled into his hand in confusion. "Jack? Who is Jack?"

"Your footman. He followed you last night. You caught him, and you struck him down."

More bewilderment. "I had no idea I had a footman called Jack. Margaret does all the hiring, with Woolwich's approval. I have nothing to do with the servants."

I lost my patience. "Whether you knew who he was or not, you struck him. For following you."

"You have run absolutely mad." Bennett wiped his eyes and gazed at me with more confidence. "I have killed no one. I saw a large man skulking after me, but then I lost him, and I thought it was my imagination. I did not strike anyone."

A liar was never more resolute than when he was telling the truth for once. Damnation.

"I might be convicted of bigamy," Bennett said,

"though I assure you I will fight it. But not murder."

He folded his lips and sat back, fixing his gaze out the window.

We arrived in Bow Street in silence. Pomeroy himself, alerted by the message we'd sent before we'd gone to Cavendish Square, opened the carriage door and escorted Mr. Bennett down.

"Welcome, sir," Pomeroy said. "You will find fine accommodations in this inn, I'm sure. Perhaps even a pot of your own for your piss. Thank you, Captain. You may let him go now."

I had climbed down after Bennett and seized his arm. My fingers clamped down as he tried to follow Pomeroy, no doubt believing Pomeroy safer than me.

"Where were you going?" I asked Bennett. "Last night — not when you visited Ella, but after that?"

"Nothing at all to do with this," Bennett said quickly. "A business matter. I promise you."

"Where?" I repeated severely.

"Tottenham Court Road." Bennett gave me a peevish stare. "If you must know."

Pomeroy flicked my fingers with his. "The prisoner is mine," he said. "When I get the conviction, I'll stand you a pint."

I let go. I no longer needed to hold on to Bennett. He'd come up before the magistrate, who would send him to Newgate to await his trial. It was finished.

With Bennett's last words to me, thrown out so I would cease pursuing him, he'd given me a large piece of the puzzle. Now, I knew.

Chapter Twenty-Nine

I called up to Jackson to take us to Tottenham Court Road, and scrambled as quickly as I could back into the carriage.

Jackson drove us northward through Drury Lane and Bloomsbury, and we ended up on the wide thoroughfare of Tottenham Court Road. Jackson halted halfway along, as I'd asked, and I invited Grenville and Brewster upstairs with me.

I had not said a word to them in explanation. Grenville had started to berate me, then lapsed into silence. He'd learned when to leave me be.

If I were wrong, then I was. Unlike with Bennett, I wanted no other to lose by my hot temper and erroneous assumptions.

The younger surgeon, Coombs's former apprentice, was not in, but the door to the main part of the house was unlocked, presumably so consultants could wait for his return. I thumped my way upstairs, Grenville and Brewster following, and tapped on the door at the top.

Mr. Coombs was indeed within. He peered at us with his wide brown eyes and readily invited us into his front room.

"How may I help you today, Mr. Grenville? Captain? Have you had any progress?"

Grenville said nothing, only stood back and let me speak.

"I have come to tell you that Mr. Andrew Bennett has been arrested," I said.

Coombs's eyes widened, and his brows climbed. "Bennett?"

"The husband of Judith Hartman, whose arm you set."

"Ah, the poor creature you found in the river. He murdered her?" Coombs's voice warmed. "Then I am glad I could help you discover her identity. And that you are bringing the man to justice."

"Mr. Bennett did not kill her," I said. "I made a mistake. I am apt to come too quickly to conclusions."

Coombs gave me a puzzled look. "Then I do not understand. I thought you said you arrested him."

"For something else entirely. Why did you treat Judith's arm?"

"Why?" Coombs's puzzlement grew. "She'd broken it, and her father brought her to me."

"Who broke it? Her husband? Or her father, in his anger?"

"I ... don't know."

"I believe you do know exactly what happened," I said.

I leaned both hands on my walking stick. I noticed Brewster, out of the corner of my eye, position himself in front of the door.

Coombs shook his head. "I am in the dark."

"I believe that Mr. Hartman brought Judith here for her arm to be set—how she broke it, I am not certain. He gave you her sister's name because he was ashamed that Judith was now Mrs. Bennett, disgracing the family. Judith appears to have gone along with this—perhaps she was regretting her choice in Bennett and wanting to appease her father. He brought her to you, far from his friends and family, so they would not see her. You set the bone, and she went away."

"Yes." Coombs nodded. "I explained this."

"Bennett found out, I'm certain. Either Judith told him, or he followed them to you. Perhaps he wanted to discover what Judith's father had been doing with his wife."

Coombs said nothing. My heart beat swiftly. Again, I was guessing, poking in the dark, but I was certain Coombs was the key to this.

"I can always ask your apprentice," I said. "I imagine he was here at the time, as your assistant."

"All right, yes." Coombs scowled at me. "Bennett did come here looking for his wife, and I told him what happened. Bennett is not a good man—I am glad to hear he has been arrested. He was carrying on with other women when Judith was his wife. Nasty business."

"Did you tell Judith this?" I asked, watching him.

Coombs lifted his knuckle and pressed his teeth into it—a habit he had—and I saw a new light come into his eyes. "Yes, I did. When she returned to me to have her splint removed, I mentioned it. I said I could furnish proofs if she wanted it. She did, and we arranged to meet again."

I saw Grenville's tiny start of surprise. A man who

didn't know Grenville might not observe that he was jolted; he hid it well. Brewster, as always, remained stoic.

"Did you meet her here?" I asked.

"Not here, no, indeed. In the City, near the Great Synagogue, where her people are."

Her people rented rooms over a shop in the Strand, but I forbore to say so.

"You met her," I said. "You told her of Bennett's promiscuity."

Coombs nodded. "I felt she ought to know. She'd left her life to be with him, poor lamb. We walked from Aldgate down toward the river—I scarce noted which direction we went. And then Bennett found us."

"Mmm." I had the feeling I knew what he would say next. "What happened?"

"He was enraged. Bennett confronted me, then shouted at Judith, telling her to go home, like a good wife. She wept, she groaned, she pleaded with him. We were near the docks at St. Catherine's. He found a piece of iron bar, discarded. He took it up, and he hit her ... She fell to the ground—it was terrible. Then he lifted her and tipped her into the river, dropped the bar in after her, and went home."

Coombs stopped, letting out a long breath.

"What time of day was it?" I asked.

"Pardon? Oh ... I scarce remember."

"I would predict, evening. Judith's sister saw her at Aldgate in the afternoon. No one saw you, or Bennett—Devorah would be sure to state if she saw *him*. I will return to my early speculation. You arranged to meet her here, in these rooms."

"No, indeed. That would have been foolish."

"Not if you wished to save her from Bennett," I

went on doggedly. "She was, as everyone has pointed out, a pretty young woman. I speculate that she was at Aldgate looking for her former intended, Mr. Stein. To reconcile with him? Perhaps. If Judith could prove Bennett did not marry her legally, she might ask Mr. Stein to forgive her and make an honest wife of her. You had already alerted her of Bennett's perfidy. She would talk to you, get the proof she needed, and set a solicitor and her father on him. When she came here … what happened?"

"She did not come," Coombs said stubbornly. His face was red.

"Again, I could ask your former assistant. Or anyone else I can find who was in the house at the time. She came here."

"Very well—yes," Coombs said, his voice a cracked whisper. "But Bennett was here too. That is not a lie. He followed her. He found her. He …"

"I do not believe Bennett killed her," I said. "I looked into Bennett's eyes when he protested his innocence. Bennett is a great liar, but about that, no."

"How can you believe him?" Coombs asked, his lips white.

"You have tools." I moved to the shelves and removed the long-handled chisel. "One blow killed her, dealt by a man who knew exactly where to strike. The other surgeon I consulted suggested such a thing."

"Who is this surgeon?" Coombs flashed. "Let him accuse me."

"He has no idea of your guilt. Why did you hit her? Did she refuse to leave Bennett for you? Even when you promised to take care of her?"

Coombs stared at me, openmouthed, and then at last his face flushed with color, and his eyes filled with rage.

"She was devoted to him. I could not understand it. Bennett was married to another woman already, and Judith would not believe me. She'd made up her mind to go home to her father, to beg forgiveness and start her life again, but when she came back here, she revealed that Bennett had talked her into staying with him. I was flummoxed. In my anger, I struck out at Bennett. Judith leapt in front of him to save him, and so I hit her ..."

Coombs's hand had come up in demonstration. As it came down again, mimicking the blow, tears sprang into his eyes and flowed down his cheeks.

"Good God," Grenville said. "Bennett *saw* you kill his wife? Why did he not send for the magistrates at once?"

"Because he is an evil, evil man," Coombs said, his voice rising. "He already had a wife. He wanted Judith's money for the keeping of *her*, then Judith's father refused to give them any. Not while he was alive, not in a will when he was dead. But that night Bennett found a new source of income — me. Money from me to keep quiet that I'd murdered her. Bennett took her off in a cart, and I never saw what became of her until you brought in her bones. He bled me dry ..."

"Why did you not say so?" I asked. "When I came here, and showed you what had become of her, why did you not tell me what he'd done? For keeping it quiet, he is as much a murderer as you."

"Because I do not want to hang!" Coombs's shrillness increased. "Not for only killing a Jew. If I steered you to him, and you found out what he was yourself — I have heard of your ability to find criminals and take them to Bow Street. Bennett would hang, and I would cease having to pay him."

He buried his face in his hands, weeping.

"Only killing a Jew," I repeated. "Is that what she was to you, in the end? Not quite a person, in your eyes? Because she refused you?"

"She was a bloody fool!"

"I agree," I said. "I would have fled you both. You killed again, though, did you not? You saw the man I hired to keep an eye on Bennett follow him, and you struck him down as well."

Coombs nodded, continuing to weep. "Yes."

"He killed Jack?" Brewster broke in, outraged. "Let me have a go at him, Captain."

"No," I said. "He is for the magistrates."

Coombs looked up, his sobs quieting. "I will tell them about Bennett. All about what he is."

"And I have no doubt he'll tell them all about you," I said.

Coombs paled, then he reddened again and he came at me. Pushing me onto my bad leg, he snatched the chisel from my hand, raised it, and swung it with precision straight at my head.

I swiftly brought up my walking stick and blocked the blow. The metal rang against the hard wood of the stick, jerking his hand up again. Coombs tried another strike, but he crumpled and fell as Brewster bowled him aside, his fist landing in the man's gut.

Coombs collapsed to the floor, groaning. Brewster shook out his hand, looking furious but satisfied.

***

Coombs was in no shape to fight the three of us as we, for the second time that day, bundled a criminal into Grenville's carriage and drove him to the magistrate's court.

I sent a message before we left to Thompson in Wapping that told him to come to Bow Street to find the murderer of Judith Hartman. Thompson arrived in a remarkably short time after we descended at Bow Street with Coombs and gave him to Pomeroy.

Thompson looked buoyed—for him. "Well done, Captain," he said, wringing my hand as we met inside the front door. "I knew you'd not fail. This is a burden from my mind, I will tell you. I'd think of her on a winter night, unknown, unwept for ..."

"It was good of you to care," I said. "Not many would."

Thompson shrugged, his narrow face flushing. "Mayhap I'm too sentimental to be a thief-taker." He shook my hand again. "I thank you, Captain. I am in your debt."

"Go to Mr. Hartman," I said. "Tell him and Judith's sister, and Mr. Stein, all that has happened. Do that, and I will consider the debt paid."

"I will do so, but that will not be enough," Thompson promised. "Consult me anytime you need assistance, Captain."

He touched his battered hat to me, and disappeared up the stairs, calling to Pomeroy as he went.

***

After that, Grenville, I, and Brewster made for Grimpen Lane, in the still-light evening, and shared brandy.

"Whew," Grenville said after he'd drunk a large measure. "What a pair of disgusting, underhanded, horrible ... I cannot think of words bad enough to call them."

"Selfish-prick bastards," Brewster supplied.

Grenville pointed the fingers around his goblet at

him. "I will agree to that. What on earth made you suspect him, Lacey?"

"Nothing," I said slowly. "And everything. I remembered his instruments — torture devices I thought them. The fact that Judith had been killed with such precision, the same precision that healed her arm, was in the back of my mind. When Bennett said his appointment last night was in Tottenham Court Road, where the only other man who'd seen his wife before she died had rooms ... I was not certain, but I had to try."

"I see." Grenville pondered this. "I imagine Bennett pointed you in Coombs's direction for a reason. If he had to go down, so did Coombs." Grenville sipped more brandy. "Those poor women. Although, I am happy they will be free of him."

"He had to be mad," Brewster said with conviction. "Bennett, I mean. My missus is furious if I even wink at a woman. I can't imagine hiding another wife and entire family from her, let alone two or three. She'd have it out of me in no time. And then she'd kill me."

"Bennett's wives were not gifted with keen intelligence," Grenville pointed out. "He seemed careful to choose those who were trusting and naive."

"True." Brewster nodded.

"Whatever their natures, they should not have —" I broke off my statement, frowning. I'd heard a creak on the stairs, or so I thought.

I rose. The room had grown dim as the sun finally decided to sink, but it was still early twilight. Daylight lingered for a long time in June.

By this light, I saw the door swing open. The man who stood in its outline was my father.

I halted. No—not my father. The vicar at Parson's Point in Norfolk had buried him nearly ten years ago, and everyone in the village had breathed a collective sigh of relief. My father was dead and gone.

But this man could have been his twin, though much younger.

Then I realized—he could be *my* twin.

Grenville had also risen, gaping. "Good Lord."

The man stood my height, had the same dark, unruly hair, and brown eyes. He had my build, but he stood straighter, without my broken limb. His face was not quite the same, I saw, in that second. The touch of another lineage had shaped it.

Brewster was on his feet, hands balled. "Who are ye?" he demanded.

"The one you ruined," the man said to me, his deep growl much like mine, though his accent held a touch of the colonies. "And so, I ruin you."

A pistol came out of the folds of his coat. He pointed it straight at me, and fired.

Chapter Thirty

I saw the kick of the gun, the flash. Heard the roar, smelled the stench of gunpowder.

The bullet never reached me. Brewster, snarling, launched himself into me and pushed me out of the way. We fell together in a heap, Brewster a dead weight on top of me.

"Lacey!" Grenville was shouting. "Hey! Stop him! Help!"

Boots on the stairs announced the man running, Grenville after him. I shoved at Brewster. "I'm fine. Get up."

A groan answered me. I scrambled out from under Brewster's heavy body and looked down at him in shock.

Blood seeped from Brewster's gut to stain his rough linen shirt. His face was dead white, eyes open and filled with pain.

"Damnation," I snarled.

I ran for the bedchamber, snatched every towel I

could find, and rushed back to the front room. I jerked open Brewster's shirt and pressed the folded towels hard to his abdomen.

He'd taken the bullet on the left side of his stomach, I saw before I pushed the towels down. The bullet had not come through into me or the floor, so it was still inside him.

"The surgeon," I said urgently. "You'll need him. Where is he?"

Brewster shook his head the slightest bit.

Grenville burst back inside. "I couldn't catch him. I grabbed a patrolman, told him to spread the alert." He switched his gaze to Brewster, and stopped. "Good Lord."

"Tell me where to find the surgeon," I said to Brewster. "You don't want *me* to take out the bullet. It's too tricky." I had done such things before, but I'd prefer the steady hands of the man so well trained.

Brewster continued to shake his head. "Denis won't like it."

"I don't give a damn." I put into my voice the note that had terrified my soldiers on the Peninsula. "*Tell me*, damn and blast you. Or Denis will be the least of your worries."

Brewster wheezed, his words growing fainter. "Captain …"

"If you don't do it for your own sake, or mine, do it for your wife's. Do you want to leave Emily alone?"

Brewster's eyes snapped open again. He had difficulty focusing, but he managed to speak. "King's Court. Off Great Wild Street."

"I'll go," Grenville said. "It's not far."

Without waiting for argument, he was off again, running faster than I ever dreamed he could.

Grenville was an athlete, however much he hid it, riding, walking, fencing, dancing, and boxing with enviable skill.

"Tell Em," Brewster whispered. "You know what to tell her."

His eyes slid closed.

I pressed down harder with the towel. I did not want him to sleep—he might die before the surgeon could even arrive.

"Brewster," I said sharply. "No, wake up and talk to me." I shook him. My voice cracked. "Thomas. Tommy …"

* * *

When Grenville returned in about twenty minutes, he not only brought the surgeon, but also James Denis.

Denis's face was dark with rage. I rarely saw him this angry—only when one of his men got hurt.

He said nothing at all, only stood aside while the surgeon fell to his knees next to Brewster, a canvas bag clinking to the floor beside him.

The surgeon looked over the little I'd done: a folded blanket for Brewster's head, the towels on his abdomen, the smaller blanket I'd spread across his legs to keep him warm, the basin of water standing ready.

"Should we put him on the bed?" I asked.

"Not yet." The surgeon spoke with clipped, decisive words. His hands, thin and deft, skimmed the wound, feeling around it. Brewster's eyes opened and widened in pain, but the surgeon quickly finished.

"Give him this." The surgeon handed me a flask.

I obediently sat down at Brewster's side, lifted his head with my arm, and poured the liquid into his throat.

Brewster swallowed. "Aw, that's foul," he whispered, but the draught stayed down.

I had no idea what the surgeon had given him. I expected brandy or laudanum, but the odor was wrong for either. Brewster's face went slack, but he breathed hoarsely, and grunted in pain when the surgeon probed him again.

"Hold him down," the surgeon said.

I put my arm across Brewster's chest. Grenville got down on the carpet, regardless of his pristine clothes, and held on to his legs.

I could not see all that the surgeon did, but there was the flash of a very thin knife and the scent of blood. Then the man reached into Brewster with the slenderest pair of forceps I'd ever seen.

His hand was steady, without a tremor. Slowly he pulled out a round iron ball and dropped it onto my carpet.

Immediately, he pressed the towels to the wound again. Surgeons I'd observed in the army would let a wound bleed a bit, to clean it. This surgeon kept the towels on Brewster and ordered Grenville to shove the basin over to him.

My carpet grew sodden with blood and water as the surgeon used nearly a gallon of the stuff to wash out the wound. He then sewed up the gash with needle and thread, his stitches smaller and neater than the elegant stitching on my wife's underclothing.

The surgeon washed the wound again when he was finished, wrapped a long bandage around Brewster's middle, and rose.

"Heave him on the bed now—carefully. Don't break the stitching. He doesn't move after that until I say so."

I carefully took Brewster by the shoulders. His eyes were open, gleaming with pain, but clouded by whatever drug he'd been given.

It was not Grenville who took his legs, but Denis. He lifted Brewster with careful strength, letting me guide us all into the bedroom. Grenville came behind with the blankets and whatever towels could be salvaged. The surgeon, I saw, with some surprise, had poured water into another bowl and now threw his instruments into it.

Denis's strength came to me through Brewster's body. I'd known the man was strong when we'd fought for our lives in Norfolk, but it came as a sharp reminder that he'd begun life struggling for survival. Denis so often sat still while he directed others to do things for him that I forgot about his brute strength, just as I forgot Grenville's agility.

I gave Denis a nod when I was ready, and we lifted Brewster as one and placed him on the bed. Brewster gave another grunt of pain, his eyelids fluttering, then he settled down.

Denis stepped back, and Grenville and I carefully laid the blankets over Brewster's inert body.

The surgeon came to look him over. "Keep him warm. If he takes a fever, give him more of this." He set the flask on the bedside table. "Not more than a swallow or two at a time."

"What is it?" I asked in curiosity.

"An extract of a native plant from the Americas," the surgeon said. "I do not know its true name. A sage of some kind." He continued before I could ask more questions. "The bullet did not penetrate any organs, so he should mend. Keep him here, and do not let him move. Feed him if he wants food, but not too much. Someone will have to nurse him."

"Em," Brewster whispered.

I laid my hand on his shoulder. "I'll bring her. You and she are welcome to stay as long as you need."

The surgeon gave me a final nod, the last of the sunlight touching his balding head. "I will return in three days."

Without further word, he walked out. I followed, but the surgeon moved quickly, and I did not catch him until he'd reached the bottom of the stairwell.

"What do I owe you?" I asked him. "Beyond what Denis pays you, I mean. You saved his life."

The surgeon looked me up and down, his eyes so cold, with no pride in what he'd just done. "As I told you before, Captain, my price is silence. I have no other."

With that, he opened the door and walked out into the darkening lane.

Grenville came clattering down after him. "Strange fellow, but remarkable." He put on his hat. "I am off to fetch the good Mrs. Brewster. Poor lady—I'll break it as gently as I can."

"Thank you. Can you also get word to Donata? Tell her what has happened and to keep Gabriella home. Tell her I will come as soon as I can."

"I've sent Jackson back to Mayfair already," Grenville said. "The surgeon's house was close enough and the streets so crowded it was easy for me to go on foot."

A knot eased inside me. Grenville was a good friend and a wise man.

Grenville continued. "Mr. Denis requests that I send you up to him. I believe he wishes to confer."

"Mr. Denis is eager to give orders in my own

rooms," I said, but I was too tired and worried for anger.

"No doubt he wants to know what happened. He saw me as I went sprinting down Drury Lane and into the heart of molly territory. I shudder to think of the newspapers tomorrow. Denis insisted that his carriage bring us back, but I have never seen him so angry. Even that business in Norfolk didn't enrage him as much I think."

Grenville nodded at me, slipped out the door, and was gone.

I climbed the stairs and entered my front room. Denis had moved there, and was lighting candles. He was not one for sitting in the dark. He'd also drawn my curtains, so that the light would not show us to those outside.

Denis pointed to the chair by the fireplace, indicating I should sit. "Tell me about this man who shot Mr. Brewster."

To remind him of my independence, I took the straight chair at the writing desk. I soon regretted my decision, because my leg was starting to ache, with a deep hurt that I knew would stay with me for days.

"I know nothing about him," I said. "He has been sending me threatening letters, he rode at Peter and me in the park, and tonight he shot at me. He looks like me and has my voice, though he sounds as though he's been living elsewhere in the world. I'd never seen him before."

Denis took the wing chair and cross his trousered legs. "A relation?"

I shrugged, pain seeping through my entire body now. "If so, I've never known of him."

Denis touched his fingertips together. "I will find him, have no fear of it. I will explain to him that I do not like gentlemen shooting one of my own."

"To be fair, he was aiming at me, not Brewster. Brewster jumped in the way."

Denis's eyes went hard. "I was talking about *you*."

I met his gaze as silence fell between us.

I did not want to belong to him; I hadn't from the day I'd met him. And yet, there now existed between us a complicated mesh of obligation, favors, secrets, and gratitude that I would never untangle. I did not know whether Denis had won the game, or entangled himself in it as well.

"I would be obliged," I began, "if you would keep this person away from my family."

"That shall be done," Denis said. "I sent two of my men to South Audley Street as soon as Mr. Grenville babbled out what had happened."

More knots loosened. "Thank you."

Denis merely rested his hands on the arms of the wing chair. He hated being demonstrative.

We waited in silence for a little while. One of the candles, wax, Donata had insisted, gently crackled as its wick drew up fuel.

My curiosity would never let me sit quietly for long. "The surgeon," I said, "who remains nameless. What on earth did he do?"

Denis's brows lifted a fraction. "He is a killer."

So Brewster had intimated when I'd first asked. *Knows exactly where to stick the knife if he has to …* Brewster had said.

"More specifically?" I asked. "Did he do away with his wife? A patient? He seems so very cool that I cannot imagine him losing his temper and stabbing a man with his scalpel."

"There is nothing amusing about him, Lacey. I will tell you so that you do not go blundering about asking *him*. He murdered, not one man, but a dozen."

I went still. "A dozen?"

I'd killed men myself, in Mysore, on the Peninsula, in other places during the long wars. I'd fought for my life, to win battles, to take my men to safety.

One man killing another in anger, in a fight or struggle in London's streets was understandable. A dozen bordered on horror.

"Why? Is he a madman?" I'd never met a calmer, more collected madman if so. "Please do not tell me he killed his patients for the scientific knowledge of it."

"Nothing so macabre." Denis's voice was quiet. "He is an extremely competent surgeon and is quite angry if one under his care dies. But he knows how to kill quickly and efficiently, exactly where to cut, what to sever. Other men began hiring him to do so. I believe he asked a reasonable fee and did the job so competently it left no trace. He was caught not because of anything he did, but because the last man who hired him panicked and told the magistrates. The surgeon did not discover this in time to leave the country, and he was convicted of two of the murders. His sentence was commuted to transportation, possibly because I asked it to be done, but more likely because of his professional skills. Someone like him would be needed in the colonies."

"You employed him?" I asked. "Is that how you knew him?"

Denis's eyes held no emotion I could see. "No, indeed. Someone else employed him to kill *me*. Needless to say, he was not successful."

"Your guards stopped him?" I asked.

"My guards were useless against him. He got past them all and into my bedchamber."

I stilled in amazement. Denis never, ever let anyone get close enough to him to so much as touch him.

Denis went on, "I am alive because he let me talk to him, and then I paid him a large sum, far larger than the other man had given him. It was that employer who went to the magistrates. He was terrified I'd send the surgeon after *him*." He shrugged. "I was tempted, but that would have been too obvious."

I pictured the situation, two men of equal sangfroid and ruthlessness squaring off.

"If you paid him, why did Brewster tell me you considered yourself in his debt?"

"Because the surgeon's professional pride did not want him to turn on his employer. I persuaded him, and he liked the idea of having me under his obligation. So ... I worked to get his sentence commuted, and I provided the means for him to escape that confinement when he wished. And so when you kept asking to send for him ..." Denis shook his head. "You do try my patience, Captain."

"An explanation might have saved you much trouble," I said.

His fingers moved on the chair arms. "I forget that you will not leave well enough alone simply because you are told to." Denis gave me a severe look. "For this man who is trying to kill you—leave that alone as well. I will hunt him and find him."

My irritation stirred. "You wish me to ignore a man threatening me and mine?"

"No, I wish you to take care of your family while I and my men find this person. Go to Norfolk as planned; do not alter your journeys without telling me."

Were I the only one in danger, his guarding me might grate, but I would do anything to keep Gabriella, Peter, and Donata safe.

"I thank you for your help," I said. "Truly."

"I have invested much time, wherewithal, and money in you, Captain. I would not like to see that be for nothing."

"Hmm," was all I could think of to say.

We waited again in silence, not very long, until we heard Grenville on the stairs, calling up to us.

Mrs. Brewster—Emily—once a lady of a bawdy house, now Brewster's devoted wife, barely acknowledged me. She threw off her shawl and plunged into the bedchamber, her exclamations drowning Brewster's tired rumbles.

We saw them settled, and I went downstairs and told Mrs. Beltan, before she went home, that Brewster and his wife would lodge there for a time. They were to have anything they wished, and I gave her coins to cover the cost.

Then Grenville and I, in Denis's carriage, went home.

Chapter Thirty-One

The first person I saw upon entering the South Audley Street house was my daughter. I entered alone, Denis's coach moving off with Grenville in the direction of Grosvenor Street.

Gabriella halted in mid-flight toward me, taking in the blood on my coat, waistcoat, shirt, and breeches.

"Father," she gasped. "Are you hurt?"

I did not bother to explain. Barnstable, equally aghast, had taken my hat and gloves. I thrust my walking stick at him as well, and opened my arms to sweep up my daughter as she came off the stairs.

I embraced her, hard, feeling her warmth, the beating of her heart, hearing her voice, so melodious. She was alive and well, whole and beautiful.

"Good heavens, Lacey," Lady Aline said, as she came down the stairs in Gabriella's wake. "You are covered with blood and ruining the gel's gown."

I pulled back. Gabriella's pink and white striped

satin now bore a smudge of dirt and blood.

"I do not mind," Gabriella said. "As long as you are all right, sir."

"I am whole. The blood is not mine. It is poor Brewster's, but he will mend, I am told."

"What on earth happened?" Gabriella demanded. "A great thug of a man came to deliver a message to Bartholomew that Lady Donata and I were not to stray a step."

"This after I gained us invitations to two extremely exclusive soirees," Lady Aline put in indignantly.

"Not tonight," I said to Gabriella. "Tonight, you will stay home, and I will tell you of my adventures."

Gabriella's face softened in relief. "I am happy to stay," she said. She laced her arms around my neck and whispered into my ear. "Truly. You have spared me an ordeal."

A flurry of steps on the stairs announced the arrival of Peter. He paused on the landing, as though expecting me to scold him for eluding his nanny and fleeing the nursery.

Instead, I crouched down and held out my arms. "There's my boy."

Peter dashed the rest of the way down. I caught him and lifted him as I came up, ignoring the protest of my knee. It was not done for a man to dote on his son, especially one not of his body, but I kissed Peter's cheek.

"I will go to your mother," I said to Peter. "So that she will not have me boiled in oil. Then we will have supper, all of us together, and I will tell you the whole story. My lady, you are included in the invitation."

Lady Aline flashed me a wistful look, as though

she'd like nothing better than to dine informally with us, but she shook her head, the feathers in her hair dancing.

"No, indeed. I moved heaven and earth for the invitations, and I must go. I will say that you were hurt and Gabriella stayed home to tend you. That will go over well—a devoted daughter might make a man a devoted wife." Aline came to me and dropped a light kiss to my cheek, taking care to not let me soil her clothes. "Do clean yourself up before you go to Donata. You'll give her the vapors."

Aline turned away, taking a wrap from her maid, who'd hurried to attend her. "What shall I do with you, dear boy?" she muttered, even as she lumbered out of the house.

I set Peter down, promising I'd see him and Gabriella in the supper room, kissed my daughter again, and ascended the stairs.

Aline was correct that I was a mess, and I continued to my chamber without stopping at Donata's. The last time I'd come home covered in muck, my wife had convinced me to come in and speak to her regardless. Today, however, I wanted to wash myself of the evening's horrors before I approached her.

Bartholomew answered my summons and my command to bring me a large basin of water and a sponge. I stripped off while he fetched the things, then I sent him away so I could bathe myself in peace. I had to promise to tell him everything, in vivid detail later, before he would take himself off.

The quiet trickle of the water as I glided it out of the basin at my feet was soothing, incongruous with the frantic events of the day.

I found myself shaking. The roar of the pistol

came back to me, then the voice of the man who'd shot it. I saw the bright blood gushing from Brewster's side, soaking rapidly through his shirt then the towels I'd held.

Blood that should have been mine.

I barely heard the door open, but I sensed her presence, the crisp coolness of it, like an autumn breeze cutting the torpid heat of summer.

I turned my head and saw her in the doorway, her peignoir floating, locks of dark hair tumbling to her shoulders.

I could not hide—I was standing bare, on a towel, in the center of my chamber, and the sponge was not nearly enough for concealment. I could only remain motionless, water and soap sliding down my large body, and stare at her.

Donata closed the door. "I remember now why I agreed to marry you."

"To pour water on your pristine carpet?" I managed to say.

She did not answer as she approached. When she reached me, Donata plucked the sponge from my hands and began drawing it over my skin.

"The man writing the letters tried to kill me," I said.

"I know," Donata answered, maddeningly calm. "Grenville's coachman told us. The account was rather jumbled, but I imagine you will give me the entire tale. For now, I am pleased to see you whole."

Her lips trembled as she finished, and she pressed them shut.

I stilled the sponge. "I will not go to Egypt," I said. "I will tell Grenville. I might not have been able to come home tonight … I don't want …"

Donata snatched the sponge from my grip,

squeezing it so that cooling water splashed me. "What absolute nonsense. Of course you will go. You have been longing to. I told you, Gabriel, never let another's threats determine your life." She dragged the sponge down my chest with a firm, almost digging, stroke. "Besides, many things will happen between now and January. Wait, and decide then."

Donata touched her damp hand to her abdomen, reminding me what would happen in the months before January.

I pushed the sponge away and gathered her to me. She came, unprotesting, though I soaked her gown.

"You are beautiful," I said.

She moved wonderfully as she laughed. "I am a mess. Not fit to be seen."

"I like you a mess," I murmured.

She was the lady for me, strong, clear-headed, exasperating, never letting me become complacent with myself.

And beautiful, as I'd told her.

Donata did not object when I lifted her and took her to the nearby bed. There I proceeded to get her, the peignoir, the pillows, and the bedcovers, quite soapy and sodden.

End

Author's Note

This venture into Captain Lacey's world taught me more about London than I'd ever known before. Every corner tells a story.

I hesitated before writing this book, because I wanted it to involve Jewish London, a subject about which I knew nothing. I had to begin research from scratch about the reintegration of Jews into England after their thirteenth-century expulsion was more or less reversed by Oliver Cromwell in the mid-1600s.

I realized that, like me, Captain Lacey would likewise know very little about Jewish London. He's a relative newcomer to London (having spent all his life in Norfolk and then in the army traveling the world). We would learn together, not only Jewish history but of the attitudes toward Jews during that time.

When I asked my fellow Regency authors about sources of information, they hands down recommended *The Jews of Georgian England*, by Todd Endelman, which is an excellent history of Jewish life in London and England from the early 1700s until the dawn of the Victorian age. I highly recommend it for informative and thoroughly interesting reading.

The Hartman family, Itzak Stein, and Mr. Molodzinski are Ashkenazi Jews, whose families immigrated from Central and Eastern Europe. The choice of their ancestry was a random decision on my part, and not one that espouses any bias, except that a large population of Ashkenazi Jews inhabited London during this period. Georgian London was also home to Sephardic Jews, who originated in Spain and Portugal before they were expelled from Iberia altogether in 1492. (There is an excellent lecture series offered by The Great Courses called *The Other 1492,* which covers Spain and the expulsion of Jews and the persecution of Jews and *conversos*.)

The Ashkenazi synagogue Lacey visits with Mr. Molodzinski in Duke's Place is no more. Built in 1690, it was destroyed in the Blitz in 1941. The nearby Sephardic synagogue of Bevis Marks, completed in 1701, has been in continuous use and has an informative website. Thanks to the series of prints of London by Augustus Pugin and Thomas Rowlindson, published in *Ackermann's Repository of Arts,* we know what the lost Great Synagogue and other buildings in the London of Lacey's era looked like.

I also learned much about public records in the Regency, which were scattered for the most part among parish registers and court records. Not until the Births and Deaths Registration Act of 1836 was an office established in Somerset House for the gathering of all birth, death, and marriage certificates — thus saving sleuths in the remainder of the nineteenth and most of the twentieth centuries much trouble when seeking a missing clue.

All in all, I hope you have enjoyed this look into Captain Lacey's London. He will return for more adventures in Book 11 and more novels to come.

Thank you for reading!
Captain Lacey's adventures continue in

The Alexandria Affair

Captain Lacey Regency Mysteries
Book 11

Coming 2016

The Captain Lacey Regency mysteries
are also now available

in Audio

from Audible and iTunes

About the Author

Award-winning Ashley Gardner is a pseudonym for *New York Times* bestselling author Jennifer Ashley. Under both names—and a third, Allyson James—Ashley has written more than 85 published novels and novellas in mystery and romance. Her books have won several RT BookReviews Reviewers Choice awards (including Best Historical Mystery for *The Sudbury School Murders*), and Romance Writers of America's RITA (given for the best romance novels and novellas of the year). Ashley's books have been translated into a dozen different languages and have earned starred reviews in *Booklist*. When she isn't writing, she indulges her love for history by researching and building miniature houses and furniture from many periods.

More about the Captain Lacey series can be found at www.gardnermysteries.com. Or email Ashley Gardner at gardnermysteries@cox.net

Made in the USA
Lexington, KY
30 October 2015